THE RECOGNITION REVELATION

Recognition Book 3

HENRY VOGEL

Copyright © 2018 by Henry Vogel

All rights reserved.

No part of this publication may be reproduced, stored in a retrieval system, or transmitted in any form or by any means, electronic, mechanical, photographic, or otherwise, without the prior written consent of the publisher.

Published in the United States of America by Rampant Loon Press, an imprint of Rampant Loon Media LLC, P.O. Box 111, Lake Elmo, Minnesota 55042. "Rampant Loon Press" and the Rampant Loon colophon are trademarks of Rampant Loon Media LLC.

www.rampantloonmedia.com

Cover design by www.ebooklaunch.com

ISBN: 978-1-938834-85-1 (ebook)

ISBN: 978-1-938834-86-8 (print)

First publication: April 2018

For the real Jana, who likes Olivia better than her namesake.

ROYAL UNEASE

Olivia

"Why, in God's name, do you want to take the ship with the experimental hyperdrive back to Xapreathea?" William asked. "After all you've been through, I thought you'd want a little luxurious rest and relaxation."

My husband was right, I *did* want to enjoy every possible luxury available to me. As the Crown Princess of the Star Kingdom that's a lot of luxury. Nothing would give me greater pleasure than to wallow in the lap of it all. Even more than the luxury, I wanted to wriggle on William's lap and show him just how much I appreciated his recent heroics. But all of it paled in comparison with my need to talk to my mother-in-law, Queen Charlotte. I couldn't say that to William, so I told a not-quite-lie, instead.

"I want to get home as quickly as possible," I said, "so Dr. Edwards can examine me and make sure our baby is completely healthy. I know it's paranoid of me, but you know how expectant mothers can be when it comes to their baby's health."

"I know Jeanine had her best doctors examine you, darling, but there's no one on Gaunner who's as good as Dr. Edwards. I completely understand your concern."

I offered a shy smile, "Thank you, darling. I'm more comfortable with Dr. Edwards."

William smiled and took my hand. "If that's what you want, that is what you shall have. Nothing is too good for my princess."

The dear man meant every word of that, too. He would do anything for me, including making a near-orbit space dive to rescue me—and Jeanine, of course—from kidnappers. How could any woman not love such a man?

"Are you sure you don't mind, darling?" I asked, wrapping my arms around his neck.

"I can never deny you anything, my dear." William kissed me lightly on the lips, "I'll tell Captain Palmer and our Chief of Staff that we're taking the fastest ship in the galaxy."

Twenty minutes later, our ship lifted from my former home world. Twenty hours later, our ship landed on my new home world. As I expected, a crowd of newsies waited for us.

"Don't worry, Olivia, I'll keep this short. Surely, even a pack of newsies will understand your desire to have Dr. Edwards examine you and the baby."

"They would," I said, "if they knew I was pregnant. We haven't made an official announcement, remember?"

"Damn me, but I had forgotten!" William cocked his head and looked at me, "Of course, we could make the announcement now."

"Are you sure that's wise, Your Highness?" Godfrey, our Chief of Staff asked. "I was given to understand that Her Majesty was quite looking forward to making the announcement, herself."

William leveled a flat stare at Godfrey. "Is my mother having the baby? No, she is not. Given that, I see no reason for her to make the announcement."

"But... But, she's the Queen!" the other man sputtered.

"And I'm the father," William snapped.

I looped an arm through one of William's arms and started toward the airlock. "I believe father trumps Queen, in this situation. Now, let's get this over with as quickly as possible so I can see Dr. Edwards."

Having grown up in the limelight, William handled the newsies masterfully. He announced the pending Royal birth, segued directly into our need to cut the interviews short, and had us in a ground car in less than ten minutes.

Once Dr. Edwards gave the baby and me a clean bill of health, I said, "Will you excuse me, William? I really should talk with your mother."

"Why? You know Dr. Edwards will send a copy of the medical report immediately."

"I know, darling, but I must report the political situation on Gaunner. After all, that was the reason we visited in the first place."

William's lack of interest in *that* discussion was reflected in his eyes. As they glazed over, he nodded, "Then, I suppose I should report the same to Father."

I knew what he was going to report to the King—everything about his adventures and nothing about the politics that precipitated them—but I didn't mind. It would please William, it would please his father, and it would leave Queen Charlotte and me free to act upon the truly important developments from our trip.

It took me thirty minutes to deliver the concise version of our trip to Gaunner to my mother-in-law. She listened carefully, not once interrupting with questions or comments, until I indicated I was done.

"I know you and Colin were very close, Olivia," Queen Charlotte said. "Please accept my deepest sympathies, both for his death and for your role in it. I doubt it helps you any at this moment, but you had no choice, my dear. Colin forced your hand."

"I know, Mother, and that does help. Some."

"You probably don't want to hear this right now, Olivia, but you have grown far beyond Colin's tutelage. Meanwhile, he remained rather provincially centered around the Duchy of Gaunner."

"The narrowness of his vision did...surprise...me. I've only been here for a few months, but I see things so differently now." I met my mother-in-law's gaze, "I attribute that to your guidance, Mother."

"And I attribute it to your keen intellect and eye for detail. On that subject, my dear, what do you consider our primary concerns with regard to Lady Jeanine in her role as Duchess of Gaunner?"

"It is unfortunate that she knows—or, at least, suspects—that we staged my spaceship's destruction and William's rescue of me from the wreckage," I replied.

"The same can be said of her knowledge of your original involvement in the coup attempt against her," Mother agreed. "But, the simple fact that she has not made that information public leads me to believe she'll stick to her agreement. She will leave us alone if we leave her alone."

I nodded, "That's my read on it, as well."

"But...?"

"But, something still bothers me. I can't quite put my finger on it, though."

Mother's face grew solemn. "It's her interest in the Star Stone. That certainly makes me uneasy. I...don't know why it does, but I cannot shake the feeling that no good will come from her interest."

Once Mother voiced her concern, I realized the Star Stone was the source of my unease, as well. And, I realized I also couldn't explain why. But, I had enough to worry about without worrying about why I was worrying about the Star Stone.

"Perhaps, we should increase our surveillance on Lady Jeanine and her husband. With the Royal Intelligence Agency at our disposal, I'm sure we can feed them enough disinformation to keep Jeanine and her friends running in circles."

"That's a good idea, Olivia, but it leaves one loose end."

"You mean the slicer you let access the Star Stone, Mother?"

"Yes. I feel as if she is the key to this whole situation. Worse, we have no idea who she is, where she came from, or how she returned from the Star Stone with her sanity intact." Mother shook her head, "I'm afraid this slicer may be far more dangerous to us than Lady Jeanine."

"You have cut off all outside access to the Star Stone, haven't you?" I asked.

"I've closed the connection she used to find you and Jeanine, but we cannot isolate the Star Stone entirely."

"Why ever not? Leaving it connected to the net could be a huge mistake!"

Mother's gaze sharpened on me. My comment had not pleased her.

"I am quite aware of that, my dear, but this matter is out of our control. The Star Stone requires those connections."

"I don't understand, Mother."

Mother sighed, "No, you don't. There are certain documents in the royal family's library that provide an explanation. Well, an explanation of sorts, anyway. I think it's time you read them. Once you have, we can bend both of our minds toward solving the slicer dilemma. Let us hope we can find a way to stop her without killing her."

I felt a jolt of alarm. "Jeanine is close friends with this slicer. If something were to happen to the woman..."

"I understand your concern, Olivia," Mother said. "But, stopping that slicer may prove more important than keeping our secrets away from William."

DROP IT IN THE NEAREST STAR

Jana

"Tell me everything," Jeanine said.

I looked across the low table at my...duchess. It dawned on me that I should feel strange thinking of Jeanine in such noble terms. I mean, I'm a rebel—and I don't mean that in the same way as someone who goes against social norms does. I mean that in the 'take up arms to overthrow a despotic and uncaring government' way. You know, the kind of rebel who risks a hell of a lot more than social embarrassment if her side loses.

So, I *should* think of Jeanine as a compatriot of the cause, a fellow rebel, even a rebel leader. I should *not* look at her and see a woman I would happily crown queen of the galaxy and serve for the rest of my life. The rebel commanders wouldn't be happy if they knew I was thinking like this. Hell, *Jeanine* would be royally pissed if she could read the thoughts running through my head. Or maybe she'd just be nobly pissed, since she was of the nobility instead of the royalty. Anyway, I pushed aside thoughts of Queen Jeanine—dammit, it even rhymes, so you just *know* she'd be perfect on the throne—and answered her question.

"The first thing you have to know is that the Star Stone is a whole lot more than the mystic, gift-from-God rock that all the stories say it is. It's some kind of ancient, alien artifact. It's an AI of some sort."

"And you got all of this during the six or seven minutes you were...what, interfacing with it?" she asked.

"Yeah, though it wasn't hard to figure out. Hell, the Stone, itself, told me as much."

Jeanine's eyebrows rose in surprise. "The Star Stone *talked* to you?"

I nodded. "If you ask me, the thing is pretty lonely. I don't think that's something its designers built into it, so I'm guessing it learned loneliness from humanity."

Jeanine's eyebrows came back down and lowered even further, either in confusion or disapproval. "And you feel sorry for it?"

The Star Stone's plans to let me fade from existence rose, unbidden. As a result, my response was more vehement than I intended. "Hell no! I do not feel sorry for the damned thing, at all! Given half a chance, I'd drop it in the nearest star and cackle with glee as it tumbled toward its fiery doom!" I paused to think for a second and then nodded. "In fact, that's not a bad plan. We should definitely do that."

"You're not making much sense, Jana," Jeanine chided. "Why don't you take a deep breath and then start from the beginning?"

"Right," I agreed, realizing I had been babbling. "I'll do that."

I took several deep breaths, managing to regain control of my emotions and order my thoughts. "A lot of what happened to me inside the Star Stone is hard to explain, especially to someone who wasn't there. But, after I drifted in darkness for a while, I managed to assert some control on the...view? Environment? Or maybe the Star Stone figured out what I was trying to do and did it for me. Anyway, I ended up in something that looked like a monitoring station. It had thousands of vid screens showing life through the eyes and ears of people who have been Recognized. The Star Stone said it could also monitor a lot of their children, too."

Jeanine stiffened and her eyes widened in alarm. "And I was one of those people?"

"You've been Recognized," I replied, shrugging.

Jeanine's tone went quiet, but intense. "What did you see and hear?"

"Uh, when the Star Stone showed me your screen, you were in a room with Colin. I heard him force you to choose which of the Holder children would be kidnapped. That's when I knew I had to leave the Star Stone and make sure the Holders were taken to safety."

"Drake told me that much. I'm just glad you were able to leave without any problems. Drake told me about the Queen's warning."

"Jeanine, I didn't just up and leave. The Star Stone was intent on keeping me for as long as possible—until I faded into nothing, if the Stone didn't lie to me about what happened to the others who came before me."

Jeanine blinked at me a few times, her face a mask of horror at my words. "I don't understand. I thought you slicers just return to your bodies if your connection is severed."

"The Star Stone is different. The interface I went through... I don't know exactly what it did, but the Star Stone said it stripped the essence of what makes me 'Jana' and left an empty husk behind."

Involuntarily, I shuddered at the memory. Concern written all over her face, Jeanine rushed around the low table and enveloped me in a hug. "My God, Jana, you shouldn't have taken such a risk for me!"

Blinking away unwanted and unexpected tears, I shook my head. "I had to. It was the only way to find out where you were!"

"I'm not worth—"

"Don't you dare put yourself down, Jeanine!" I pulled back and glared into her eyes. "You are totally worth risking my life for. Besides, it was the Star Stone! The ultimate slicer challenge!"

"Well, I thank God the Star Stone decided to let you go. I'd never have forgiven myself if—"

I shook my head vigorously. "That damned Stone didn't let me go. I escaped!"

"You what?"

"Escaped! And I'll bet the Star Stone is hopping mad that I did, too, because it has no idea *how* I did it." I stifled a giggle. "It will probably never guess, either! I just—"

Jeanine clapped a hand over my mouth. "Don't tell me. Don't *ever* tell me! If you do, you're also telling the Star Stone."

My eyes widened in shock at what I'd almost done. "Oh, crap! I can't believe I almost did that!"

Jeanine got a thoughtful look. "Since I'm nothing more than a direct line to the Star Stone, I don't think you should tell me anything else about the Stone or any plans you have for it."

"Um, okay, but how can we coordinate—"

"Stop right there, Jana! Say nothing more about the Star Stone when I'm around!" Jeanine thought for a moment, then her expression cleared. "Drake hasn't been Recognized and his parents are commoners. He can speak with my voice and, of course, I trust him implicitly."

"You want me to tell him about all of this?" I asked.

Jeanine nodded. "Definitely. Go to his office right now. I'll call ahead and tell him the situation. On your way, grab anyone you need to help you plan and get busy. Just don't *ever* tell me what you're doing. Clear?"

Nodding, I let Jeanine bundle me out of her office. Deep in thought, I went in search of Tilly. I had no idea what we could do to get rid of the Star Stone, but I felt certain I was going to need as much help as I could get.

∼

A member of the palace's ever-observant staff noticed my

expression as I exited Jeanine's office. Without hesitation, she asked, "May I help you, miss?"

"Yes, please! I'm looking for Lady Smythe-Warrington." Before he left, William told the staff of Tilly's title and, much to Tilly's disgust, everyone on the staff now used it. "I'm on my way to Captain Haral's office and need her to meet me there."

The woman smiled brightly at me. "Don't worry, miss, we'll find her. Do you know the way to Captain Haral's office?"

"I do," I replied. "Um, I forgot to get breakfast this morning. Could you possibly have some food sent to his office for me?"

"I'd be happy to. After all, breakfast is the most important meal of the day!"

The woman was already speaking into her comm as she turned away. Confident that Tilly and food would be at Drake's office soon, I headed that way.

Tilly, looking disgustingly well-rested and impeccably dressed, met me in Drake's outer office. Drake was there waiting for us.

As he ushered us in, he said to his receptionist, "Sally, don't disturb me unless it's Jeanine or a life-and-death emergency."

"Yes, sir."

"I asked to have some breakfast delivered," I said. "Could you please allow an exception for that?"

Drake flashed a grin that didn't rise to his eyes. "For you, Jana, anything."

Drake's office was large and ostentatious, though it was still surpassed by Jeanine's ducal office. It had the same basic layout and Drake settled us into the sitting area to one side of his desk.

Without preamble, he said, "Jeanine told me to drop everything and meet with you immediately. That's all she said. As you might guess that has me concerned. What's this about?"

He and Tilly turned expectant looks my way, but I wasn't quite ready to come to the point yet. Turning to Tilly, I asked, "You've never been Recognized, have you, Tilly?"

Drake's brows drew down in what I guessed was anger. "What the hell difference does that make? Answer my question!"

"I will, Drake, but you have to be patient for a minute." I turned back to Tilly. "Well?"

Tilly was nonplussed by the question, but shook her head, "No. I've never even seen the Star Stone in person."

"And your mother? Or, for that matter, your father?"

Tilly's eyes flashed, joining Drake in anger. "No! And I don't appreciate this interrogation. You asked me to be here after all."

I held my hands up in a placating gesture. "I know, and I'm sorry, but you'll understand why had to ask that once you hear my explanation."

Of course, that's when my breakfast showed up. The young girl—I think her name is Mary—immediately felt the undercurrent of tension in the room. She glanced nervously at each of us, and each of us offered up a strained smile.

"Should I take this away, Captain Haral?" the girl asked.

"No, Mary," he replied. "I know Jana is quite hungry."

"That looks delicious," I said, as the girl placed dishes in front of me. "Thank you."

Mary curtsied and quickly left with her empty cart.

The second the office door shut, Drake and Tilly turned hard eyes my way. Tilly spoke first, "Spill it."

I told them what I had told Jeanine, wrapping up with, "I've been thinking a lot about the children of Recognized parents and am pretty sure the Star Stone can only see and hear through kids whose mother was Recognized before they were born. Whatever the Star Stone puts into a Recognized person's body has nine months to...I don't know if infiltrate is the right word or not, but it's all I can think of. So, nine months to infiltrate the baby's body. A Recognized father's only direct bodily interaction with the baby is at the moment of conception. I think the Star Stone can plant a marker that way, but that's probably it."

My two friends looked at me, aghast, as I wrapped up. Tilly

assayed a slight smile, "Well, that certainly explains all your questions before we got started."

I returned her smile. "I'm sorry, but I had to be certain."

Drake looked down and rubbed his temples, an expression of weary resignation crossing his face. "Well, so much for the family Jeanine and I were planning."

"I wouldn't go quite that far," I said. "At least, not yet."

"Did you listen to what you just told us?" Drake asked. "I will not inflict the Star Stone on any child of mine!"

"I understand, Drake, and completely agree with you. That's why the three of us are meeting right now." I looked back and forth between my two friends. "We need to find a way to wash the taint of the Star Stone from Jeanine, and then we need to destroy the damn thing. Or we could destroy the Stone. Jeanine's system will probably cleanse itself after that. I don't think it matters which we do first."

"Destroy the Star Stone?" Tilly asked. "Are you serious? I mean, it's right there in the Royal Palace on Xapreathea, the most heavily guarded planet in the galaxy. I don't care how well-equipped your rebellion is, there's no way an attack like that could succeed!"

Drake nodded, "She's right. A truly determined suicide attack might get through, but who knows if it will be able to destroy something like the Star Stone. By your own admission, it's some kind of alien artifact. For all we know, it's indestructible."

"I doubt it," I replied. "But you both have very good points—that's why we're not going to attack Xapreathea. Like you say, it would be suicide. Even if we destroyed the Star Stone, it would also destroy the rebellion. No, we need another approach."

Tilly arched one eyebrow. "Like what?"

I grinned at her. "Funny you should ask, since you're going to be integral to my plan."

Tilly pulled as far back from my grin as she could. "Oh, no! Please, tell me you're not thinking what I think you're thinking!"

"I'm not thinking what you think I'm thinking."

Suspicion tinged Tilly's next word. "Really?"

"Well, yes, I *am* thinking what you're thinking—but, it's not step one."

Drake looked back and forth between the two of us, frustration evident on his face. "Since I'm not on the same wavelength as the two of you, could you stop speaking in code and just tell me what you're planning?"

Tilly jerked a thumb my way. "Jana wants me to steal the Star Stone."

Drake's head swiveled in my direction. "You can't be serious?"

I met Drake's disbelieving stare. "I can, and I am. But, I don't expect Tilly to do this all by herself, and it's entirely possible we won't even need her to do that. It all depends on what else I can find out about the Star Stone."

Tilly's eyes narrowed. "Find out how?"

I shrugged, "I need to go back into the Star Stone."

"Absolutely not," Drake declared.

"What he said, only doubled," Tilly said. In case that wasn't entirely clear, she added, "Absolutely, *absolutely* not!"

I paused between bites of breakfast, "I'm getting the feeling you're against my idea."

"After hearing what you learned while you were inside the Star Stone, getting rid of it makes perfect sense," Tilly said. "It's the idea of you interfacing with it again that we're against. The idea is idiotic!"

"Don't hold back, Tilly. Tell me what you really think of my plan."

"Ha, ha." With her face surrounded by hair the color of midnight, Tilly's light-bronze skin made her dark eyes truly stand out. Those eyes were currently locked on mine and blazing with intensity. "By your own admission, you barely got away from the Star Stone last time, and that was by sheer luck."

It was my turn to bridle. "Or, as I like to call it, deductive reasoning."

"Luck!"

"Logic!"

"*Ladies!*" Drake's voice cracked across us like a whip. "This bickering is pointless and it won't get us any closer to solving the problem of the Star Stone."

Tilly bit back whatever she was going to say next. The human mind works oddly in times of stress. Despite all the real issues we had to worry about, I found myself wondering if she could have kept the alliterative theme going. Nothing appropriate sprang to my mind, but Tilly was a smart woman. Who knows what she thought up?

"The argument is useless," I agreed, "but my idea is extremely sound."

Tilly shook her head emphatically, "That's just your slicer pride speaking, Jana. You simply can't bear the thought that the Star Stone beat you at your own game."

"It *didn't* beat me," I replied through gritted teeth. "If it had, Jeanine would probably be dead, and I'd still be inside the Stone, slowly wasting away to nothing."

"Fine, the Star Stone didn't beat you," Tilly rolled her eyes. She leaned forward to emphasize her next words. "You slipped in and out of it like a digital wraith. You *won*. There's no good reason to risk giving it another chance to capture you."

"I can think of plenty of good reasons to take the risk."

Tilly pounced on my claim, "Oh, really? Name just one."

"Jeanine."

Tilly was silent for a heartbeat, then nodded, "Right. Objection withdrawn—on one condition."

"What's your condition?" I had a good guess, but Tilly might as well voice it, herself.

"I'm involved in everything—planning, execution, infiltration, all of it! *And* I get some kind of veto power against anything I decide is truly outrageous."

That was about what I'd expected, but I still raised an

eyebrow and asked, "Does that mean you want in on recruiting, too?"

That drew Drake's interest far more than our short-on-details negotiations had. "Recruiting was an important part of my job with the rebellion. What kind of people are you looking for?"

"Slicers, obviously," I replied. "I'm planning on going back into the Star Stone, but I'm not going in alone if I can help it!"

Drake studied his hands for a few seconds and then looked me in the eye. "You know that you're the only top-level slicer we could convince to join the rebellion, right? Honestly, you're the only top-level slicer we could even *find*!"

"I know, Drake. And, returning honesty for honesty, I went out of my way to make sure you guys found me. I wanted to join the rebellion, otherwise, you'd never have gotten close to me."

"I'm not surprised, Jana. But, if we could only find you because you wanted to be found, how can the two of you have any hope of finding any of those slicers?"

"I know how a slicer thinks and how a slicer hides. I'll find them because I'm one of them." I smiled at Tilly. "And because I'll have a kickass lady thief working with me."

"I'm completely out of my depth in both your fields, but I trust you know what you're doing." Drake flicked on his data pad. "What can I do to help?"

"We'll need money," I said.

"Of course," he replied. "How much?"

I ticked off on my fingers, "We'll need specialized equipment—both for me and, I'm guessing, Tilly—and it will have to be untraceable. We'll need secure, high-speed connections to the net. A center of operations. Transportation, including a spaceship at our beck and call." I realized just how expensive this was going to be and finished lamely, "Um, let's just say we need a lot of money, Drake."

Drake tapped on his pad for a few seconds. "Can I assume you have an anonymous bank account I can send funds to?

Jeanine's finance people assure me they can move money around without leaving a trail. This is my first chance to test their claim."

"Yeah, of course." I called up an account number on my portable pad and showed it to Drake.

He tapped the number in and then looked up. "You never gave me an amount, Jana."

Swallowing hard, I almost blurted the number I had in mind. Afraid to suggest such a large amount, I cut it by a third and said, "Twenty million?"

Drake didn't ask me if I was crazy, which is certainly the first thing *I'd* have done in his place. He just stared at me for a few seconds and then said, "I'm going to bump that up to one hundred million. I don't want you worrying about a tight budget."

One hundred? Million? Jana Ward, I thought, you are definitely out of your financial league!

Aloud, I asked, "Are you sure, Drake? That's a lot of money!"

"Do you remember the part where Jeanine claimed two duchies? Neert is the single most prosperous duchy in the Star Kingdom. Gaunner is somewhere in the middle. Regardless, Jeanine's governments collected a lot more than one hundred million credits just during the time you've been in my office. At least, that's what Jeanine tells me." Drake caught my gaze and held it. "Money isn't important, Jana, and a hundred million isn't even petty cash around here. Jeanine is all that matters to me, and I cannot put a price on her well-being. Okay?"

Tilly and I both nodded our understanding.

Seeing our heads bobbing in unison, Drake smiled, "Spend money like there's no tomorrow. If you run through half of what you've got, alert me and I'll transfer more. Is that clear?"

"As crystal, Drake."

"Anything you need for this job—from high tech equipment to bribes to clothing necessary to fit in wherever you need to go —buy the absolute best you can get."

"Got it!" Tilly and I chimed.

"Good. Was there anything else?"

"A spaceship and a trustworthy pilot? I mean, obviously we can buy a ship, but I don't know anything about them and don't know anything about hiring pilots, either. Any suggestions you can offer would be extremely welcome."

Drake's eyes lost focus for a few seconds, as if he was considering something. With a decisive nod, he looked down at his pad. "I can supply a ship and a pilot."

"Great! Then I guess we should go pack."

He shook his head. "It'll take at least a day for Kelly to get here with the *Rising Star*. You should spend that time planning your next moves."

My eyes flew wide in surprise. "You're letting us use the *Star*? Your *Star*?"

Without a second thought, Drake said, "Yes."

That, far more than the essentially unlimited line of credit, told me just how important our mission was to Drake. That ship used to be his life.

"Don't worry, Drake," Tilly said. "We'll take good care of the *Star*."

"More importantly," I said, "we won't let you down."

ADEQUATELY RUTHLESS

Jeanine

I looked out at the gathered nobles of my duchy. Well, of my *spare* duchy, as Drake has taken to calling Gaunner when we're alone. Forty-six men and women with strained smiles and wary eyes returned my gaze. Many of those faces were haggard, the result of answering my summons on such short notice.

Once I was certain I had everyone's attention, I asked, "Is there anyone who doesn't understand why you're here?"

Once again, my gaze swept over the nobles, this time looking for any hint of confusion over my question. I saw resignation reflected in every face before me, but not one hint of confusion.

I gave a single nod and gave my own weary smile. "Good. I'm glad Olivia didn't leave any titled morons to vex me."

A nervous laugh ran through the nobles as if they felt obligated to laugh at their new ruler's lame joke. Only, I wasn't joking.

"She left no morons, but she left at least two dozen *idiots* who had to be stripped of their titles and, in two cases, executed."

The weak laughter stopped as if I'd flipped a switch. I thought that would get their attention.

"Despite rumors to the contrary, I didn't enjoy performing that execution. Nor did I force Olivia to kill her mentor, Colin. The man did that all by himself."

The heads of a few of the more astute nobles bobbed up and down in unconscious agreement. I noted who they were and mentally moved them to the top of my list for one-on-one meetings. Running one duchy is hard enough—especially when you were raised as a commoner. I was going to need all the help I could get if I had any hope of running two duchies.

"I won't claim my people have rounded up everyone involved in the failed revolt, but the ones captured at Baron Chilton's hunting lodge have proven extremely cooperative. I'm certain watching me execute their leader had something to do with that, but my interrogators have also administered quite a cocktail of truth drugs. I am as confident as it's possible to be that none of you had anything to do with the revolt."

I heard the quiet releasing of unconsciously held breath, followed by the rustle of clothing as the nobles settled into more relaxed postures. The sword they'd felt dangling above them disappeared with my words.

"I summoned you to Gaunner so you could hear those words directly from me. And to tell you that I am *not* planning a purge of the Gaunner nobility. Perhaps Olivia would have done as much to the Neert nobles, had she ever gained power over them. Having finally spent some time with her, I believe she's ruthless enough to do something like that, but only if it was absolutely necessary. Because wiping out a major part of a duchy's government for petty personal reasons is just plain stupid. Whatever else you can say about Olivia, she's not stupid."

Now that everyone was relaxed, I noticed most of the heads nodding in agreement. Good.

"Am I correct in assuming I have been adequately ruthless in putting down this revolt? Note, I said 'adequately' rather than 'needlessly' ruthless."

Every noble nodded, most of them emphatically.

"Furthermore, I think my actions ever since I found myself thrust into the galactic limelight have demonstrated that, like Olivia, I am not stupid."

It was kind of comical watching the rapidly nodding heads make a sudden shift to decisive shaking. Some nobles moved so quickly I wondered if they'd given themselves whiplash.

"I'm glad we're all in agreement on both points. Trust me when I say that I would rather not be forced into further displays of ruthlessness. I'd much rather rule this duchy with intelligence and compassion. And, I'd much rather rule it *with* your enthusiastic cooperation. As such, I'll be scheduling meetings with each of you so we can discuss the needs of your people and of your holding."

I looked down for a moment and replaced my solemn expression with a smile. I'd practiced this smile with Drake until he agreed the smile was welcoming. When I raised my head again, I watched the nobles for their reactions. To my relief, my smile sparked real smiles in return.

"My assistant will contact you soon with your appointment time. Thank you for coming to Gaunner on such short notice. The palace staff will see to your every need while you are here."

With one last smile, I turned and left the room.

Reluctantly, I headed for my next appointment. I had avoided visiting the Holder family for the last several days. Servants and guards took care of their every need while giving the family a chance to come to grips with everything that happened to them during the short revolt.

Reports told me the children were doing fine, which wasn't a surprise. They aren't old enough to know what's going on. Those same reports said Mike and Carol Holder appeared calmer and less fearful than when I'd seen them last—right after Captain Pennington and his crew pulled them from their house.

I had originally hoped the Holders might become friends—people well outside a duchess's normal social circles who could help keep me grounded and aware of the needs of my citizens. Perhaps it's because I wasn't raised among the nobility, but I naïvely thought someone like me could have friends like them without those friends finding themselves dragged into political schemes and machinations. I had been horribly wrong about that and Sasha, the Holder's four-year-old daughter, was targeted for kidnapping as a result.

Mike and Carol were less than thrilled with their newfound fame—especially when it drew unwelcome attention to their children. As a result, they drew back from Drake and me when we met with them the night the revolt was put down. And who could blame them? I sure as hell couldn't. If our situations were reversed, I'm pretty sure I'd have reacted just as they had.

I stopped before the door to the palace apartment I'd provided for them. Looking back at the two guards trailing me, I said, "Please stay out of sight. I'd like to at least pretend everything is normal."

The guards nodded and took up positions along the same wall as the door and five meters down from it on either side. With a nod of thanks to them, I knocked on the door. Carol answered, and I found myself holding my breath, waiting to hear her greeting.

She nodded as if she'd been expecting me, and said, "Lady Jeanine, what a pleasant surprise. Won't you come in?"

I released my breath quietly, smiling to hide my disappointment at her formal greeting. "Only if it's not an imposition, Mrs. Holder."

With a quick smile—all mouth and going nowhere near her eyes—Carol replied, "It is we who impose on you, my lady, by taking you away from your important work. As always, we are at your service."

Well, I guess that told me everything I needed to know about how this conversation was going to go. With a nod of thanks, I entered the apartment.

Unlike my previous visit, both of the children were awake. Young Will smiled at me but stayed in his father's lap. Sasha, on the other hand, hopped up and ran toward me with open arms.

"Duchess Lady Jeanine!" she cried. "Are we gonna play Princess today? Is Mr. Drake with you?"

"Sasha, stop that this instant!" Carol commanded. "Lady Jeanine has more important things to do than play with you."

Watching Sasha's face crumble almost broke my heart. I wanted to go down on one knee, give her a hug, and play Princess with her more than I could say. But, I wasn't going to gainsay her mother—especially after recent events.

I did go down on one knee, though, and said, "I'm afraid your mother is right, I don't have time to play right now. I really wish I did, though, because playing Princess with you is a lot of fun."

Sasha perked up a little at my comment, but she still looked extremely disappointed. If you've never run across a disappointed four-year-old girl, that's a lot of disappointment. "Okay."

Her mother bent over her, and said, "Why don't you take Will and go into the back room for a moment? Mommy and Daddy have to have grown up talk with Lady Jeanine."

"Aw, Mommy!"

Carol stood and crossed her arms, giving her daughter a 'mom look.' At least, that's what the look meant when I'd seen it on vid shows. "You heard me, young lady!"

The little girl wasn't happy with the instructions, but she took her brother's hand and led him into another room. Only after the door shut, did Carol take a seat next to her husband. They both looked at me and waited for me to speak.

Drawing a breath, I said, "I hope you both know that I would give anything in the world to make this whole situation go away. Unfortunately, that's beyond my power."

Mike Holder nodded politely and said, "We understand, my Lady."

I understood the unspoken part of his comment, too. They understood the situation, but that didn't mean they were ready to forgive me for my part in dragging them into it. I waited for a beat, in case either of them wanted to say something more. They didn't.

Unwilling to torture any of us by dragging this out any longer,

I continued, "I'm told the repairs to your home are complete. You can move back in whenever you wish."

The couple merely nodded. To fill the void, I found myself adding, "The overseer told me everything looks exactly the same as before. You'll never know anything even happened."

Carol frowned, "But we *do* know it happened! We know our safe little home, in our safe little neighborhood, was invaded. For God's sake, my lady, men and women were gunned down in my *living room*!"

Closing my eyes, I nodded in sympathy. "I understand."

"No, my lady, you really don't," Carol insisted. "How can I even sit in that room without imagining the horrors that took place there? How can I sleep in that house without wondering if powerful people are targeting my family again? How can I ever feel safe in that house again? How can our neighbors ever feel safe living near us? How can our lives ever be the same again?"

"I don't see how they can be," I admitted. "What can I do to help make you feel safe?"

"Leave us alone, my Lady," Mike replied. "We understand this wasn't your fault. We understand you wish you could make it all go away. *And*, we understand that you can't do that. So, please, just don't do anything."

"I'll abide by your wishes, of course," I said. "Someone will be along shortly to help you move back home." Just before opening the door, I looked back at the couple. "My offer of help remains open for as long as I am the Duchess of Gaunner. If you change your minds, simply call the palace and identify yourselves. You'll be put through to me immediately."

As the apartment door slid shut behind me, I forcibly pushed the Holders from my mind and turned my attention to the myriad duties before me. I had fifty billion other subjects counting on me to rule wisely and could no longer dwell on the misfortunes of one family.

THE CLUB

Jana

Wanting to keep our movements hidden from the Star Stone and knowing Jeanine was a direct line to it, Tilly and I slipped unnoticed from the Gaunner Palace the day after our meeting with Drake. And I mean *literally* unnoticed—not even Drake knew we were gone. The ease of our escape disturbed us so badly we left a detailed description of the vulnerabilities we exploited and implored Drake and Captain Reel to fix them.

Undiscovered by any of the guards, Tilly had mapped out the hidden passages Colin used when he abducted Jeanine and Olivia. She discovered three unguarded routes that led from the residence wing to exits beyond the wall surrounding the palace. Each route was circuitous and passed through areas where guards patrolled, but any reasonably competent kidnapper or assassin could have slipped in and out of the Palace using one of them. For a thief of Tilly's caliber—even hampered by her less-than-nimble slicer companion—it was no trouble at all.

Of course, the head of Palace Security, Captain Reel, knows his job. He was aware of the holes in his defenses. Unfortunately, he was also shorthanded after the recent purge of disloyal men among his guard ranks. In time, he'd build the guard back to their full strength. Until then, he was forced to plug gaps with security cams and sensors. Those, of course, were linked into the Palace network—and that made them vulnerable to *my* particular set of skills. I left a detailed list of the weaknesses in their network security, along with the names of a couple of reputable specialists they should hire.

There was much more to our departure plan than simply getting out of the Palace—including hacking the planet's subspace relay so I could tell Kelly to meet us with the *Rising Star* in a different star system, having Tilly acquire false identifications for us, and me arranging a ride off-planet.

We rented a cabin on a tramp freighter willing to carry passengers and, as I record this, are already a day out from Gaunner. It's been a peaceful trip, too, other than us having to deflect a few come-ons from some of the men in the crew. No amount of makeup can make Tilly unattractive and, well, I'm a woman, which is apparently all some men look for during an interstellar voyage.

"Don't put yourself down like that, Jana!" Tilly insisted.

Sigh. Guess who heard me dictate that last bit into my journal?

"Are you saying I'm *not* a woman, Tilly?"

My friend vented her own sigh, "You're quite aware of what I mean. You're no less attractive than I am!"

"Said the woman who never has to buy her own drink at a club and has her pick of the best-looking dance partners. And partners of a more intimate nature, including the crown prince, himself." In the driest tone I could manage, I continued, "But, yeah, I'm just as attractive as you."

Tilly glared at me, apparently serious in her delusions concerning my beauty, and then made a sudden change of tack. "How many guys have introduced you to their mother?"

"What?"

"Just answer the question."

Tilly's eyes burned with an emotion I couldn't identify, so I humored her. "Three. Why?"

"None of the guys I've hooked up with have ever introduced me to their mother. Not one." Tilly's shoulders sagged as she blew out her breath. "I lived with William for a month, just two doors down from his parents' suite, but I've never met Queen Charlotte."

I waved this off. "Be happy for it, Tilly. Meeting a guy's mother isn't as much fun as you obviously think it is. I end up walking on eggshells because I know she's watching me like a hawk and judging my every word and action."

"Yes, Jana, the guy's mother is judging you because she knows her son thinks he might want to spend the rest of his life with you. Whether the guy knows it or not, he's watching his mother for signals of acceptance or rejection. Did any of them ever break up with you shortly after you met his mother?"

"One. I wasn't surprised though."

"Because you picked up his mother's signals, too. Those other mothers though—I'll bet they were disappointed when things didn't work out between you and their son."

"So? I don't see where you're going with this."

"Jana, you're take-home-to-mother beautiful. You're plan-for-a-life-together gorgeous. You're bear-my-children desirable. You're what smart, caring guys *really* want." Tilly leaned her head back against the bulkhead and closed her eyes. "I, on the other hand, am just a notch in a bedpost. No guy worth having will take me home to meet his mother because every guy worth having wants you."

I was certain Tilly was just kidding around and almost dismissed her rant with a flippant remark. Then, a tear spilled out of the corner of her eye and the words froze in my throat.

I pulled her into a hug. In my most soothing tones, I whispered, "Hey, now, don't cry! There are plenty of guys in the galaxy who would love to take you home to meet their mothers. You just haven't met any of them yet."

"But why not? I go out a lot. I meet plenty of guys. Why hasn't just *one* of them been interested in me in *that* way?"

I didn't think this was the time to go into the difference between regular guys and kinds of guys who traveled in the same circles Tilly did. Sure, she needs to mingle with that crowd for professional reasons, but at that rarified level of society every woman was an exotic beauty—either naturally, like Tilly, or through careful sculpting like...well, like a lot of the Beautiful People who dominate the society news sites. In those circles, would a guy take Tilly home to meet his mother if he could take an equally beautiful baroness home, instead?

Even though I had a huge to-do list, I mentally added helping Tilly find a guy worthy of her to the list. I'd have to be careful, since I doubt Tilly would welcome my help any more than I would if I was in her place. If I was careful, though, I was pretty sure I could keep this off her sensor screens.

Neither of us said anything about Tilly's revelation after that, but it made our already-tight friendship even tighter. We both understood each other just a little bit better and our minds seemed just a tad more in sync.

Two days later, we docked at a way station in a system so barren no one had even bothered naming the star. Kelly and the *Rising Star*—now flying under the name *Dragonstar*—were waiting for us. Two hours after our transport docked, we had everything aboard the *Dragonstar*. Traffic was so light we received an immediate departure clearance. Kelly jumped us a few light minutes outside of the system, leaving a false departure vector. Chances were no one was watching us, but we all agreed it was better to play it safe.

When we were far from any other human, Kelly said, "Drake's message was pretty mysterious, and your follow up just deepened the mystery. It's time for you to tell me what's going on."

"Absolutely," I agreed, "but why don't you plot a course to Xapreathea, first."

Kelly stared at me for a few seconds, nodded, and began working with the nav system. Tilly, on the other hand, was more vocal.

"We're going to the capital of the Star Kingdom?"

"Yes."

"Home to our most dangerous enemy, Queen Charlotte?"

"Who, by your own admission, doesn't know you," I replied, "and definitely doesn't know me."

"And home to our second most dangerous enemy, Princess Olivia, who most certainly *does* know me!"

"But not me," I countered.

Tilly visibly took control of herself and then, in a calmer voice, asked, "I'm sure you have a good reason for going to Xapreathea, Jana. Why don't you share it with Kelly and me, so we'll all understand why we're flying into the dragon's mouth?"

"I'm pretty sure the best slicer in the galaxy lives there. We're going to need his or her help when we take on the Star Stone."

"That's a lot of risk for something you're only *pretty* sure about."

I shrugged. "It's the best I can do, Tilly, but I really do think we need this slicer's help."

"If you say so…" Tilly looked thoughtful for a minute. "Wait a minute, I thought Protosloth lived on the planet Zeenus."

I couldn't help laughing, "That guy isn't the best slicer in the galaxy. I wouldn't even put him in the top two hundred."

"But he's the one all the newsies quote when they have a big slicing story," Tilly protested.

"Yeah, because the newsies could *find* him. He's just smart enough to realize he can line his pockets using the publicity he gets from being the most quoted slicer in the galaxy. The rest of us keep an eye on him and make sure he doesn't do anything stupid, but we're more than willing to let him color the public's perception of the slicer community."

"Okay. Then, who is the best slicer in the galaxy?"

"The Fox."

"Who's the Fox?"

"I have no idea," I replied, "but we're going to find out."

Tilly insisted on coming with me to meet the Fox even though it was an entirely virtual meeting. I could have refused, but after our terrifying high-rise escape from police the last time we were on Xapreathea, I felt as if I owed it to Tilly to give her a good look at *my* world. In preparation, I crafted an avatar for her and taught her basic slicer manners and protocols. She found the latter fascinating and the former, well...

We connected to the *Star's* onboard network and my avatar appeared next to Tilly's default one. I wore my usual avatar—a stylized primitive woman, someone whose look matched my name, Dreamwalker. I drew bits and pieces from the lore and history of a hundred different planets, ensuring no one could determine my home world just by my avatar's appearance. I also took a cue from virtual games and added a bare midriff, a push-up halter that showed lots of cleavage, and a slit skirt that showed lots of thigh.

"Damn, Jana, you look hot in that avatar!" Tilly declared. "I bet all the boy slicers drool over you."

"Most of the boy slicers think I'm a boy, too," I replied.

"Say what? Why would they think that?"

"Because a lot of guys wear female avatars, and their avatars are usually straight from sex-fantasy central casting. Mine is kind of subdued in comparison, the kind of thing a high-end slicer would craft once he got past his porn star phase."

"Uh, why do a lot of guys wear hot-girl avatars? Are they trying to attract another guy or something?"

"I think most of the male slicers are interested in women, but I've got no idea why men wear female avatars. They just do."

"It never occurred to you to ask one of them?" Tilly asked.

"That would be a dead giveaway that *I'm* a woman."

"And that would be bad, because...?"

"Because it's knowledge about my true identity. It's not much knowledge, but you never know what other slicers already know about you. If any of them ever figures out who I really am, they'll turn me into their thrall."

"Their what?"

"Slave."

"You're kidding, right?"

"I'm deadly serious. Trust me on this."

"Wow, and I thought *thieves* were paranoid!" Tilly looked thoughtful for a moment, then said, "If your identity is so secret, how come so many people know who you are?"

"Most of the people who know *who* I am do not know *what* I am. But I also have the protection of one of the most powerful women in the galaxy—Jeanine—so I don't have to be quite as secretive as many of my fellow slicers." I flashed a conspiratorial smile at her, "Besides, how do you know 'Jana Ward' is my true name?"

Tilly's default avatar actually looked hurt that I might not have given her my birth name, so I added, "I was just kidding, Tilly. I gave you my real name when we met. But, when we're in the net, you must *always* refer to me as Dreamwalker. And never, ever use pronouns that include a sexual identification—scrub things like 'Jana' or 'she' or 'he' from your vocabulary the second you enter the net."

"Maybe I'll just keep my mouth shut and watch the mistress in action," Tilly said. "Enough of this, though. Let me see my avatar!"

"Okay, but remember what I said about guys and their avatars," I warned. "Especially guys who are new to the net."

Tilly's default avatar got a suspicious look on its face. "What did you do, Ja- um, Dreamwalker?"

I deployed Tilly's new avatar over the default one. "See for yourself."

Honestly, I was quite proud of my work on the avatar. It was an exaggeratedly sexualized woman, with voluptuous curves, enormous breasts, long, curly, blonde hair, and barely enough clothes to cover the essentials.

"You can*not* be serious!" Tilly exclaimed. "This avatar is ridiculous!"

"That's the idea," I replied. "Anyone competent who sees it will assume you're a newb, a guy, and not worth their trouble to mess with. You might get hit on by some other newbs, but I'm confident you can handle those."

Tilly sighed. "Fine. We're in your world now, so I'll defer to your judgment. Once I get the hang of the net, though, I want a better avatar!"

"You can have a better one as soon as you can craft it, yourself. Until then, you're stuck with that one."

"Have you picked out an equally embarrassing name for me? Titanic Tits, or something even worse?"

"You can pick your own name, but I reserve the right to veto it if I think it's too revealing."

Tilly gestured to her avatar's mostly naked form, "You gave me *this* and you're concerned about revealing stuff?"

"Stuff about who you really are, Tilly. So, avoid any name that refers to thieves, thievery, burglary, or anything like that."

She thought for a while, then asked, "How about the Pick? *I* know I'm referring to picking locks, but it's generic enough that it won't be obvious to others."

I grinned, "It's great, as long as you don't mind other slicers making jokes about picking your nose."

"Blech," she shuddered. "Okay, how about...um...how about Smoke? As a thief, I can go just about anywhere and I'm impossible to catch."

"Better. You'll get jokes about being smoking hot, and slicers will offer to 'smoke' you, but that's about it."

"Are slicers really that juvenile?"

"The ones who are juveniles are," I replied. "And a lot of the more experienced slicers will make those jokes, too. I don't know if it's just a guy thing or if they're using the jokes to further hide their true identity, but don't expect a lot of sophisticated humor from the slicer community."

"Got it. I can handle the jokes, so I'm going with Smoke. Assuming Dreamwalker approves."

"It's fine by me, Smoke."

"Great! Let's go find the Fox."

"We'll never find the Fox, just like the Fox could never find me."

"Then, what's the point of this whole exercise? If we can't find the Fox, why—"

"I can't find him—or her—but I can arrange a meeting at The Club."

"The Fox would meet us in the real world? That seems like a risky proposition for a paranoid slicer."

"The Club isn't in the real world, Smoke. It's a virtual location that's modeled after real-world clubs, down to the bar, the dance floor, loud music, and private rooms. It's the one place in the net where big-name slicers can meet without fear of discovery."

"Isn't it overrun with star-struck newbs looking to meet their slicer heroes?"

"Nope. The Club is one of the best-secured sites in the net. It takes real skill just to find it, and a lot more skill to get inside. By the time a slicer actually joins The Club, they're usually beyond hero-worship. There's still plenty of respect shown to the best of the best, but that's about it."

"How am I going to get in?"

"I'll bring you as a guest."

"The mighty Dreamwalker has spoken. Smoke will obey. How do we send a message to the Fox?"

"We've all got message drops at The Club. I sent a meeting request to the Fox as soon as I entered the *Star's* net. By the way, remind me to thank Drake for adding a subspace communicator to the *Star* next time we see him."

"When can we expect an answer?"

"It depends on how often the Fox checks his message drop."

The Fox replied within minutes and proposed an immediate meeting. It's what I'd have done in the Fox's place. Why give a potential opponent more time to prepare for your arrival than necessary?

I showed Smoke how to hitch onto my avatar and then we headed for The Club. We flowed past the crowd of insider wannabes, those who had found The Club but couldn't get inside. We slid through the security wall and entered The Club.

I think my reception startled Smoke. Many of the avatars bowed as I passed. Others simply offered respectful nods. All of them cleared a path to my table.

"Good God, Dreamwalker," Smoke hissed, "you really *are* slicer royalty!"

I just smiled and settled in to wait for the Fox.

It wasn't a long wait. Within seconds, a serving bot appeared at our table with two drinks.

"Compliments of the gentleman at table one," the bot announced as it placed two filled shot glasses on the table.

Smoke, obviously curious about the possible effects of virtual alcohol, reached for the glass before her. Catching her hand in mine, I invoked one of my own bots. A full shot glass appeared on the serving bot's drink tray. "Give that drink to the gentleman at table one, offer my compliments in return, and invite him to join us."

As the bot left us, Smoke gently pulled her hand free from mine and asked, "Why don't you want me to try the drink? It's just an image in the net—it can't be poisoned, right?"

"No—at least, not the way you're thinking. Nothing in the net can harm your physical body. It *could* install a tracer or a logger in your avatar, though, which would let Fox track our avatars back to our real-world location or send him a record of everything we do in the net."

Smoke nodded her understanding. "So, The Club is just like a real club—you never accept anything from someone you don't know extremely well."

"It's not that bad. I made sure your avatar had my best detection and destruction software installed in it. Only a few slicers in the galaxy are good enough that they might get something past the filters. Fox is at the top of that list." I ran a quick scan of slicers currently in The Club. "None of the others are here, so you should be fine if anyone else offers you anything."

Smoke made a face. "I think I'll pass. Besides, what's the point of a drink that doesn't have any effect on you?"

"Oh, it'll have an effect, just not the one you're expecting."

"Yeah? How?"

"Most of the drinks invoke a bot that sends signals straight to your brain's pleasure center. The weakest ones will give you a mild euphoria. The strongest ones... Let's just say you want to work your way up the drink list before you even think about trying a Screaming Orgasm."

"It's that good?"

As if in answer, two ecstatic cries rose above the crowd noise. At the same time, the mob between us and table one parted. A handsome male avatar strode out of the crowd and toward our table. He was tall and dressed impeccably in a form-fitting suit. Warm blue eyes regarded us from below neatly trimmed black hair and above a mouth that quirked up on the left side, giving the impression of a man who found the world around him amusing in ways you'd never quite understand. He held the drink I'd sent in his right hand.

"Wow," Smoke whispered, "now *that* is a man who can give me a screaming orgasm any time he wants."

"First, he can hear you," I said. "Second, you've just given away something about yourself—specifically, your sexual preferences. Third, remember that Fox designed that avatar for this effect. Chances are, Fox looks nothing like that."

Keeping my eyes on the table, I whispered, "Isn't that right, Fox?"

Laughter bubbled up from the middle of our table and a deep baritone said, "Indeed, Dreamwalker. Are you going to introduce me to your charmingly voluptuous friend?"

Smoke looked at the table and covered her face with her hands, obviously embarrassed. "God, let me die now."

"That's no way to act," Fox said, sliding into the chair across from me. "I, for one, found your comment refreshingly open and honest. You find so little of that here in The Club."

Waving a hand in Smoke's direction, I said, "This is Smoke. As you might've guessed, Smoke has never been to The Club before."

Fox reached across the table and gently pried Smoke's right hand from her face and kissed it. "I am charmed, Smoke, to make your acquaintance. I might add, you have good taste in friends."

Fox and I always got along well. We mostly knew each other from The Club, where we respected each other's privacy and each other's skills. It helped that Fox had a sterling reputation among slicers and, as best I knew, only accepted jobs that met his high ethical standards. High for a slicer that is.

Fox gestured to the glasses before Smoke and me. "You haven't touched your drinks."

I motioned to the glass in Fox's hand. "Nor have you."

"Would it help if I swore to you that I put nothing in those drinks?" he asked.

"About as much as it would help if I swore I put nothing in your drink," I replied.

Fox grinned, "Do you so swear?"

Returning his grin, I said, "I swear I put nothing in your drink."

To my surprise, Fox drained the glass in a single gulp. A slow, satisfied smile spread across his avatar's mouth. "That *is* good! Is it your own creation?"

"Yes. Would you like a copy of the bot?"

"I'm not feeling quite that trusting, yet," Fox replied. "However, I also swear that I put nothing in your drinks."

I knew this was coming, but I wasn't particularly happy about it. Fox had displayed trust, which would be vital if we were going to work together. But, I'm not sure I could slip anything past his filters. Meanwhile, I remain positive he could slip something past mine.

The question was, did I trust Fox?

No, that wasn't the question. The real question was, did I have any other choice but to trust Fox?

I didn't.

Raising the glass, I said, "To trust."

Then, I also drained the glass in a single gulp. Smoke followed my lead, and we both smiled at the pleasant feeling spread through us.

"Excellent, Fox—not that I expected anything less from you."

"I'll happily match your offer and give you a copy of the bot that created the drink."

"Perhaps I'll accept it sometime in the future. If we end up working together, I'll definitely accept it."

Fox raised one immaculate eyebrow, "Before we do the job?"

Considering what I was going to ask Fox to do, I thought that was a pretty reasonable request. "Yes, before the job."

Fox's other eyebrows rose to join the first. "This job must be truly important to you."

Nodding, I said, "It's important to me, to you, to Smoke, and...oh...everyone else in the Star Kingdom."

"Now you have me *really* curious, Dreamwalker. Please, share the details."

"May I deploy a privacy shield, Fox?"

"By all means, please do. May I add my shield to yours?"

"Of course."

Fox and I concentrated and two shimmering bubbles

surrounded my table. All sound from The Club cut off as if someone had flipped the switch.

Waving a hand, I said, "Opaque."

My bubble turned white, blocking anyone outside from seeing inside. Fox studied this new development briefly and then nodded in satisfaction.

I had spent days considering what I would say to Fox. None of my ideas were particularly satisfying. In the end, I decided to go for direct simplicity.

"I need the best slicer in the galaxy for a very dangerous job. Specifically, I want to raid the Star Stone's database—or whatever the hell that crystal abomination uses for data storage—so we can figure out how to remove its bots from everyone who's been Recognized. After that, I want to steal it and drop the damned thing in the nearest star."

Fox regarded me for a few seconds—that's a *really* long time in the network—before saying, "I can't tell if you're serious or seriously insane."

"Believe me, I understand your reaction," I replied, "but, I am absolutely serious. I've already interfaced with the Star Stone and, after what I learned, consider it the single greatest threat to humanity in the galaxy."

Fox grimaced, "See? That sounds crazy!"

Smoke glared at Fox, "Dreamwalker is telling the truth, and you should listen."

Fox glanced at Smoke. "Well, Dreamwalker, you've obviously convinced someone that you're not crazy. Convince me."

I could only think of two ways to convince Fox. The easiest, but least likely to succeed, was to simply tell him the full story of my trip inside the Star Stone. The problem is, I'd have to give away far too many details about myself as part of the telling. After hearing it, I doubted it would take Fox more than a couple of hours to figure out my real identity. Was I ready to have the galaxy's best slicer know everything about me?

Conversely, the best way to convince Fox would be to take

him into the Star Stone. He would definitely believe me after that, but could I teach him how to escape the Star Stone before we ever entered it? How could I teach him to find his soul's connection to his body without having the actual connection there to find? If I waited until we were inside the Star Stone to teach him, I'd also be telling the damned Star Stone exactly how I got away from it. Could it use that information to block us from getting away again? I had no idea, but I didn't like the idea of revealing that secret to the Star Stone.

In the end, it all came down to who I was willing to put at risk to get Fox's help—me or him. And, considered from that point of view, there was only one choice.

I met Fox's gaze and said, "My true identity is Jana Ward."

YOU TOOK A HUGE RISK

Tilly

Fox and I looked at Jana or Dreamwalker or whoever the hell she was right now in absolute stupefaction. I found my voice first.

"Why did you waste all of that time telling me how to avoid giving away my identity or your identity, if you were just going to blurt it out in casual conversation?" I demanded.

"I had to do it, Smoke," Jana replied. "It's the only way to convince Fox I'm serious."

"A smart woman like you couldn't think of a different way to do that?" I rolled my eyes for added effect. "And, worse, haven't you gone and...thrallified...yourself to Fox?"

Jana offered a gentle smile, "Enthralled."

"Don't try to distract me with sex!" I insisted. "Fox's avatar is hot and all, but you're the one who told me avatars usually don't look like their owners."

Jana shook her head, "I'm not talking about sex and I'm not trying to distract you. When someone makes you their thrall, you become enthralled."

"Okay, fine, you're enthralled. But—"

"I'm not going to make Dreamwalker my thrall," Fox interrupted, his tone mild. "I have no interest in virtual slavery."

Even though no one has to breathe in the virtual world, I saw Jana release a held breath. Then, she said, "I didn't think you did, Fox, but I couldn't be sure."

"You took a huge risk, Dreamwalker," he replied. "Are you sure there wasn't another way to convince me to pay attention?"

"I could've taken you with me to infiltrate the Star Stone. You'd have gone along, too, out of curiosity and absolutely certain you could pull out at any time." Jana stared hard into Fox's eyes. "By the time you learned otherwise, I might not have been able to get you out. And I'm not willing to risk your life to get your help."

I looked back and forth between Fox and Jana. The two slicers were obviously having a 'moment' but I interrupted, anyway. "You could've just told him the story. I'm pretty sure your slicing of the Star Stone would sound authentic enough to convince him."

Jana glanced my way, "Maybe, but my way was faster. After hearing the story, Fox would have figured out who I am pretty quickly. I just cut out a step."

I rolled my eyes again, "And put your life in his hands."

"Which worked out fine, Smoke. You heard Fox—he's not going to make me his thrall."

"Exactly," Fox added.

"I cannot believe what I'm hearing!" I cried. "Are both of you seriously deluded? In my world, just because somebody says they won't do something doesn't mean they won't do it. I can't believe a bunch of slicers who have words like 'thrall' in their day-to-day vocabulary never, ever break their word."

Jana shrugged, "I believe him. Or her. Whichever."

We both looked at Fox, waiting to see if he would clarify on that. He didn't.

"You say you have a story to tell, Dreamwalker?" he asked.

If Jana—no, Dreamwalker. I'd better stay in the habit of using that name when we're inside the net. Anyway, if Fox's change of subject disappointed Dreamwalker, she hid it well.

"I assume you heard about the recent kidnapping of Princess Olivia and Lady Jeanine?" she asked. At Fox's nod, Dreamwalker continued, "I sliced the Star Stone hoping it would help me find Jeanine. It did, but I learned a lot more than where my Duchess was being held—and what I learned terrifies me."

Dreamwalker went into more detail telling the story to Fox than she had when she told me. Part of that is because she went into technical details that I assume Fox understood, but might as well have been a foreign language from my point of view. But part of it was because she didn't try to make things sound safer and easier than they actually were. I assume she gave me the abridged version so I wouldn't worry. Well, it sure as hell worried me, now.

When Dreamwalker finally finished her tale, she said, "That's it, Fox—the whole story."

He leaned back in his chair and looked hard at Dreamwalker. "Well you're right about one thing—I would have been able to track down your true identity after hearing that story."

I gave him the evil eye—which probably didn't work worth a damn with this avatar—and snarled, "That's all you have to say? Dreamwalker bares her soul, not to mention her true identity, to you and all you can think of is to brag how you could have tracked her down?"

Fox turned an amused smile on me. "Would you prefer if I'd questioned her sanity?"

"No, you asshole, I prefer you to ask what you can do to help," I declared. "At the very least, you could tell us what we have to do to convince you to help."

Dreamwalker laid a hand on my shoulder, "That's enough, Smoke. Getting Fox's help was a long shot and, in all honesty, my story is hard to believe."

"I haven't said that I won't help," Fox interjected in a mild tone of voice. "I've just been trying to figure out a good test to see how determined the two of you are."

Dreamwalker raised one eyebrow, "And?"

"I think I've come up with something sufficiently challenging for you. You've told me your true identity. I haven't investigated it yet, but I don't doubt it will check out. If you're really serious and you're really determined and you're not insane, maybe you can track down *my* true identity. If you do, I'll help you."

"Oh, is that all?" My voice fairly dripped with sarcasm.

"Yes, that's all. If you know anything about Dreamwalker, you should know she is one of a handful of people in the galaxy who has any chance of succeeding."

Dreamwalker nodded, "I accept, of course."

With a nod, Fox stood, "If there's nothing else, I'll leave you to get started."

Dreamwalker waved her hand and her opaque bubble vanished. Fox waved his hand and his transparent bubble also vanished. Without another word, he turned and walked back into the crowd.

The moment Fox disappeared into the crowd, Dreamwalker grabbed me by the hand and pulled me to my feet. We headed for the exit at a fast walk. As when we entered, the crowd parted before us and we were out of The Club in just a few seconds.

Dreamwalker did something—shifted planes or transferred to a different network or something, it's totally beyond me—and suddenly, we were alone inside a small, bare room.

Stepping back for me, Dreamwalker said, "Stand still while I scan you for tracers, loggers, viruses, or anything else that could follow us back to our bodies."

I did as instructed and Dreamwalker's eyes lost focus. She walked around me, running her gaze up and down my avatar. Finally, she stopped and gave a single nod.

"You're clean. I didn't think anyone in The Club put anything on you—I installed copies of my best protective bots in your avatar—but better safe than sorry."

"What about you?" I asked. "If you tell me what to look for, I can try scanning you."

"No need. I've already checked myself." Dreamwalker took my hand again, "Ready to get back to your body?"

"And give up this cartoonish, walking advertisement for sex you gave me as an avatar?" I asked. "Hell. Yes."

Dreamwalker laughed and, the next thing I knew, my consciousness was back inside my body. Or, I guess it's my focus or attention that was back inside my body. At least, that's how Jana explains it. I'm just a thief and have no idea what she's talking about once she gets technical. Her distinction is reasonable, though, since the true danger of the Star Stone was that it *did* pull her consciousness into it. The net just seems like a real world, but it's only in our minds. That's probably confusing as hell, which is about what you should expect since the whole concept is completely beyond me.

Regardless, I was happy to see my own body and not that ridiculous avatar.

As Jana and I sat up, I said, "You're making me a new avatar before I go back into the net. I want something classy, like your avatar."

Jana grinned at me, "Maybe, since you did behave yourself and didn't do anything to give away our identities."

"Unlike a certain superstar slicer I could name," I growled.

"It was necessary."

"What was necessary?" Kelly asked, looking up from her data pad.

Jana motioned for me to answer the question. "You tell her, Tilly. I've got to prepare for our search."

"Search?" Kelly asked. "Do I even want to know how this went?"

"No, and yes," I replied. At Kelly's quizzical expression, I added, "It's complicated."

"As Drake would say, uncomplicate it for me. Now."

By the time I finished my explanations and answered Kelly's questions to the best of my ability—if not to her satisfaction—Jana was concentrating deeply on...whatever it was she was concentrating deeply on. I'm going to go out on a limb and guess it had something to do with slicing and tracking down Fox and other stuff I don't understand."

Glancing at Jana, Kelly asked, "Did she say if she wanted me to change course?"

I was shrugging when, to my considerable surprise, Jana responded, "No, stay on course to Xapreathea."

Jana never looked up. She gave no indication that she had been listening to anything we were saying. And, by the time Kelly and I looked Jana's way, her attention was once again focused on her work. Kelly and I looked back at each other and shrugged.

"I'm going to go check on the *Star's* systems," Kelly said, heading toward the pilot's compartment.

"Is there anything I can do?" I asked.

Without looking back, Kelly said, "Make dinner. I'm starving."

"Aye aye, Captain Cutthroat!"

Kelly stopped and slowly turned around. "Did Jeanine tell you about the nickname she gave me? I'd gotten the idea the two of you aren't that close."

"We're not, though I think the potential is there. Right now, I'd say we're sort of friendly acquaintances."

"Jeanine isn't the type to tell personal stories like that to acquaintances," Kelly said.

"She's not," I agreed. "But she and Jana have become very close. As have Jana and I. So—"

Without looking up, Jana interjected, "I told her, Kelly. Jeanine didn't mind."

"That's good enough for me," Kelly said. Without another word, she turned and headed for the pilot's compartment.

I headed into the galley and started working on dinner. As I cooked, my mind whirled with questions. What was Fox's true identity? Could he be trusted? Would he really help us if Jana tracked him down? Could Jana track him down? Could he figure out my identity from Jana's identity? If he could, what would he do with that information? Threaten to tell the police I'm a thief unless I—what? Stole for him? Paid him large sums of money? Provided kinky sexual favors? And, was he anywhere near as gorgeous as his avatar?

My imagination was just drifting into a combination of those last two questions when Jana came into the galley and interrupted me. "That smells great! I hadn't realized how hungry I was until I smelled the food."

"It's an old family recipe I learned from my great grandmother's private chef."

Jana shook her head in wonder, "The nobility really do live different lives than the rest of us. My old family recipes get passed down by parents, not private chefs."

"Just make sure you include me in that 'rest of us' you're talking about," I said. "I only travel in high social circles for business."

"Uh huh," Jana said, her tone skeptical. "What business led to you hooking up with Prince William?"

"So," I said, changing the subject, "do you think you can find Fox?"

Jana gave me a knowing look, but didn't call me on my change of subject. "Yes."

"You sound pretty positive, Jana. What do you know that I don't know?" I cringed at my silly question. "Ignore that. It would take forever for you to tell me all the stuff you know that I don't know. And I still wouldn't understand most of it even after you told it to me. Let me rephrase the question. What do you know about finding Fox that you haven't told me?"

"A lot," Jana grinned. "Mostly, I know I planted a tracer on Fox and he hasn't discovered it yet. Or, he's discovered it but is leaving it in place because he wants us to find him."

"But, you swore you didn't do anything like that!" I exclaimed. Shaking my head in mock disapproval, I said, "It pains me to learn that you're just as dishonest as I am."

"I make my living breaking into secured networks and taking data from its rightful owners," Jana said in a dry tone. "What part of that sounds honest to you?"

"It's not what you do, it's why you do it that makes the difference. I steal for personal profit. You slice for idealistic reasons. That makes you honest, in a slightly tarnished way." Afraid we were going to wander away from my original question, I returned to it. "And, that's why I'm surprised that you lied to Fox about putting something in his drink."

Jana shook her head, "I didn't lie. There wasn't anything in his drink."

I furrowed my brow in puzzlement. "Then how did you plant a tracer on him?"

Jana grinned, "It was on the glass. When he picked up the glass, the tracer attached itself to him."

"Ingenious! I bet he never thought of that, Jana!"

"Oh, he thought of it, Tilly. The glasses he sent us had tracers on them. Only, I neutralized them after we left The Club."

"Well, damn, aren't you slicers a sneaky bunch! You're hardly any different than a pack of thieves."

"Thanks," Jana said, "I think."

"How long do you think it will take to track him down after we land on Xapreathea?"

"If he's actually on Xapreathea—which I'm almost positive he is—I should be able to find him in a couple of days." Jana turned thoughtful for a moment. "That's assuming he doesn't go to ground, change his identity, move to another planet, or do any of the other things slicers do when they think someone is getting too close to their true identity."

"How much longer will it take to find him if he does any of that stuff?" I asked.

Jana shook her head, "If he runs, I'll never find him."

I didn't like the sound of that. "Then let's pray he doesn't run!"

SOMETHING DISTURBING
Olivia

I finished my morning retch, cleaned up, and got dressed. Morning sickness did not become me. I doubt it suits any woman. Some of my friends among the nobility would finish that sentence by decrying that something so common should affect women of their rank. Thank God I'm not one of those shallow twits who believe nature should change itself to suit their image of themselves. On the other hand, if biology suddenly gave the Princess of the realm a pass on morning sickness, I would not complain.

I emerged from our sleeping chambers to find a servant waiting with William. My husband ignored the attractive young woman in the way only those born into wealth can. I doubt William gave her any more thought than he would a pretty painting he saw every day.

After giving William a quick good morning kiss, I turned toward the servant. "Yes, Marie?"

Marie dipped a quick curtsy. "Her Majesty, Queen Charlotte has called for you, Your Highness. May I escort you to the subspace communications chamber?"

"Thank you, Marie. Please, lead on."

As Marie and I entered the hallway, William's assistant arrived at the door. He bowed and murmured, "Your Highness."

I nodded and said, "William awaits within, Peter. You may enter."

I barely noticed the door opening and closing behind me as my mind began sifting possible reasons behind Mother's call. She and King Bernard were making a Royal Progress through one of the duchies. I should probably know which one—especially since they'd have dragged William and me along if I hadn't used my morning sickness and the stress of the recent kidnapping to beg off from the trip—but I couldn't find it in myself to care.

A moment later, Marie opened the door to the subspace communications chamber. "Shall I wait in case you need me, Your Highness?"

"That won't be necessary, Marie. I'm sure you have too much work to waste time being at my beck and call."

My father always taught me to respect those who made our lives easier. He taught me that showing respect to servants made them feel appreciated and encouraged loyalty from them. Marie's warm smile, given in response to my words, once again proved the wisdom of my father's advice.

"As you wish, Your Highness. Should you need me, press the call button and I will return immediately." She curtsied again and pulled the door to the chamber closed.

Matilda, Mother's assistant, nodded from the screen and said, "I'll inform Her Majesty you're here."

A moment later, my mother-in-law appeared and offered me a maternal smile. "I'm sorry to rouse you so early, my dear, considering your condition. Unfortunately, it's late evening here on Ontarie and I'm quite worn out from all the festivities we've attended."

I offered a small smile. "That's all right, Mother. My stomach has already offered up its morning sacrifice for the baby. I dearly hope the child doesn't demand another."

Mother laughed, "Have I told you how much I love having

such a droll daughter-in-law? In all seriousness, how are you doing, dear?"

"As well as can be expected, for someone who was forced to kill her mentor." I blinked rapidly against the tears that welled up. "William has been most attentive and caring, and not just because of the pregnancy. I do believe that planning and leading my rescue has done wonders for his attitude and self-confidence."

Mother gave a smile maternal pride, "I, too, noticed a change in my son. Perhaps Bernard and I should have let William do something truly dangerous years ago. Then again, had we done so, I might not have you as a daughter-in-law."

"Thank you, Mother. I love you as well. But, I know this isn't why you called."

"You're quite right, Olivia. I've received the final report concerning the events surrounding your abduction."

My eyebrows rose in surprise. "William and I told you everything, Mother. What was there to investigate?"

"Relax, dear, the investigation had nothing to do with you or William. Or Jeanine and Drake, for that matter. No, the investigation centered around the slicer who apparently entered the Star Stone successfully and, more surprisingly, exited safely." Mother's brow furrowed, "I can't say why, exactly, but my feelings of unease concerning this slicer have grown since we discussed them."

I found myself nodding, "I've noticed the same thing, Mother—at least, when I'm not suffering from morning sickness."

"Well, if both of us find something...disturbing...about this slicer, then I was correct to order an investigation. I could believe one of us was unreasonably concerned, but *both* of us?" Mother shook her head, "Absolutely not."

"What did your investigators discover?"

Mother frowned, "Not as much as you might expect. For example, they started with the security vids from the car I sent to the Neert Palace on Xapreathea. The driver gave a ride to two young women whom he described as a beautiful brunette and an attractive, but unassuming, blonde."

"That's not a very useful description, but at least you have the security vids."

Mother shook her head. "Alas, we do not. Something interfered with the security cam while those two young women were in the car. The cam recorded nothing but static. The security cams at the spaceport where the experimental ship is kept were better—but not where the two young women were concerned. They appear as nothing but blobs of static."

"How is that possible, Mother?"

"The man in charge of the investigation tells me there are highly classified devices that can do that. He would have sworn only the Royal military and the Royal Intelligence Agency had access to them. Upon learning differently he ordered an investigation into the security breach and found nothing." Mother met my gaze through the subspace communications screen. "Whoever stole the designs for that device is, in the words of my investigator, supremely talented and extraordinarily dangerous."

"What about the ship's pilot? He spent over twenty hours with them. Surely, he could provide descriptions?"

"He certainly did better than the driver, but the pilot also spent the majority of the trip in the pilot seat. I'm told this is standard for experimental ships, and doubly so for this ship. Apparently, the pilot must pay close attention to the course and any stellar objects along that course. If we could track these two women down by the size of their breasts, the shape of their backsides, and the tightness of their clothing, the pilot's description would be invaluable."

I offered a wan smile. "The pilot is a young man, so I'm not surprised at what he noticed."

"Yes, you're right. His commanding officer suggested a reprimand, but I refused to punish the man simply for being a man. Besides, it's not like he was told to pay attention to their overall appearance. His orders were to fly them to Gaunner, which he did. He also flew them to near orbit and then, according to your report, flew you, William, Jeanine, and Drake back to the Gaunner Palace. Is that correct?"

I grimaced, "It is, Mother, but I'm afraid it was a short flight and I paid little attention to anyone except William. I can corroborate the brunette's exotic beauty and the blonde's tendency to fade into the background. I'm told she was recovering from a severe case of hyperspace sickness, so it's hardly surprising that she wasn't particularly outgoing. I am sorry that I, too, have failed you."

"No apologies are necessary, dear. You went through a trying ordeal and had just been reunited with your heroic husband. No woman in the galaxy would have noticed more than you did." Mother stifled a yawn, "This was a long shot, Olivia. I doubted you would have anything more to tell me than anyone else, but I had to ask. I don't know who these two women are, but we desperately need to find out."

"I'll try to remember as much as I can, but I wouldn't hold out much hope."

"I understand, dear. Don't let this trouble you too much. Now, why don't you go lie down for a bit? Even though it is early, you look a tad tired to me."

"I'll do that. Do give the King my best wishes."

"I will, dear. Do the same for me to my son. Farewell."

Mother tapped a control, and the screen went dark. I turned off my machine and wandered back to our Palace suite. I must have had a thoughtful expression on my face when I walked into the suite because it attracted William's attention.

"What did my mother have to say that has you so distracted, Olivia?" he asked.

"Hm?" I responded. "Oh, that. She asked me about the two women who helped you and Drake with the rescue."

"You mean Tilly and Jana?"

"You know who they are?" I asked, my tone incredulous.

"Well, I don't really know Jana, but Tilly…"

William's face reddened, and I suddenly had a good idea how he knew Tilly. Not wanting him to stop talking about her, I assured him, "Anything that happened between you and Tilly was before we were together. I am fully aware that you have far more experience with women than I have with men. Rest assured, I won't hold anything you did with Tilly against you." I let my voice drop into a sultry tone, "But if you tell me everything you know about those two women, I'll definitely hold something *else* against you."

Just in case William's mind had not started working properly, I undid the top two buttons of my blouse. My husband's eyes lit up and a broad grin spread across his face. It turned out, he knew quite a lot about Tilly and enough about Jana to tell me she was the dangerous one. Then, true to my word, I rewarded my husband's brains out.

BACK IN THE GAME

Jeanine

Do you have any idea how paranoid you get when you know, beyond all shadow of a doubt, that someone hears everything you say? When someone sees everything you see? You find yourself wondering if they feel what you feel. If they know what you think. If, in fact, you have any secrets from them at all.

It doesn't help knowing it isn't a some*one* who's seeing and hearing everything. The some*thing* that's doing it is far worse.

Why is it worse? Because I don't know what it can do with the information.

Can it communicate my secrets to Queen Charlotte or Princess Olivia?

I don't know.

Can it alert my enemies when I'm distracted or sleeping?

I don't know.

Ever since Jana told me about the Star Stone's connection to all Recognized nobles, I've found myself all but paralyzed with indecision. The simplest decisions—what to wear or what to eat—become burdens. And I know that sounds ridiculous but don't judge me until you've been where I am. Don't judge me until you find yourself looking over your shoulder, metaphorically and for real, because you know something *is* watching.

I'm not the only one affected by this. It's driving Drake up the wall, and I don't blame him. I can't discuss anything with him. No, that's not true. *He* can't discuss anything with me because I've turned every sensitive decision over to him.

Security?

He's in charge, now.

Trade negotiations?

He handles them all without any input from me.

Working with the rebellion?

You don't even have to ask. Of course, I have *nothing* to do with that, anymore.

Coordinating with Jana and Tilly to discover more about the Star Stone?

Drake is handling it.

Hell, I didn't even realize they had left the planet until a day and a half after they were gone. I would have liked a chance to say goodbye—Jana's one of my closest friends in the galaxy and I have a feeling Tilly will be once I get to know her better—but that would have been a foolish security risk.

I'm cut off from everyone and everything that truly matters. That includes physical intimacy with my husband.

Drake stopped spreading kisses over my stomach. "You know, babe, you might actually enjoy this if you relax. It feels like I'm kissing a rock. A beautiful rock, but still a rock."

Keeping my eyes squeezed tightly shut, I murmured, "I'm sorry, Drake. It's just…you know."

I felt Drake's warm breath blow across my stomach as he vented a sigh. "Yes, I know. That damned crystal voyeur has you tying yourself in knots. You feel like you can't be the duchess your people deserve because you don't know what that thing will do with the information it gets from you. I get it."

Drake moved up next to me and wrapped his arms around me. "But, unless the Star Stone is planning on releasing sex vids of you and me, who cares if it watches us make love?"

"I care," I whispered. "For women, sex is as much mental as

physical. I can't slip into the right mood knowing that...thing...is watching everything we do—and doing it through my own eyes! I desperately want to make love to you, Drake, but—"

"You're not ready for a three-way." Drake shook his head in mock disappointment. "I guess I shouldn't suggest we invite... Hm, who should our third be? Not Olivia, I want to survive the experience, after all. Jana? No, that would just be wrong. She's become too much like a little sister to me."

Despite myself, I giggled. "Oh, come on, Drake—you *know* who you'd invite!"

Drake eyed me suspiciously, "Please, tell me you don't mean Kelly! That would be worse than wrong in so many ways!"

Still smiling, I rolled my eyes, "You're right about that. Tilly, on the other hand..."

"I've never considered her before, but I like the way you think, wife! Tilly, it is." Drake's eyes unfocused for a moment, then he grinned. "We could make a whole role-playing thing out of it. You and I would be making passionate love as the beautiful burglar slipped into our room. Hearing our cries of ecstasy, she finds herself overcome with desire, throws off her clothes, and leaps into bed with us!"

I gave Drake's chest a playful slap and asked dryly, "If you've never considered her before, how do you explain how quickly you came up with that fantasy?"

"I'm a man, babe. That's how our minds work."

I laughed loudly for the first time in what felt like years, even though it had only been days, Drake took advantage of the moment and lowered his mouth to my neck. When he began nibbling, I laughed and gasped and, somehow, didn't think about the Star Stone again until *much* later.

My good mood evaporated quickly as soon as I stepped into my office. The mood swing wasn't caused by the work waiting for me, but by the work that *wasn't* waiting for me—the work I couldn't do because of my connection to the thrice-damned Star Stone. An hour later, I caught myself pretending sales tax receipts were secrets of vast importance to the safety of the Duchy.

I heard the door open and, assuming it was Mary with my lunch, said, "I'm not hungry right now, Mary. Just leave the tray on the cart and I'll get it when I find my appetite."

"It took a little work," Drake replied, standing just inside the door, holding his hands behind his back, "but we were able to find your appetite last night."

I looked up in surprise. "I'm sorry, I thought—"

"I was a teenage girl." Drake grinned, "But, hey, if that's what it takes to put you in the mood."

I offered a slight smile in return. "That's sick, Drake."

"Probably. Kinky, at the very least. But it did draw out your smile even if it was a particularly pathetic one."

I plastered a big, insincere grin on my face. "Is this better?"

Drake recoiled in mock horror. "Gah! That's horrible. Take it away."

Once again, despite myself, I laughed. How could I not love a man who could do that for me? "What do you need, dear? As you can plainly see, I'm very busy working with vital ducal secrets."

Peering at the display on my data pad, he said, "I wasn't aware tax receipts were such a sensitive subject."

"They're not, but I'm pretending they are."

Drake brought his hands from behind his back and put a box in front of me. "Maybe it's time to stop pretending."

"I don't understand."

"Open the box, Jeanine."

Fingers trembling with excitement, I undid the fasteners and lifted the box's lid. A standard data pad was nestled inside, with some kind of odd device next to it. "Now, I *really* don't understand."

"Let me show you." Drake put the data pad on my desk, connected the device—which looked like nothing more than a small data screen—to it and grabbed a stylus from a container on my desk. "Watch."

He turned on the pad which also powered the device. Holding the stylus against the device, he drew the letter 'I' and tapped the edge of the device twice with his finger. In rapid succession, he wrote l-o-v-e-y-o-u, tapping once after each letter, and twice after the 'e'. The data pad displayed the sentence he wrote—'I love you'.

"That's sweet, Drake, but I've got plenty of data pads I can write on."

"They're all connected to the net. This one isn't—and it never can be. It's a stand-alone unit. I had to have it built special by someone Jana recommended."

"I'm still lost, Drake. What's the point?"

Drake cleared the screen and handed me the stylus. "Write a message using the small input pad. Tap the edge after each letter and tap twice at the end of a word."

Sighing with frustration at this silliness, I looked at the little pad and thought about what I should write. Before I could begin, Drake slid a sleep mask over my eyes.

"Hey, I can't see a thing, Drake! What the hell?"

"Can you write letters from memory, without watching?" he asked.

"Yes." I couldn't keep the irritation out of my voice. "So what?"

"You're not thinking it through, Jeanine. If you can't see what you're writing, neither can the Star Stone. But, since you're the one writing the message, you don't need to see it. You already know what it says. Since I'm not Recognized, I can read your message and figure out a way to respond without giving away your question." He gently massaged my shoulders. "Try it. Please?"

Trying to keep my hopes low, I carefully wrote a message.

"Yes, babe, I can read it just fine."

I tore off the sleep mask and looked at the pad before me. The message wasn't perfect—I'd written 'Can yuu reab this' instead of my intended message, but I thought it was pretty good for a first try.

"You'll get better with practice, Jeanine. Soon, I expect the biggest problem will be figuring out how to respond without giving away your question."

"Isn't there an ancient code that uses taps to spell out a message, Drake? If all else fails, maybe we could learn that and you could tap replies on my back."

"We can keep that in the back of our minds while we work on other options," he replied. "But, what do you think of this setup?"

"It's slow and cumbersome and carries a real risk of miscommunication, but it's a lot better than nothing!" I stood and kissed Drake thoroughly. "Thank you!"

"Better save that thanks for Jana. I knew just enough to ask if there was some way you could communicate without speaking or looking at your message. She came up with the rest."

"But would she have thought of it without your prompting?" I kissed him again, silencing his reply. "That was a rhetorical question. The important thing is, I'm back in the game!"

FOX HUNT
Tilly

When I set up shop in a new place, it's a pretty straightforward process. My burglary tools are small, easily concealed, and always with me. That means I just unpack my clothes, install a little security, and I'm ready for business. Jana, on the other hand, needs an amazing amount of stuff to set up her slicer lair. Okay, so it's really just a big apartment, but I like the sound of 'lair' better. It's more mysterious and mystery appeals to a burglar.

Of course, Jana couldn't personally buy any of the stuff she needed, or even rent the apartment. As she put it, "Fox will track down any ID tied to me and he doesn't need any more advantages than he already has. Since he'll probably track Tilly down through me, we're going to need you to take care of all of this stuff, Kelly. He might connect us through Jeanine, but we'll just have to take that risk."

Kelly grinned, "I've already got that covered. Jeanine had official Neert IDs set up for each of us. We had to scramble a bit for Tilly because she wasn't part of the crew until a week or so ago, but they should hold up. I mean, they are *real* government IDs issued by a real government. It's Jeanine's government, but it's plenty real."

I felt an unexpected tingle of warmth inside. "I'm part of Jeanine's crew?"

"Well, Drake's and Jeanine's crew," Kelly clarified, "but hell yes you're part of the crew. Anybody who puts their life on the line for those two is automatically 'good people' in my book. And, in case you're wondering, it's a pretty damned thin book."

I blinked rapidly for a few seconds while watching Kelly closely. She was remarkably guileless—I could read everything she was thinking right from her face. I am just not used to that kind of open honesty from people. Okay, I do travel in criminal circles where honesty is usually in short supply, but I grew up around nobles and the elite commoners who hobnobbed with them. That crowd could teach criminals a thing or two about dishonesty. As a result I'm totally unprepared for life as part of Jeanine's crew of honest folk. And Drake's—I don't want to forget him with Kelly around.

It's going to take a serious shift in mindset for me to fit in with these people. Fortunately, I've gotten some practice at it with Jana. She's more open than the criminals I know but plays things a lot closer to the vest than the revolutionaries Kelly hangs out with. And, yes, I realize just how odd it is to think members of a rebellion are less secretive than Jana and me. Anyway, it's given me some practice at being sort of open and sort of honest. Believe it or not, I sort of like the feeling.

So, we let Kelly rent the apartment and buy all the equipment Jana needed. Jana told her exactly what to buy, but Kelly paid for stuff, signed her real fake name on all the documents, and arranged for all the services Jana needed—stuff like net access and subspace connections and the like. This left me at loose ends for a while, so I renewed a few contacts in the Xapreathea underworld. If we have to go underground, I want to know we've got ground to go under.

I have a good reputation among criminals—well, among the nonviolent criminals. I don't know what the psychos and sadistic bastard killers and hitmen think of me—if they even know who

I am—but other thieves are usually willing to work with me. That includes the thieving support staff—getaway drivers, fences, gear suppliers, people like that. They know I'll keep my end of the bargain and, equally important, usually have a line on very profitable jobs.

It dawned on me that made me sound downright honest—for a criminal, I mean, since I doubt those I'm stealing from particularly appreciate the theft. Unless they're really strapped for cash and want to collect the insurance money on the stuff I steal. Then, they love me. I've done more than a few jobs along that line—having people hire me to steal their own stuff—and admit those are choice assignments. Nothing makes a job easier than knowing the full layout of the house, having the schematics for the security system, and personal assurances from the 'victim' that nobody will be home when I break into the house. On the other hand, those are not particularly exciting jobs, and any burglar who tells you they aren't in it for the thrills is lying.

Anyway, two days after we landed on Xapreathea, we had everything in the apartment and Jana was happily ordering Kelly and me around. She told us what to open, what to put where, what to connect to what, and what to leave alone, because Jana didn't trust us with the truly technical stuff. Even the stuff she thought was nontechnical turned out to be pretty damned technical to me. More than once, she told me to do something or other with the whatchamacallit and plug it into the dohickey after inserting the dongle and... You get the idea.

Most of the words Jana used in her directions were normal ones. I understood each of them perfectly well. It's the way she combined them into sentences that confused me. I'm a smart woman—stupid thieves don't last very long, particularly with the kind of jobs I usually pull—but Jana could make me feel dumb without even trying. I think Kelly feels the same way.

More than once, Jana would finish giving us instructions and Kelly and I would exchange glances, trying to remember whose turn it was to ask for clarification. Then, one of us would ask,

"Would you say that again, Jana, and this time use a language we understand?"

Jana always rolled her eyes, muttered curses about working with normies—I think that's slicer slang for normal people, you know, ninety-nine point nine nine nine and a lot more nines percent of the human race—than she would explain again using small words.

Eventually everything was unpacked, installed, connected, and working to Jana's extraordinarily exacting specifications. Kelly and I wanted to go celebrate at a bar. Jana wanted to celebrate by slicing. Since she was going to The Club to meet Fox, I decided to skip the bar. There was no way in hell I was letting Jana face that man without her wingwoman watching her six.

I guess Fox felt the same way because he had another guy with him when he joined us at Jana's table. "Dreamwalker, Smoke, this is Braincase."

The other guy, whose avatar looked a lot like a male version of my over-sexualized avatar, screwed his face up in distaste. "You *know* I hate that name! Dammit, N—"

"*Fox*!" Fox snapped. "I'm *Fox*. Got it?"

"Then you can call me *Enigma*."

Fox and his companion glared at each other for a few seconds. "Fine. Ladies, this is Enigma."

"Thank you, Fox," the newly renamed Enigma said. Turning to us, he added, "And I'm pleased to meet you both. I'd know you, Dreamwalker, without the introduction. Fox talks about you a lot."

"Does he now?" Jana the Dreamwalker asked, cocking her head and regarding the other slicer. "What does he say?"

"Lately," Fox said, cutting off Enigma before he could speak, "I've been telling him what you told me last time. About the Star Stone, I mean. Nothing else."

In other words, Fox had kept Jana's identity secret. Or, he claimed he had, anyway.

"If it's true," Enigma said, "it's a fascinating story and—"

"It's true, Enigma," I snapped. "Every. Last. Word."

Enigma turned his attention on me. "Were you with Dreamwalker?"

"Sort of." That sounded lame, even to me.

"Smoke kept watch over my body while I interfaced with the Star Stone," Dreamwalker said.

Enigma nodded. "I'll want to hear your side of the tale after Dreamwalker is done."

"If you don't mind sharing that information, Smoke," Fox clarified.

I shrugged, "Sure."

"And," Fox said, turning to Dreamwalker, "assuming you don't mind telling your tale again."

In response, Dreamwalker began the tale. Enigma interrupted with questions now and then, but he paid rapt attention to her tale and did the same for my much shorter story. He got a faraway look when we both fell silent, obviously mulling over our stories.

"Well?" Fox finally asked.

"Hm?" Enigma turned to Fox. "Well what?"

"What do you think of their stories?"

Enigma shrugged, "You know I'm just going by gut instinct, right?"

"And you know I trust your gut instincts," Fox replied. "Do you believe them?"

Enigma looked at Dreamwalker and me, then turned back to Fox. "Absolutely."

Fox gave that response careful consideration, then looked at Dreamwalker. "We need to meet in person."

"Perfect. If you're at home, Smoke and I can be in your building's lobby in about twenty minutes."

Fox and Enigma both raised their eyebrows in surprise. "You've figured out my identity already?"

"Not yet," Dreamwalker replied. "I've got it narrowed down

to eight people in your building, though. Assuming you live at eight thirty-six Strathmore."

"I'll be damned." Fox shook his head in obvious admiration. "You are impressive, Dreamwalker!"

"Wait until you meet her," I said.

"I can't wait. And, yes, I am at home. Enigma is visiting. How will we recognize you?"

"That's easy," she replied, "just look for the gorgeous brunette. I'll be the blonde standing next to her."

THE FOX'S DEN

Jana

It took me about two minutes to get ready. I threw on some clean clothes, ran a brush through my hair, and that was it. Tilly took longer. When she emerged from her room, she wore a bleeding-edge-of-fashion skirt so short I'd never have worn it in public, a shimmering blouse that didn't even have buttons above her navel, and a strappy pair of high-heeled shoes that probably cost more than my entire wardrobe.

Folding my arms, I said, "You do realize we're just going to visit another slicer, right? We're not going to a club or any fancy restaurants."

"How do you know?" Tilly responded. "What if you deduced the wrong address and Fox just agreed to meet us there to throw you off? Then, he won't have an apartment to invite us into."

I hadn't thought of that possibility. Then again, I was virtually positive I had the right address. "Unlikely, but I suppose it could happen."

"And, you did tell Fox and Enigma to look for a gorgeous brunette and the blonde next to her. I might have dressed more casually if you told them to look for two pretty women, a blonde and brunette."

I shook my head, pretending more frustration than I felt.

"Fine. And it's not like I want to wait while you change into more appropriate clothes."

Tilly grinned, "I knew you'd like it."

"Well, I don't," Kelly said. "This whole operation depends on you two. What if this Fox and Enigma turn out to be a couple of girl-grabbing psychos?"

"We don't have a lot of choice, Kelly," I said. "I'm going to need Fox's help, not only as a recruiter but as a slicer. I have no idea what type data, if any, we can extract from the Star Stone. But I do know we'll have a much better chance of finding what we need if I'm working with the best slicer in the galaxy."

"Yeah, I understand that. But why can't you handle all of this at that Club you and Tilly go to?"

I knew Kelly was truly concerned about us and wasn't trying to be difficult, so I tamped down exasperation and responded with the question of my own. "Would you trust someone who claimed they wanted to join the rebellion but refused to meet with you in person?"

Kelly glared at me for a second, shook her head, and started hiding weapons on her body. "Okay, you win. But I'm tagging along, too."

"I told Fox there would be two of us."

"And there will be two of you. I'm going to tail you. If Fox has more people working with him, I'll spot them. Wherever he takes you, I'll follow. And, if I get the slightest twinge of a bad feeling about this, I'll come in and get you."

This was becoming a lot more complicated than it needed to be. I suppose I should be flattered that everyone wanted to keep an eye on me, but I felt more like I was fifteen and trying to convince my parents to let me go on a date with a seventeen-year-old boy.

That was a memory I didn't want to dredge up again—especially since Mom and Dad were right to be concerned. Don't worry, that story had a happy ending. A knee to the guy's groin stopped him and a threat to his father's credit rating kept him in check after he stopped rolling around in agony.

Anyway, I didn't think this was going to end the same way. My gut told me I could trust Fox—at least enough to meet with him in person. But, Kelly had a point. Drake and Janine were counting on me. That meant I had to be careful and take precautions.

I nodded to Kelly. "I think that's a good idea. If Fox takes us to an apartment in the building and everything seems on the level, do you mind if I tell Fox you're there and see if he'll invite you in?"

Kelly considered that question for a few seconds. "Tell you what, if *Tilly* thinks everything is on the level, she can tell Fox about me and see if he'll let me join you."

I cocked my head and asked, "Why Tilly? Not that I mind, I'm just curious."

"I'm sure you've got great instincts for trouble in the net. Tilly has great instincts for trouble in the real world. If she didn't, she'd probably be in prison right now."

"She's right, Jana," Tilly added.

"Whatever. Can we get going now? We're going to be late as it is, and I hate being late."

Tilly headed for the door, "She's not kidding, Kelly. I have never met anyone who was so anal about being on time in my entire life, and many of my jobs require split-second timing."

I followed her to the door, "I'm not *that* bad."

"Uh huh," she said, stopping in the middle of the doorway.

I waited for Tilly to move. She just stood there. So, I just stood there and waited. Tilly smiled at me and didn't move. I smiled—okay, it was more like a grimace—and waited some more. Tilly still didn't move.

"Okay, you win," I spat. "Now, move!"

Tilly turned and walked out, but not without adding, "Told you!"

Once we were outside, I turned and walked towards Fox's

building. Next to me, Tilly sashayed. I swear, there wasn't a single guy along our route who didn't stare—openly or surreptitiously—at Tilly. She jiggled and wiggled and did it all as naturally as breathing.

"You're attracting a lot of attention, you know," I murmured.

Tilly cocked her head, smiled brightly at a particularly brazen admirer, and said, "That's the idea, Jana. I spend all my professional time hiding in shadows, it's why I like to be very visible when I can be. You ought to try it sometime."

"Yeah, right."

"I'm serious, Jana. If you'll let me help you, you can look just as exotic as you claim I do."

I'll admit, that had some appeal to it, but this wasn't the time for it. "We can worry about that later. Right now, you are making Kelly's job a lot harder."

"Wrong," Tilly sang.

"That's crazy! How can she pick out people looking for us when everyone is looking at us?"

"You said it yourself, Jana. Everyone is looking at me. Since you're the person Fox is watching for, anyone looking at you stands out."

"Um, thanks?"

"I'm not saying you aren't worth looking at, Jana. We've been over just how beautiful I think you are. But, I'm dressed to attract attention and you're not. I'm walking to attract attention and you're not. Fox might have tracked down my identity though I doubt he cares all that much about me. It's certain he knows what you look like. Hell, you told him who you were and I guarantee the first thing he did when he got home was find pics of you. If he has any minions surrounding his lair, they'll be watching for you."

When Tilly put it that way, it didn't sound so bad that everyone was looking at her and ignoring me. I think. Anyway, her reasoning seemed sound to me.

Ten minutes later, we entered the lobby of eight thirty-six

Strathmore. My eyes swept the lobby, looking for one of the half-dozen people I thought might be Fox. I spotted the most likely candidate, a nice-looking man about my age named Nathan Fox. Using his last name as his avatar name was risky but he'd protected his secret well—until now. Nathan was watching me while his companion—an intent-looking man close to our age—had his eyes locked on Tilly.

Well, damn, Tilly was right. She did draw every eye except for those specifically looking for me.

I smiled and waved at the two men and set off in their direction. Fox waved back and the two men headed our way.

"Hug Fox like he's an old friend," Tilly said.

"Okay. Why?"

"This lobby has six security cams. I doubt anyone will ever check the vids, but it's best if we act like we've known each other for years."

When we were a few feet from the men, Tilly opened her arms wide and smiled fondly at the man who must be Enigma. Then she said, "It's been way too long since I've seen you. Give me a hug!"

Enigma, whose eyes had been roaming all over Tilly, broke into a huge grin and enveloped her in his arms. Fox and I both opened our arms and broke into more tentative smiles.

"Jana!" Fox said.

Not to be outdone, I said, "Nathan! I've been looking forward to seeing you again."

I tried to act natural, going so far as kissing Nathan's cheek, but we were both a little stiff. It's a slicer thing—we're not used to meeting each other in person. Next to us, Tilly all but melted against Enigma, who was enraptured. But what guy wouldn't be?

Nathan and I broke apart quickly. Tilly and Enigma took their time.

After a few seconds watching them, Nathan said, "Do you guys want a room?"

Watching their hands roam, I'd originally thought the same

thing. Then, I realized what they were doing. In a fierce whisper, I asked, "Are you two frisking each other for weapons?"

They broke apart, neither one of them looking even remotely embarrassed.

"Would you like to come down to my apartment?" Nathan asked.

"Down?"

"I've got a basement apartment. Actually, two of them linked." Without waiting for an answer, Nathan set off for the drop chutes. "I'm sure, Jana, you can think of many reasons why I do that."

I could, though I didn't like basement apartments myself. With a nod to Tilly, I followed Nathan into the drop chute.

Fox's—make that, Nathan's—apartment was the only one in the basement. That's a smart move for a slicer since privacy is extremely important to our work. The door looked normal at first glance, but I gave it a closer examination and realized it was anything but. It was reinforced metal held in place by a reinforced metal frame and was probably surrounded by reinforced metal walls hidden behind standard paneling. I spotted two obvious security cams and two more hidden ones. If Nathan was like me, he had one or two other cams I missed. I didn't look for alarms. They'd be embedded in the door frame and the door. That didn't count the motion sensors I was sure we'd find inside the apartment.

Nathan pulled out an old-fashioned mechanical key and unlocked the door. That opened a hidden retinal scanner, which read his retina print. With a soft whoosh, the door slid to one side.

"After you, ladies," Nathan said, half bowing and waving his arm toward the apartment.

I caught Tilly's arm and said, "No, no, please lead the way."

Enigma laughed and walked through the door. I released Tilly's arm, and she followed him. Nathan and I eyed each other for a couple of seconds before sidling through the door together.

It was a surprisingly intimate thing, facing each other and being forced well inside each other's personal space.

Watching us, Tilly said, "You two are going to have to trust each other sometime, or this is never going to work."

"I've already trusted Nathan," I insisted. "I told him my true identity."

"Then, I met you in person and invited you into my home," Nathan countered.

"And I willingly entered your home," I shot back.

"Only in the hopes of convincing me to follow you on a slicing mission into the Star Stone," Nathan snapped. "You know how much trust that involves."

I crossed my arms and met Nathan's building glare. "That only counts if you actually come with me into the Star Stone."

He crossed his arms and leaned in toward me. "Why do you think I invited you here?"

"You've decided to come with me into the Star Stone?" At his nod, I leaned in towards Nathan, "So you expect me to use your slicing rig? That level of trust makes your level of trust look ridiculous!"

"Oh for God's sake," Tilly cried, "go into one of the bedrooms and screw each other, already! Once you've cleared the sexual tension and established trust, maybe we can get on with the mission."

I felt the heat of a deep blush while also watching Nathan's face turn red. "Tilly! I can't believe you said that!"

"I can't believe she had to," Enigma said.

Nathan growled, "Alfonso! You're not helping."

Tilly glanced at Nathan's friend, "So, your name is Alfonso. I like that more than Enigma."

Alfonso grinned back, "I chose that avatar name because I'm told women like men of mystery."

"Now, who needs to find a bedroom?" I asked.

Tilly flashed a wicked smile and purred, "Now there's an interesting idea!"

Alfonso nodded, "Tempting, but I *am* here to make sure Nathan stays safe."

"I'm fully capable of taking care of myself, Alfonso," Nathan retorted. He waved toward the back of the apartment, "Go have fun. I don't care. Besides, I know I can trust Jana."

"You do?" I asked.

"Of course, I do. You told me your true identity, for God's sake! How can I not trust you?"

Tilly made a face. "Is it just me, or have things suddenly gone sickeningly sweet?"

"It's not just you," Alfonso said. Turning his attention back to Nathan, he asked, "I guess this means you and Jana are going slicing together?"

"Yes, but only after she's had a chance to examine my equipment." Tilly and Alfonso burst out laughing, and Nathan blushed again. "My *computer* equipment, dammit. And you both know that's what I meant!"

I felt heat climb my cheeks, again, as I suddenly caught the joke. "*I* knew what you meant, Nathan. And *my* mind stayed out of the gutter, unlike certain companions of ours. Where do you keep your slicing rigs?"

Nathan pointed down the hall and led me in that direction.

"That reminds me," Tilly said, "we've got a heavily armed friend in the lobby—just a precaution in case you turned out to be woman-grabbing psychos—who's waiting for a call from me letting her know everything is okay. Do you mind if she comes down here?"

Alfonso looked at Nathan and raised an eyebrow, "What do you think?"

Nathan shrugged, "As long as she leaves her weapons at the door, I don't care. Alfonso, do you think you can handle two women at once?"

Without waiting for an answer, Nathan turned and headed toward a room at the end of the hall. Inside, he had an entirely normal-looking network connection. Knowing that was just a cover, I waited for Nathan to show me his real equipment. Slicing equipment, I mean. Damn Tilly and Alfonso and the thoughts they put in my head!

Nathan did something against the far wall. I couldn't see what it was because he blocked it with his body. I respected his professional privacy and didn't crane my neck to see around him. A second later, a section of the wall slid aside and revealed a slicing rig that would be the envy of anyone in the galaxy—including me. Nathan stepped to one side and motioned for me to inspect the setup.

I took my time, started up the machines, checked the displays, ran a few commands, before pulling out a data stick. Holding it up, I asked, "Do you mind?"

Nathan picked up an old junker of a data pad—interestingly enough, it was the exact same model I'd given to Drake and Jeanine the night I first met them—and said, "Load it on this, first."

Appreciating his caution, I did as he asked and then handed the data pad back to him. "Check the code for yourself. Run the commands if you want and ask me anything about them."

While Nathan checked out the data pad, I heard the door open and close. A third voice joined the two already out in the main living room. Obviously, Kelly was out there, now. Ignoring them, I turned back to Nathan. He had his own data stick out and loaded his own commands into the data pad. His software analyzed my software. After a few minutes, it delivered a satisfactory result to him.

"Nice work, Jana. Your code is elegant. More importantly, I have no objection to loading it into my system."

I did just that and my software analyzed his software. And, thanks to Tilly and Alfonso, my mind went right to the gutter after I thought that. I pulled my thoughts back to the task at hand and waited for the results. As expected, Nathan's system was pristine and had no booby-traps.

Withdrawing my data stick, I said, "Let's do this."

"Do you think your connection to the Star Stone is still open?"

"The one Queen Charlotte authorized? Not a chance. But, Tilly and I set up our own connection shortly before we had to leave for Gaunner. If Her Majesty isn't *too* paranoid, it might still be in place."

"And if it's not?"

"Why do you think I brought Tilly?"

"Okay... Where should we meet on the inside?"

I thought for a second and said, "Let's meet at The Club?"

Nathan nodded and handed me a network cable. We both plugged in and entered the net.

SCOUTING THE STAR STONE'S INTERFACE

Jana

Hundreds of virtual eyes watched us enter The Club together, tracking our movement across the floor towards Fox's table. We left silence in our wake as fellow slicers speculated what our arrival together meant. Low voices erupted as we settled into the seats at Fox's table. With a wave of a hand, Fox invoked a privacy bubble, cutting off all sound. I made a small gesture with my hands and a second, opaque bubble blocked us from sight.

"Is there any reason we're meeting here, instead of going straight for your connection with the Star Stone?" Fox asked.

"Yes. You're not ready, yet."

Fox bristled at that comment. "I'm as ready as you were when you entered that thing!"

"I wasn't ready, either. But I didn't have any other choice."

My admission mollified Fox enough that he gave a quick nod of acknowledgment. "Fair enough. You're the one with experience in this, so I'd be a fool if I didn't pay attention to what you have to say. What do I need to know?"

I sighed and combed a hand through my hair, "Something I can't teach. The best I can do is tell you how I discovered the way out of the Star Stone and put you in the right frame of mind to discover it for yourself."

"Does this have something to do with that soul stuff you mentioned?"

"Yes, and it's not a load of crap. I don't know if 'soul' is the right word, but it fits as well as any." I leaned on the table, bringing my virtual face within inches of Fox's virtual face. "Do you have someone in your life you love?"

Fox snorted and sat back. "Don't tell me Tilly and Alfonso were right and you're just trying to lure me into bed. If so, I can save you a lot of time, Dreamwalker. I'm not in the market for a girlfriend right now."

"I'm going to ignore your comment and your tone because you have no idea what you'll be facing if you follow me into the Star Stone. There's a good reason I asked that question, and it had nothing to do with hooking up with you." Taking a moment to calm myself and douse my anger, I continued, "When the Star Stone told me I would never leave and, much worse, would fade away to nothing after a few days, it took everything I had to avoid panicking. While the Star Stone blathered on about its previous prisoners, I racked my brains trying to figure a way out."

Even now, more than a week after that encounter, the terror I felt in that moment was still raw and painful. As I'd programmed it to, my virtual body reacted the same way my real body would and gave an involuntary shudder. I closed my eyes and tried pushing the fear back into the dark recesses of my mind where it came from.

I felt a hand enveloped mine and Fox asked, "Are you okay?"

"Is it that obvious?" I asked, knowing the answer was yes. Why else would he ask?

"I'm sorry I was so dismissive, Dreamwalker. Even a clueless guy like me can tell something frightening happened to you inside the Star Stone. I never noticed it in the past because you always glossed over it. Why?"

"I was afraid I'd get the exact reaction I got from you. I know how odd my story sounds, how unbelievable talk of souls and having your entire consciousness pulled out of your body sounds to anyone who hasn't experienced it. I kept a lot of details to myself because I was certain you'd never have met with me, otherwise."

Fox shrugged, "You're probably right. But, having met you face-to-face and watched you here in The Club, I think I believe you. So, I will sit back, keep my mouth shut, and listen to your entire story."

"Thank you. Where was I?"

"Talking about love."

"Right. What put me on the right track was wishing I had my parents around to talk to. I used to talk my problems through with them when I lived at home. I still do it sometimes when I visit. They don't always understand what I'm talking about—especially if I'm talking about slicing—but just telling them helps me see my problems in different ways. Asking them for advice makes it easier for me to find answers on my own." I gave a wan smile. "I quite literally thought about how much I would love to discuss escaping from the Star Stone with my parents. That made me realize that my desire to speak with my parents was entirely logic-driven. I felt no love toward them. I felt no need for them beyond how I might benefit from having them around."

"And you made the leap from that to realizing love was your way out of the Star Stone? That's an impressive chain of reasoning!"

I shook my head, "It's not as impressive as you think. The Star Stone had already told me of one man—a religious leader— who entered the Star Stone and got away. He'd have no trouble believing in his soul or searching himself for it. The ones who stayed and faded from existence were all scientists, people whose thoughts wouldn't extend beyond their logical observations of the real world."

"So, the religious man believed and escaped, while the rational men didn't believe and died." Fox considered that for a moment, "Yeah, I can see why you kept that to yourself until now. Even after reading the truth from your real eyes and your virtual eyes, I have a hard time accepting that."

"Try living through it," I muttered.

Fox gave a rueful laugh, "Point taken. Anyway, to answer your question of a few minutes ago, yes, I have people I love. They're my parents, my baby sister—who would like you—and, hell, even Alfonso. He's been my best friend for as long as I can remember."

"That's a good list—better than mine was. But before we try entering the Star Stone, I want you to think very carefully about the risks involved."

Fox burst out laughing, "What kind of slicer would I be if I worried about the risks?"

It was my turn to take Fox's hand. "I'm serious, Fox. Yes, we slicers take a lot of risks and, if we screw up, may face long prison sentences. If you enter the Star Stone, you'll be risking your life. If you can't find that connection back to your body I don't know if I can pull you out using my own connection back to my body."

Fox captured my gaze with his, "And you'll feel guilty if I don't come back."

"I wasn't going to mention that, but since you did... Yes, I'll feel incredibly guilty if *we* go in and only *I* come out. So guilty I'll immediately turn around and go right back in after you. And I'll keep coming back after you until you come out with me or neither of us comes out." I offered a tentative smile, "See? I can play the guilt card, too."

Fox returned my smile, "Then, I guess we both have to come back safely. Now, is there anything you can tell me about this connection to your body? Something that'll make it easier to find or easier to see?"

I shook my head, "You'll know it when you see it. It's hard to miss, just like it was hard to find."

"Good enough. I'm ready when you're ready."

Was I ready? Yes, I decided I was. Much as I didn't want to return to the Star Stone, I felt as if I didn't have a choice. I owed it to Jeanine, to Drake, to William, and, hell, maybe even to Olivia.

I stood and waved away my opaque bubble. "Link your avatar to mine and let's go visit the Star Stone."

Fox was quiet after we left The Club. I expect that's because he's used to being the one making the decisions, the one choosing the route through the network. Slicers of our stature rarely give up control, even in such a minor way as Fox had. I couldn't remember the last time I linked to another slicer's avatar and would probably share Fox's unease if our situations were reversed. When Fox broke his silence, it was for an excellent reason.

"Slow down when you get close to your interface with the Star Stone. From the story you've told, you didn't do anything to hide or camouflage the interface. Am I right, Dreamwalker?"

"You are. That's why I'm not sure the interface is still in place. Queen Charlotte knows I set something up, and she doesn't strike me as the kind of person who likes leaving loose ends lying around. In her place, I'd have had the Royal Guard search for it and, when found, remove it."

"I'd have done the same but Queen Charlotte is probably fifty times more devious than us. What if she left it in place but had network traffic sensors and alarms installed?"

I pulled to the side of the data stream for a moment and considered Fox's question. It made sense, especially when viewed from Queen Charlotte's point of view. It wouldn't take a vast intellect or any great leaps of logic for her to figure out who had tripped any alarms her slicers set. Once they determined we weren't using a subspace connection—something any reasonably competent slicer could do—she would know I was on Xapreathea. It's a big planet with a huge population, but I'd really rather not pit my ability to hide against the Royal Intelligence Agency's ability to find me.

"Okay, Fox, you've raised a valid concern. Why didn't you bring this up earlier?"

Fox's avatar shrugged, "Because it just occurred to me. I let myself get caught up in the excitement and the mystery of the greatest slicing challenge of all time and only considered the deeper implications of your story while riding in your wake."

Had I let my concern for Jeanine override my caution as a slicer? Did I really need to ask? I most certainly had been acting with a haste and lack of caution atypical for me, or any other elite slicer.

"I have been pushing for action, haven't I?" I asked. "I still believe quick action is required, but not at the expense of caution and safety. Should we return to our bodies and consider other options?"

"Not yet, Dreamwalker," Fox replied. "We're already here, so let's see if your connection is still in place and scout for alarms and sensors at the same time. At the risk of sounding immodest, I can't imagine Queen Charlotte has anyone good enough to fool both of us when we've got our guard up."

"So, we scout but we don't enter the Star Stone?" Fox nodded, and I continued, "I agree. And, I'm damned glad I have you along. I might have blundered right into Queen Charlotte's trap."

"I don't know, Dreamwalker. I think your slicer sense would have reasserted itself when you got close to the interface."

Fox linked his avatar to mine, again, and I set off toward the connection. Shortly, I found myself automatically slowing down and concentrating on the environment around me. I guess Fox was right about my slicer sense.

"Fox, stay linked to my avatar. That should let you turn all your attention to finding sensors and alarms."

"That was my plan, Dreamwalker."

For the most part, I let myself drift with the data current. Like the first time I entered this data stream, everything flowed toward the connection with the Star Stone. Wordlessly, I pointed out the Star Stone's odd data packets flowing with us, but otherwise left Fox to his own devices. It didn't take me long to find the first alarm—a simple affair easily avoided. The next sensor and alarm were better camouflaged, but only the most optimistic slicer would think I couldn't bypass them easily.

All told, I found eight sensors and twelve alarms. Several of them were cleverly hidden inside other sensors and alarms. One alarm was actually three alarms, one of them embedded in the external alarm, and another one embedded in that internal alarm. I'd seen work like that before, but not often. Whoever Queen Charlotte had working for her was good—very good.

I stopped short of the interface between Xapreathea's network and the Star Stone and waited while Fox studied it. After a bit, he nodded, and we returned to our bodies.

Disconnecting the network cable, I sat up. "How many sensors and alarms did you find, Nathan?

"Eight sensors and twelve alarms. They were all good work, but not good enough."

"Yeah, I was particularly impressed by the three layer alarm."

Nathan nodded, "That one was daunting. What do you think the whole aim of that level of security is?"

I'd been thinking about that. "At the very least, tripping one of those alarms or sensors would tell Queen Charlotte that I was in the system and probably on the planet. If she really wanted to capture me, she could turn the RIA loose. They'd find me, too. They have too many resources not to."

"You're probably right, Jana, but what if her goal is protecting the Star Stone, rather than capturing you?"

I hadn't considered that possibility, but felt a chill running up my spine at the thought. What if she knew what the Star Stone really was? The Queen could simply wait until we passed through the interface and into the Star Stone, destroy my interface, and effectively trap us inside the Star Stone.

The horror that idea evoked made me draw my knees up to my chest, wrap my arms around my legs, and begin rocking in agitation. I rested my forehead against my knees and closed my eyes, trying to regain my composure.

Suddenly, two arms wrapped themselves around me and held me still. "Hey, Jana, it's okay. Whatever you're worrying about didn't happen. Would it help if you told me?"

In a whisper barely loud enough for Nathan to hear, I told him. "I think Queen Charlotte may want to trap me inside the Star Stone. I'm the only person she knows of who interfaced with the Stone and returned. If she knew I passed through that interface, she probably knows she could destroy it and block my only way back to my body."

Voicing that thought made me shudder again. Nathan's embrace tightened, and I felt his breath tickle my ear as he whispered, "But there have to be other data feeds into the Star Stone. It would just be a question of finding one of them, right?"

"Maybe," I replied. "But the separation caused by going through the Star Stone's interface isn't like anything else. What if severing that network connection also severs your mind's connection with your body? What if there's no way back after the network connection is severed?"

"I guess we're just going to have to make sure we have a way into and out of the Star Stone that no one else knows about. You told me you brought Tilly along for just this sort of thing. Is she some kind of network engineer?"

I couldn't help it, I burst out laughing, and, God, did it feel good. I released my knees, stretching my legs out before me and feeling my fear of being trapped in the Star Stone recede. "No, Tilly is not a network engineer. I'll leave it to her to explain further."

Nathan's arms loosened, though he didn't let me go. "Are you okay?"

I looked up into his eyes and nodded. "Thank you."

He gave a lopsided smile and caressed my back. "Anytime."

Then Nathan kissed me.

When we broke apart, I asked, "Didn't you tell me you weren't looking for a new girlfriend?"

"I wasn't," he replied. "But I found one, anyway."

"Don't I get a say in this?"

"You already did, Jana. If you weren't interested, you wouldn't have returned my kiss."

"I do love a smart man!" Then I kissed Nathan, and he returned it.

CHIC THIEF
Tilly

We heard the soft murmur of voices from the back room. They rose slightly, tailed off, rose again, and then stopped. Alfonso, Kelly, and I waited for our two slicers to join us in the living room. When there was no sign of them, Alfonso and I exchanged mildly concerned glances and headed down the hallway toward Nathan's... Slicing lair? Computer room seems a far too pedestrian name for the workroom of the galaxy's premier slicer. Anyway, we went to that room's doorway.

It turns out we had nothing to worry about. Jana and Nathan were deeply engaged in humanity's second most popular method of interfacing. Theirs was as passionate and all-consuming a kiss as I've ever seen.

Holding my hand out to Alfonso, I said, "You owe me a hundred credits."

Jana and Nathan sprang apart at the sound of my voice. Both turned reddening faces our way as Alfonso said, "I shouldn't be surprised things moved so quickly between these two. Jana's got that whole brainy beauty thing going. That's absolutely impossible for Nathan to resist."

"You had a bet on whether Nathan would kiss me?" Jana demanded of me.

I shook my head, "No, we were both positive you two would end up tongue wrestling. Alfonso just thought it would take Nathan a few hours to work up to it. I, on the other hand, had full confidence in your irresistibility."

Alfonso handed me one hundred credits and growled, "Apparently, women are better at predicting how men will behave than men are at predicting how women will behave. I could have sworn Jana was going to keep you at arm's length for at least another hour or two."

"Can we change the subject?" Nathan asked.

"God, yes!" Jana added.

"Fine," I said, "what do you want to talk about?"

"We need some ancient documents," Nathan replied.

Alfonso spoke before I could. "You want me to arrange a museum robbery? Which museum?"

"Not a museum," Jana said, shaking her head. "We need engineering documents."

"Then why are you talking to us?" I asked. "I'm pretty sure slicers of your stature can get that kind of stuff without even leaving this room."

"Nope. The stuff we want is so old it's not even in the databases, Tilly. I know, because I checked for it back when we discovered that network connection to the Star Stone."

"You never told me you did that, Jana."

My friend shrugged, "You were busy with other plans and I didn't want to distract you. Besides, we didn't really need those documents, then. I just wanted to check them out for historical purposes. Now, I want to check them out for safety purposes."

I crossed my arms and gave Jana a hard stare. "What kind of safety are we talking about?"

Jana wouldn't meet my eyes, so I knew it was something serious. Switching my gaze to Nathan, I asked, "Would you like to enlighten me?"

Nathan's eyes flicked to Jana, who gave a slight nod. With a sigh, he said, "Jana can describe it better since she's actually been inside the Star Stone, but she's concerned about using the network connection you two installed a while back. It has something to do with the possibility that Queen Charlotte will destroy the connection after we've passed through it."

I had not gone into the Star Stone with Jana, but I'd heard her tell the story several times. It didn't take a genius to figure out she was afraid the two of them would be trapped in the Stone. That was my greatest fear, too.

I uncrossed my arms and ran a hand through my hair. "Good, I approve of this caution."

Before I could continue, Alfonso asked Nathan, "I guess you want me to arrange for someone to steal these documents?"

Nathan nodded, "Do you know someone who can handle something like this? Someone who can do it without leaving a trace? And who will also keep their mouth shut after doing the job?"

"I don't, but some of my contacts do," Alfonso replied. "Don't worry, this is one reason you keep me around."

Curious about Alfonso's contacts, I asked, "Who do you have in mind for this job?"

Alfonso dismissed my question with the wave of a hand. "The name won't mean anything to you unless you have underworld contacts."

I crossed my arms again, raised one eyebrow, and glared at Alfonso. "And what makes you think I don't have underworld contacts?"

"Glamorous babes like you aren't the type to slog through the muck of the underbelly of civilization."

"As generalizations go, yours is fairly accurate. But only *fairly* so." I flashed my sweetly predatory smile at Alfonso. "Now, who do you have in mind?"

Alfonso rolled his eyes, "Fine, have it your way. I'll have to go through a couple of contacts to get to him, but I thought I'd get the Shadow Cat. Satisfied?"

I gave a thoughtful nod, "Shadow Cat is a damned fine sneak

thief. He could definitely do this job, except he always goes off planet this time of year. I'm not sure which tropical paradise world he's visiting right now, but he won't be back for at least another month."

Alfonso gave me an appraising look, "And you know this how?"

"He's a friend of mine. Well, as much of a friend as you can have in this business."

"So, you have underworld connections, as well?" At my nod, Alfonso continued, "I most humbly offer my apologies for underestimating you. If Shadow Cat isn't available, can you recommend another sneak thief?"

I smirked, "Why bother with a sneak thief when you can have a Chic Thief?"

Alfonso's eyes widened in surprise. "You know her?"

I patted Alfonso's cheek, "Darling, I *am* her."

FIND ONE, YOU FIND THE OTHER

Olivia

The soft murmur of voices cut off as I entered the conference room. Eleven pairs of eyes followed me to the seat at the head of the table. I sat, keeping my back straight and folded my hands on the table before me. A quick glance showed everyone's attention was on me. I expected no less from the department heads of the Royal Intelligence Agency.

"Thank you for taking time out of your busy day to meet with me," I said.

We all knew they'd had no choice—when the crown Princess and soon-to-be mother of a royal heir requests a meeting with you, you attend that meeting. So, why bother with the thanks? It showed these men and women I understood the disruption I caused by calling this meeting. It served as reassurance that I would not lightly intrude upon their business.

"For that reason, I'll come straight to the point and keep this meeting as brief as possible." That comment drew pleased smiles and a few nods of thanks. I touched a button on the data pad before me. "Please examine the images and vids in the folder I just sent to you."

Viewing the contents of the folder, the expressions of the men changed from bored attentiveness to alert interest. The women displayed interest, as well, but theirs was more of a 'how does she do it' level of interest. I'd expected these reactions and planned my presentation accordingly.

"The woman in those vids is Tilly Smythe-Warrington. She is the great-granddaughter of a minor noble in a minor house on a minor planet. Miss Smythe-Warrington's grandmother married a commoner, as did her mother. As you can see from the vids, Miss Smythe-Warrington is quite comfortable among the elite of Xapreathean society, including a month-long dalliance with Prince William a year ago."

The eleven pairs of eyes looked everywhere but at me after that admission. Why men and women who are privy to some of the deepest and darkest secrets in the Star Kingdom found my admission uncomfortable is beyond me.

I rapped my knuckles on the table, drawing startled glances from the department heads. "William's sexual escapades prior to my arrival in his life do not concern me. Tilly Smythe-Warrington, however, *does* concern me. According to my sources, she is an extraordinarily accomplished thief who has broken into innumerable highly secured offices and residences. She has done this without once drawing any attention to herself."

A man at the far end of the table spoke up, "Do you suspect her in a theft from the Palace, Your Highness? I assume you wish us to find her. Is that why?"

I shook my head, "No, this has nothing to do with any of her thefts. It has much to do with this woman."

I tapped another button on my data pad, sending another folder to the department heads. They examined the single image it held with nothing more than clinical interest. From the men's expressions, it was obvious they would rather return to viewing Tilly's vids. The women were no more interested.

"I want you to find Tilly Smythe-Warrington because I want you to find the woman in the image before you. As much as I would like to provide you with something better than a computer-generated image, this is the best we have."

That admission sparked some interest among the department heads. In our heavily monitored society, it is almost unheard of to rely solely upon computer-generated images.

"The image was created based upon descriptions from a single person." I saw no reason to tell them William was that person. "While I hope one of your departments can find actual vids of this woman—her name is Jana, we have no last name for her—I do not hold much hope that they will. We already have several vids that *should* provide clear views of Jana's face. They do not. Some kind of interference distorted each of those vids."

"Are you saying this Jana is protected by a team of slicers who erase evidence of her passing?" a woman asked.

"No, Jana is the slicer."

"And she has completely covered her tracks? By herself?" the same woman asked. "No slicer is that good."

I didn't blame the woman for doubting that a single person could hide from the machinery of state this thoroughly. If William hadn't told me everything Jana did during my kidnapping, I probably wouldn't believe it, either.

"According to the experts I've consulted, there is definitely one slicer capable of this kind of work. That slicer uses the name Fox. I'm afraid that's all we know about that slicer—or, it's all we *knew* about the slicer. It seems obvious that Jana and Fox are the same person."

"What if they're not? What if we go looking for Fox and don't find Jana?"

"That is why you have the file for Miss Warrington-Smythe. By all accounts, they are close friends. If you find one, you will find the other."

The same woman who had spoken earlier said, "My resources are tied up on other matters, Your Highness. We're performing those tasks at the behest of Queen Charlotte and, no offense, but I cannot pull them away from those tasks on your word. I will, of course, put them on this search of yours as soon as they complete the Queen's work."

I'd expected push-back and came prepared. "That's quite proper and I respect my position below Queen Charlotte in the royal chain of command."

Once again, I sent a file to the department heads. Eyes widened as they read the orders Queen Charlotte signed at my request.

"As you can see, Her Majesty is fully supportive of my search. May I assume you will bend all of your resources towards finding Tilly and Jana?"

Murmurs of assent came from the eleven men and women before me.

Standing, I said, "I believe Jana is the most dangerous person in the galaxy. Find her quickly. When you do, take her into custody as soon as possible. Interdepartmental cooperation will be properly rewarded. Interdepartmental competition—or, worse, sabotage—will be severely punished. Am I clear?"

All eleven heads nodded.

Without another word, I left the room.

ON THE RUN

Jana

Less than twenty-four hours after I told Tilly about the diagrams we needed, she put them in my hands. Fortunately, she didn't need my help this time. Of course, she also didn't need to ascend the exterior of a skyscraper to escape police pursuit, either.

"Really, Jana," Tilly said, "this job was so simple even *you* could have done it. My talents were completely wasted on such an easy bit of breaking and entering."

I offered her a contrite expression, "I *am* sorry, Tilly. Next time, I'll see if I can't arrange for a lively chase so you can perform a few death-defying escapes."

Tilly lifted her nose into the air and sniffed, "See that you do."

"Meanwhile, Nathan and I are in your debt." I handed the rolled-up set of diagrams to Nathan. "I hope you, Alfonso, and Kelly will excuse us while we spend the next several hours poring over your fine gift to us."

"That sounds positively boring, dear." Tilly emphasized that with an exaggerated yawn. "May I assume my services will not be needed for the evening?"

"You may," I replied. "Why, do you have a pressing engagement somewhere?"

"I thought I might pick up a new outfit—something short and slinky—and visit a club or two."

"That might not be such a good idea. If the Royal Intelligence Agency is looking for us, it would be best if we both stayed out of sight."

Tilly rolled her eyes. "God, Jana, you can be such a mother hen sometimes. I know how to be careful *and* I've got that necklace thing you gave me that distorts my face so cams don't record it. Won't that do?"

"Only if no one is watching the live vid feed. If they are, you'll stand out like... Well, like me at one of those clubs. Only worse."

Tilly's face screwed up in disappointment, "I hadn't thought that through. Someone on the staff always watches those cam feeds. I guess I'll just stay here and catch up on my reading."

Nathan, who had watched this exchange in silence, said, "If you tell me the clubs you want to visit, I should be able to intercept their feed to the RIA facial recognition software."

"Are you sure that will work?" I asked. "Won't the RIA notice the missing feed?"

"It won't be missing, Jana. I'll just route last night's vids to the RIA, instead. They'll get data, but it won't include Tilly."

I mulled that over for a moment. "Can you make sure last night's feed doesn't include some other wanted fugitive?"

Nathan looked offended. "Yes, and that was the first thing I was going to check." He turned to Tilly, "What clubs did you have in mind?"

Tilly rattled off four or five club names and Nathan went to work. Twenty minutes later, he was back. "You're all clear, kid. Go have fun."

"And don't forget to turn the facial scrambler off when you enter a club and turn it back on when you leave," I added.

"Are you going to give me a curfew, too, Mom?" Tilly asked.

Before I could come up with a good answer, Tilly turned and sashayed to the door. Looking over her shoulder at Alfonso, she asked, "Are you coming?"

Alfonso grinned, "Well, someone should keep you out of trouble."

Tilly tossed her hair, "You're welcome to try."

Alfonso waved at us and headed for the door. "I do so love a challenge."

After they left, Kelly looked up from the book she'd been reading. "You want me to follow them and make sure they don't get in over their heads?"

"No," I said. "All silliness aside, Tilly knows what she's doing. She'll be careful."

"As will Alfonso," Nathan added. He looked at me and held up the rolled up diagrams, "Shall we get started?"

"Yep. Might I add that you really know how to show a girl a great time?"

Most people would think I was kidding about that. I wasn't. You don't become one of the best slicers in the galaxy if you find this sort of thing boring. To me, it's a puzzle to study and solve, a challenge to my intellect. From the energy radiating from Nathan, he felt the same as me.

The next several hours flew by. We were so engrossed, we didn't even notice when Tilly and Alfonso returned. Well, we didn't notice until they barged into the room and told us all about their evening out. Nathan and I pretended like we needed a break and listened to their story. Honestly, it sounded dreadful—people packed wall-to-wall, pounding music, strobing lights warring with deep shadows. Blech. The drinks they had sounded good, but I can have good drinks at home and skip dealing with all that other crap.

After a while, Tilly and Alfonso stumbled off to get some sleep, leaving Nathan and me to get back to our examination of the diagrams. We'd been making good progress before the interruption and it didn't take long to get back into it. A few hours later, we had what we felt was a solid network map showing five different data feeds to the Star Stone. At least, we were pretty sure they went to the Star Stone but would have to make a few network runs to verify that.

We were both too keyed up to go to sleep, so Nathan pulled out a bottle of wine he'd been saving for a special occasion. He popped the cork and poured. We offered a glass to Kelly, but she decided it was time for her to turn in. Left to ourselves, we cuddled on the couch and drank our wine.

It was... Pleasant. Oh God, no, that sounds so tame. Sitting on the couch with Nathan's arm around me and my head on his shoulder wasn't just pleasant. It was *right*.

At least it was until someone triggered one of Nathan's alarms.

In eerie silence, barriers slid down the inside of the doorway. They locked into place with a soft snick. Whoever was coming after us wouldn't get through the door easily.

Jumping to my feet, I said, "I assume you have the same materials lining the exterior walls?"

Nathan snatched the data pad from the table next to him and replied, "Of course. Wake the others and go to the hidden room with my equipment in it."

I set off toward the bedrooms, saying over my shoulder, "You didn't show me how to open that."

He tapped the data pad screen. "It's opening now."

"You're going to join us in there?"

"Just as soon as I arrange a few surprises for our unexpected guests."

"It would help if you figured out who they are, too."

"I'll bet all the money in my hidden accounts that it's the Royal Intelligence Agency, Jana."

I agreed with his assessment but didn't bother responding. Instead, I banged twice on Tilly's door, then the same on Alfonso's and Kelly's doors. None of them called out questions, but I heard each of them moving in response to my knocks.

Tilly emerged first, dressed in her black bodysuit and fastening her tool belt around her waist. For someone just yanked out of sleep, she looked disgustingly beautiful. I doubted I could look that good with hours of professional help.

Kelly was next, dressed in nondescript clothing and carrying her backpack of weapons. She, at least, had the decency to look tousled, as if she had just woken up.

I was surprised Alfonso was the last one to put in an appearance. I mean, guys usually pride themselves in dressing quickly. Once I saw him, his tardiness made sense. He was dressed in black clothing similar to Tilly's bodysuit though not as tight, had a gun belt slung about his waist, a backpack over one shoulder, and carried a large, black gym bag in his left hand.

"This way," I said, heading to the back room. "Nathan will be with us in a minute."

"Have you got any idea who's here?" Tilly asked.

"It's a safe bet it's the RIA," I responded.

"We were extraordinarily careful," Alfonso said. "I don't know how they found us."

"I believe you, but it doesn't really matter how they tracked us down—at least, not right now. What matters is getting out of here safely. Alfonso, do you know Nathan's escape route?"

"Yeah, and he keyed it to my retina print. Let me by and I'll open the escape tunnel."

We three women moved to one side of the hall so Alfonso could pass, then fell in line behind him. True to Nathan's word, the entrance to his hidden room was open. Alfonso entered that room, felt around the side wall for something, and then put his face up to the wall. A light shined through an invisible pinhole scanning Alfonso's retina. Soundlessly, part of the back wall slid aside revealing a narrow passageway.

"Follow me," Alfonso said as he entered it.

Kelly, holding a blaster she had pulled out of her backpack, did as Alfonso instructed. Tilly glanced my way, a question obvious in her expression.

"Go ahead," I said. "I'll wait for Nathan."

She hesitated for a second and then gave a quick nod. "Be careful, Jana. You're the only best friend I've got."

Without another word, she strode into the tunnel.

"Nathan," I called, "please tell me you're heading this way."

"Almost, Jana. Give me thirty seconds."

A bang sounded against the front door as our unexpected guests tried to make an impressive and destructive entrance. I couldn't see the barrier, but it didn't sound like it gave a millimeter. It reverberated again but still sounded as if it was holding fast.

Nathan appeared in the hallway, his pace steady but unhurried. He entered the back room, took my hand and drew me into his hidden room. Next, he tapped something on the data pad. The secret door slid shut, but Nathan did not head for the tunnel.

He cast a wistful gaze over his slicing equipment, sighed heavily, and, with a resigned flourish, tapped one last time on the data pad. The equipment sprang to life and made disturbing grinding sounds. As each unit finished grinding, wisps of smoke issued from inside.

"I'm sorry you lost your home because of me," I said.

"Don't be. You know this sort of thing comes with our choice of careers. Besides, Jana, I'd rather be running from the RIA with you than spending more undisturbed nights alone in this apartment."

"That may be the cheesiest thing any man has ever said to me."

Taking my hand again, Nathan pulled me into the tunnel. "I'm a slicer, not a poet. I meant every word though! I've felt more alive since you told me your true identity than ever before."

As the second hidden door slid shut behind us, I said, "Isn't it a little early in our relationship for statements like that?"

"We only just met so I'll understand if you're not sure about me. All I can say is *I* am sure about you."

The thing is, I *was* sure about Nathan. I just wasn't sure I wanted to admit it to anyone, least of all him. No, that's not right. I wasn't sure I wanted to admit it to *me*.

Unbidden, I remembered another couple on the run. I remembered how deeply Jeanine and Drake cared for each other. What I *didn't* remember was any reticence about sharing their feelings with each other. And hadn't I recently found myself wishing I had a 'Drake' of my own?

Casting caution to the winds, I said, "I love you, too."

I WON'T ASK HIM TO DO THIS

Jeanine

I paid close attention to the older man in front of me. His much younger and much more attractive wife stood next to him, pretending to do the same.

"And that, Your Grace, is why I sought this appointment," said Baron... Baron... Morton? Yes, Baron Morton.

Okay, I wasn't much better than Baroness Morton. In our defense, the good Baron was at best a bore and at worst a blowhard. He wasn't the least bit interesting nor particularly intelligent. Worse, he had no feel for the needs of his people. The few times I tuned in on his words, the message was invariably about his needs, his desires, and his profits. Not once did he explain how the subjects of his barony would benefit from the changes he requested.

My office door opened quietly and Drake looked in. Relief washed over me at the sight of him walking my way, a purposeful expression on his face. Baron Boring droned on, so I must have kept that relief off my face. Then again, the Baron seemed so enthralled by his own words, that he might not have noticed if I stripped naked on top of my desk.

Drake nodded at the Baron and Baroness before whispering in my ear, "Get rid of this guy."

"I'm terribly sorry, Baron," I interrupted, "but an extremely important issue has arisen which requires my immediate attention."

Amazingly, the Baron heard what I said and responded, though not in the way I might have expected. "I understand completely, Your Grace, but my needs are extremely important, as well. If you'll just bear with me for another few moments, I'll—"

Drake had walked back around my desk as Baron Morton spoke. Now, he caught the man by the arm and forcibly brought him to his feet. In a coldly formal tone, he said, "I am not a noble, Baron Morton, but even I recognize a polite dismissal when I hear one. As of this moment, Lady Jeanine has far more important demands on her attention than your requests."

"But, I traveled four hyperspace jumps to—"

Baroness Morton caught his other arm and led him toward the door, "And we can return and discuss your matters later when Her Grace hasn't any pressing matters calling for her personal attention."

I smiled gratefully at the Baroness and remained silent until my office door shut. "What's happening, Drake?"

In response, my husband opened the desk drawer and pulled out the specially constructed data pad and writing tablet he had given me and began setting them up on my desk. While he did that, I pulled the opaque mask from the drawer, settled it over my eyes, and waited for Drake. Seconds later, he positioned my hand over the writing tablet. He began tapping on my back and I translated the taps into his message.

Message from our friends.

We had developed our own shorthand code so Drake delivered that message with only a few taps. 'Our friends' meant Jana, Kelly, and Tilly.

Knowing the Star Stone could not divine meaning from a single word, I skipped using the writing tablet and asked, "What?"

They've been discovered and are on the run, Drake's fingers drummed on my back.

"Who?"

The RIA.

"Dammit!" Even as I said that, I began writing a question on the tablet. *Has Jana made contact with that slicer?*

It was Drake's turn to speak a single word response, "Yes."

I rapidly spelled out my next question. *Did the slicer turn them in?*

"No." Drake's fingers added, *He's on the run with them.*

How long has it been since they were discovered?

Only a few hours, babe.

It always amused me when Drake tapped out an endearment like that. It also told me that our friends had not been captured nor did it appear capture was imminent. Drake would never have wasted even the few seconds necessary to spell out 'babe' in either of those cases. In a way, endearments had become shorthand for 'the situation could be a lot worse.'

How did you get word so quickly? I asked.

It took Drake a while to tap the response because it didn't involve everyday concepts. *Tilly and I set up several means of communication before they left. Kelly and I did the same. All either of them needs is a few minutes to send a message to us.*

I nodded my understanding before spelling, *Can they get off Xapreathea?*

"No."

Drake's voice broke as he uttered that one-word death sentence. For that is what it was. If the Royal Intelligence Agency captured our friends, we would never see them again. We would never know their fate, but we would pray for a quick end rather than suffering years of torture and deprivation.

What about the Neert Palace on Xapreathea? I spelled.

It will be watched, Drake tapped. *Besides, if the RIA suspects traitorous activity within the Palace, they may disregard its sovereignty.*

Royal permission is required, but Queen Charlotte will give it without a moment's hesitation.

What about the Rising Star? *She's a fast ship, could they—*

"No." Drake followed that pronouncement with the tapped explanation. *Xapreathea is heavily guarded by the Royal Navy. I couldn't get past them, and I'm a much better pilot than Kelly.*

You and I got away from Gaunner before I was recognized.

Drake's fingers tapped, *We had Jana's program interfering with Gaunner's planetary defense network and Grant's precision hyper jump calculations to get past the space-based defenses.*

I considered that for a moment. *Jana is right there and has the help of another slicer. They can hobble Xapreathea's defenses in real time. Can't Grant calculate a course for them? Then, we just have to send it to them.*

"It doesn't work that way," Drake replied. Tapping on my back, he added, *Hyperspace calculations that complex have to be done just before you use them. There are too many variables—from space stations to orbital weapons platforms to construction docks to large ships—to consider. Grant would have to be on the* Rising Star *during her take off window.*

You know Grant better than I do, I spelled, *will he go to Xapreathea and do that?*

Yes, but it's too dangerous. He's already done way too much for me. I won't ask him to do this.

"No," I said, "but I will."

WE LOST HER
Olivia

"We found them, Your Highness," Lord Darren, head of the RIA's Surveillance Department, said. "And then we lost them."

The man stood at attention before me, his eyes locked on a spot somewhere over my head. I studied his expression for a moment. It was calm, bland even, not the expression you'd expect from a man delivering bad news to the second most powerful woman in the galaxy. I'd have given a lot to know what was running through the mind behind that expression, but it didn't really matter.

I raised one eyebrow. "How did you find them so quickly? I was given to understand this search could take weeks."

"It was nothing more than simple luck, Your Highness. One of the young women studying the cam feeds is, in her off time, active in Xapreathean social circles. She visited the club where the fugitive was found the night before last. Miss Sontag was observant enough to recognize herself amongst the throngs shown in the feed from the club. She alerted the officer in charge, who contacted me."

I nodded, "I hope you commended Miss Sontag?"

"I did, quite profusely."

"Good. Please convey my approval as well. Also, forward her service file to me. I am always looking for good additions to my personal staff."

"I shall do so immediately upon leaving, Your Highness."

"Now, why were the fugitives not taken into custody, immediately?"

Lord Darren stiffened as if gathering his resolve. "That was my decision, Your Highness. The woman you seek—the slicer, Jana—was not among those visiting the club. It was Lady Smythe-Warrington and a petty criminal who has never before come to the attention of the RIA. I had them followed in the hopes they would lead us to the slicer, allowing the capture of both women at the same time."

"Something you failed to do."

"That is correct."

He didn't bluster. He didn't make excuses. He didn't pass the blame. As always, Mother chose her people well.

"Please, Lord Darren, explain how this happened."

Without embellishment, he told me of the sophisticated alarm systems guarding all approaches to the apartment Tilly entered. He described the reinforced walls and, as his team later found out, the reinforced ceiling and floors. Those stymied his men until it was far too late to capture the fugitives.

"Whoever designed the escape tunnel even had explosives that collapsed the tunnel after they passed through it." He wrapped up, "Full responsibility for this debacle lies with me and me alone, Your Highness. In all ways, my people performed their jobs in an exemplary manner. I underestimated our quarry and her allies—whoever they might be. My miscalculation allowed them to slip through our fingers."

I considered his words for a moment. "Please have a full report sent to me as soon as possible. Better, have Miss… Sontag, wasn't it? Yes, have the woman who set this in motion deliver the report personally. Assure her that I wish to meet and compliment her, nothing more."

"I will see to it, personally."

"Now, you may rest easy, as well, Lord Darren. Given the situation, I believe your decisions were logical and your orders were reasonable."

"Thank you, Your Highness."

"I have one other question before you leave."

"I am, as always, at your service."

"I suggested you look for converted Helldiver blockade runners—the same ship Drake Haral modified into his personal ship, the *Rising Star*. Did that search yield results?"

"Far too many results, Your Highness. I'm afraid there are eight hundred and sixty-three converted Helldivers scattered around Xapreathea's many starports. My people are working diligently to winnow the list, but my resources are stretched thin at the moment."

"Understood. If you had the budget to hire temporary staff, would that help or hinder?"

"Untrained staff would hinder, Your Highness. We have neither the time nor manpower to train them properly. Perhaps I could entice some retired personnel to rejoin my staff for the duration of this search though that would prove far more expensive than typical temporary staff."

"I care only for results, Lord Darren. Money is no object. Pay what you believe is reasonable to attract the people you need. Feel free to offer bonuses to those already on your staff. Just find that woman."

"It shall be as you command, Your Highness."

I gave a slight nod. "That will be all."

Lord Darren bowed and left my office.

In all honesty, my calm reaction to Lord Darren's visit surprised me. There was a time—a time well within recent memory—when such a report would have left me in a cold fury. The former version of myself would have vented that fury upon the unfortunate person bearing the news. Today, such a reaction never crossed my mind nor did I have to repress it. I truly was calm.

In years past, my longtime mentor and assistant, Colin, would have complimented me on this reaction. Or, rather, my lack of reaction. Those days, like Colin, have passed. I still felt a pang of loss over him, made all the worse because his death came at my hand, but the pang also passed as other matters occupied my mind. Matters such as how I might turn this development to my advantage.

A thought occurred to me and I felt my lips curl into a smile. Without hesitation, I buzzed my assistant.

"Yes, Your Highness?" he asked.

"Place a subspace call for me, Samuel. I wish to speak with Her Grace, the Duchess of Neert and Gaunner."

"I'll call Lady Jeanine at once, Your Highness, and send for you when I connect with her."

I cut the connection, leaned back in my chair, and let my smile stretch into a grin. At long last, it was my turn to ruin *her* day!

THAT'S RIDICULOUS

Jeanine

With misgivings I took great pains to hide, I settled into the seat of the subspace communicator. A flunky in Royal livery nodded politely at me from the screen.

"I'll inform Her Highness of your arrival, Lady Jeanine."

The flunky departed, leaving me alone for a few seconds. I assumed Olivia wouldn't call unless she had bad news to deliver —bad news for *me*. She would watch me closely as she delivered the news, searching for signs of concern. If she found it—or even if she didn't—I felt certain she would offer her deepest condolences. She wouldn't do this because she was sympathetic, but to show she understood exactly how much her news affected me.

How can I say this with such certainty? It's simple. I'd have done the same thing were our positions reversed. Men can be cruel or vicious, but they rarely hide those emotions behind sympathetic expressions and consoling words. That is why women are far more dangerous than men.

I was as prepared as possible for Olivia's message when she appeared on the screen before me. "Good day, Your Highness."

"Let us dispense with titles, Jeanine. It will make our conversation easier."

"Okay, Olivia, what do you want?"

"You do come straight to the point, don't you? I always liked that about you, Jeanine."

"And you always dance around the subject, Olivia, forcing others to press politely for the information you're withholding. I have no interest in such games, so please just come to the point."

I'll be damned if Olivia didn't grin in response. "We are like-minded women, you and I. It's a pity we aren't close friends."

"Yes, if only I could look past your many attempts to kill me, we could have been best girlfriends. If only you were not a vindictive bitch who blamed an innocent woman for your brother's overconfidence and overreach you'd probably have asked me to be in your wedding." I paused for just a moment before continuing, "Oh, that's right, I *was* in your wedding."

Olivia's grin vanished and her eyes narrowed. "Well, that's more than enough pleasantries, I believe. I've called to tell you that your friends, Jana and Tilly Smythe-Warrington, are on the run. They are at the top of Xapreathea's most wanted list. At my instruction, the RIA has turned its full resources toward finding and apprehending them. I have stressed the importance of bringing them in alive, but you know how field operations sometimes go. I cannot guarantee their safety."

And there it was. In less than a minute, Olivia had given away virtually everything Drake and I had been hiding from the Star Stone. Now it knew that Jana was on Xapreathea. It would know she was there for it. It would know she was planning a slicing run against it.

Because of Olivia, Jana's one advantage against the Star Stone —surprise—was gone.

Because of Olivia, the Star Stone would have time to make preparations for her.

Because of Olivia, one of my dearest friends would face dire threats to her very existence.

Olivia would not care about that. In truth, she would be thrilled if she knew just how much danger she put Jana in. As her next words showed, I had not hidden my reaction from Her Royal goddamned Highness.

Olivia maintained her part in this game. Her mouth formed a sympathetic smile while her eyes remained cold and calculating. "I know how much Jana means to you, Jeanine. Why don't you help me help her? Tell her to surrender peacefully. She'll face a few questions, but nothing more. Once she has answered those to my satisfaction, I will issue an edict of exile and let you take her to Neert."

"Take what's left of her, you mean."

Olivia shook her head in mock sorrow. "That will be entirely up to Jana. If she cooperates—something you could encourage her to do—then she should be little the worse for wear. I would truly hate to see Jana injured in—"

"What's Jana's last name?" I interrupted.

My question startled Olivia out of her almost-rapturous contemplation of what might happen to Jana. "I beg your pardon?"

"You heard me. You keep speaking of Jana as if you know her. Or, at least, as if you know who she is. I merely asked you to prove that. But you can't do it because you have no idea who Jana is and only a vague idea of her capabilities."

Olivia's eyes flashed, all calculation melted out of them by that sudden heat. "I may not know much about your little friend, but I know more than enough about Tilly Smythe-Warrington. Perhaps I cannot bring pressure upon someone near and dear to Jana, but Tilly is a totally different matter. If Tilly cares about her family, and if you and Jana care about Tilly, I strongly suggest you do as I say. I will go as far as to guarantee the bodily safety of both women. Anything else is up to them."

"Well, with such a fine and generous offer, I'm sure they'll jump at it. Or, you could call off your hounds because Jana's mission is beneficial to everyone—especially pregnant princesses."

Olivia's eyes widened, "You dare threaten my unborn child?

What happened to your noble talk during our shared captivity, when you spoke of not making war upon innocents? I see that kind of talk lasts only until it's inconvenient to you. You're not so different from me, after all, Jeanine."

I leaned toward the screen, "Everything Jana is doing will be beneficial to your unborn child. Everything you are doing will be detrimental to your unborn child. How do you think the Star Stone knew I even existed? How do you think it knew to burn your brother? Are you truly so naïve as to believe the 'gift from God' story the Star Kingdom tells children?"

Despite the light years between us, Olivia pulled back from the screen as if alarmed by my intensity. "What are you raving about, Jeanine?"

I thought about disconnecting and letting Olivia wonder if the pressure of the last few months had driven me insane. But the Star Stone was already aware of how much I knew about it. It was aware of how much Drake and Jana knew as well. And it was aware Jana was on Xapreathea and that the only thing that would bring her to that planet was itself.

"Haven't you wondered how William and Drake knew to come to Baron Chilton's hunting lodge in search of us?" I asked.

"I... William said Jana told them where to look."

I'd forgotten William had met Jana. Well, that explained how Olivia learned what little she knew about Jana, including her friendship with Tilly.

"Did you ever wonder why Jana requested access to the Star Stone?"

"Yes, but I can't believe it had anything to do with finding us."

"You can't be serious, Olivia! How do you think Jana discovered our location?"

Olivia dismissed this with an impatient wave. "She's a slicer, I assume she got the information from Gaunner's net."

"How? Your old mentor knew where all the security cams were. He avoided them. That's why none of our guard captains had any idea where to look. Yes, Jana picked up a quick comm broadcast, but that's it. She got our exact location from the Star Stone. The Star Stone had that information because it has put... something...into our bodies. Something from the Recognition ceremony that lets it see what we see and hear what we hear. Furthermore, it can find us with unerring accuracy. The Star Stone told Jana where we were. It even let her overhear Colin's order to kidnap the Holder child, giving Drake time to send my guards to defend the family."

Olivia blew out her breath in exasperation, "That's ridiculous, Jeanine. It makes the 'gift from God' stories sound reasonable."

"Really? How do you explain the fact that Jana knew exactly where to find us, but only after returning from her slicing run against the Star Stone? The very same slicing run your mother-in-law advised against."

"I have no idea, Jeanine. I'm not a slicer. I don't know what Jana might have found in the Star Stone or even if she entered the Star Stone. For all I know, she found everything she needed in Gaunner's net and simply claimed she had sliced the Star Stone and, against all odds, returned safely. God knows, she wouldn't be the first person who embellished already impressive accomplishments."

"To what end? Jana had nothing to prove to us. Why would she do such a thing?"

"I really don't know, Jeanine. Perhaps I'll ask her after she surrenders or is captured."

I knew my last attempt was doomed to failure before I made it, but I had to try. "Whether you believe me or not, the Star Stone is part of you. It flows through your blood, and that means it flows through your baby, too. Who knows whether it can do anything to affect the development of that child? I don't, but I'm not willing to risk the innocent life forming in your womb. Are you?"

"I'm too old for fairy tales and so are you." Olivia's face

smoothed as she prepared to end the call. "My guarantee of safety for Jana and Tilly is good for exactly one day. I strongly recommend you tell them to surrender because they will find themselves unable to leave this planet or evade the RIA. Good day, Jeanine."

Olivia tapped something before her and the subspace screen went blank.

Minutes later, in my office, I gave Drake a quick summary of my conversation with Olivia. From his expression, he immediately understood the consequences of it.

"So much for our plan to keep things hidden from the Star Stone." He stopped pacing and looked at me, "We've got to get Jana, Kelly, and Tilly off that planet as soon as possible. Knowing the three of them, they'll insist on bringing Fox and his friend, too. I'll tell them to get back to the *Rising Star* immediately and lift off."

I shook my head, "I don't think that will work. Olivia swore they'd never get away, and she looked pretty damned confident about it. She probably already has everything in place to ensure that, too. I can't imagine her telling me unless she did."

"I know you, babe, there's no way you're going to abandon them to Olivia and her government thugs. What do you have in mind?"

I considered getting out the writing tablet and having Drake use the tap code, but the Star Stone already knew everything I had wanted to keep hidden from it. Whatever it was capable of, I felt certain direct control of Recognized individuals—even those born to Recognized mothers—wasn't in its bag of tricks. Otherwise, it would have compelled me—its greatest enemy next to Jana—to do its bidding.

From what Jana told Drake of her conversation with the Star Stone, I got the idea it could manipulate emotions. I also made the potentially dangerous assumption that people who were Recognized as adults were immune to such manipulation or, at least, less susceptible to it. God knows I hoped that was true.

I yanked myself away from that train of thought and considered what I should do next. "What are the odds the RIA has found the *Rising Star?*"

Drake thought for a moment before saying, "Pretty slim. Converted Helldiver blockade runners are pretty common throughout the Star Kingdom—so common there could be as many as a thousand of them on Xapreathea right now. Olivia's agents might have identified all the Helldivers, but they won't have had time to dig through their registrations, yet. Even then, the *Rising Star* will be hard to identify. Its new name—I think Kelly chose *Dragonstar*—is legally registered in the Duchy of Neert. That will attract suspicion, but so will the other Helldivers registered through Neert."

"I sense another 'but' in there."

"But they'll have every Neert-registered Helldiver watched. You can be sure lots of heavily armed government troops will descend on anyone who approaches one of those ships."

I considered that. "Tilly is a thief. Do you think she can find a way to sneak everyone on board?"

Drake shrugged, "Your guess is as good as mine. Even if she could, I don't think it will matter. In Olivia's place, I'd have the Royal Navy on high alert, ready to intercept any ship making an unauthorized departure from Xapreathea."

"That's why we're sending Grant to Xapreathea, remember? If he can calculate a hyperspace jump from just outside the planet's atmosphere, they can get away just like you and I did from Gaunner after your old crew broke me out of Olivia's palace."

Drake nodded, still not happy with the idea of sending Grant into danger. "Have you called and asked him, yet?"

"I was just about to do that but wanted to fill you in on my conversation with Olivia, first. Do you want to stay for the call?"

Drake sighed, "Yeah, I think I'd better if for no other reason than it'll save you telling me about it later."

I had the tech manning the subspace communications array

place the call. A few minutes later, she put it through to me and Grant's curious face appeared on the screen.

"Hey, Skipper!" Grant grinned. "What can I do for you and her most illustrious Grace Lady Jeanine Duchess of Neert and Gaunner?"

As I outlined the situation facing our three friends Grant's grin vanished, replaced by a somber and concerned expression. "Grant, I need the best astrogator in the Star Kingdom on their ship with them when they take off. You'll have to find a way to jump out of the system before the Royal Navy blasts the ship to atoms. Can you do it?"

Grant scratched his head and looked thoughtful. "Maybe... Xapreathea has something like ten times the space traffic of any other planet in the kingdom. I can plot a course to get them into hyperspace a lot sooner than normal, but I don't think I could pull off another edge-of-the-atmosphere jump like I did back on Gaunner. There's just too much stuff flying above Xapreathea."

Drake leaned over my shoulder, "From the time you break atmo, how long do you think it will take before you can make the jump?"

Grant's eyes went out of focus for a moment, then he answered, "Twenty minutes? Maybe fifteen if we're lucky."

Drake dropped his forehead on my shoulder, "The Royal Navy will destroy them within five minutes."

"I'm sorry, Skipper, that's the best I can offer." Grant's eyes shifted to me, "Have you got a ship waiting for me? I can be onboard in a matter of minutes."

"You just told me it was impossible to get away before the Royal Navy destroys the ship."

Grant shrugged, "We might get lucky. I'm willing to risk it. Kelly would do the same thing for me."

The matter-of-fact way Grant said that astounded me. I found myself blinking back tears at his ready willingness to put his life on the line for the slimmest of chances he could save his friend.

Damn Olivia.

Damn the Royal Navy.

Damn Xapreathea and all the space traffic around it.

I nodded, accepting Grant's offer. "I won't forget this."

RETURN TO THE STAR STONE

Jana

In an adventure vid, our escape from Nathan's apartment would have turned into an extended action scene complete with a hail of blaster bolts and a high-speed chase through the center of the city. In reality, we reached the end of the escape tunnel without any problems. Nathan collapsed the tunnel behind us and then we drove away in a car he had waiting in a garage. No blaster fire. No high-speed chases.

Over the next two hours, we changed cars twice before Nathan drove us into an underground parking area on the edge of an industrial district. Since the district was undergoing conversion into an upscale residential area, our arrival wouldn't raise any suspicion.

Thirty minutes later, Nathan and I were unpacking and setting up a new slicing station. Alfonso and Kelly were inspecting the perimeter defenses and alarms while Tilly fixed an early breakfast for us. When the food was ready, Tilly insisted we all gather at the table.

She overrode all protests by declaring, "We need a council of war and that means we all need to sit together. Now stop bitching and come to the table."

We spent the first few minutes savoring the food. But, as our hunger eased, we turned our attention to the problem at hand.

"Alfonso and I were extremely careful last night," Tilly said. "Considering my profession, I think you'll agree I know how to remain unnoticed. Alfonso does too if last night is any indication. I can't think of anything we did that would have tipped off the RIA."

"We believe you, Tilly," I said. "But any speculation along this line is premature. Once Nathan and I have the slicing station set up, we can find out what happened."

Kelly joined the conversation, "It doesn't really matter how the RIA found us. Based on my experience in the Neert Space Patrol, you'll spend a lot of time searching for answers and discover the blame can be assigned to bad luck. We have much more important things to do."

Alfonso frowned, "Such as?"

"Jana and Nathan need to learn what the RIA is doing to find us again. Equally as important, they need to find out what the RIA is doing to block our way off Xapreathea." Kelly turned her attention from Alfonso to Nathan, "And I need access to external communication. I need to leave another message for Drake and Jeanine."

"What about the Star Stone?" I asked. "It's the reason we're here, after all."

Kelly shook her head, "I'm afraid it's just going to have to wait. We have more important things to worry about than a big, sparkly rock."

Everyone else around the table was nodding in passive agreement. I slammed both fists down on the table, "No! Nothing is more important than finding out more about the Star Stone. *Nothing*. Not our escape, not even our lives."

My friends stared at me as if I had grown horns and a tail. I met their stares with a glare. "I'm serious. You have not been inside the Star Stone. You have no concept what it can see and what it can do.

I only have a vague idea of its capabilities but it is not a friend of the human race. I believe it has spent thousands of years manipulating mankind from the top down. Whether it's setting us up to be pliant slaves for its creators or working to get us to destroy ourselves or something I haven't thought of yet, the Star Stone must be investigated, understood, and countered, and then destroyed."

Kelly cut a concerned glance towards Tilly, who met it and matched it. Alfonso stared at me in complete incomprehension. Nathan looked surprised at my outburst but looked as if he was considering what I'd said.

Tilly spoke first, "We're all short on sleep, especially Jana and Nathan. I think we can spare a few hours to get some rest, don't you?"

I ran a hand through my hair and glared at my friend, "I'm not being irrational, Tilly."

Tilly met my glare with a mild look, "I never said you were. In all the time we've worked together, you've always been supremely rational. All I'm saying is a little sleep would help us all. Nathan, do you believe we are in any immediate danger?"

He shook his head, "No, we've probably got two or three days before we have to worry about discovery."

"That settles it," Tilly said, her tone brooking no argument. "Finish your breakfast and then get some sleep."

"I do want that external line of communications before everyone retires," Kelly said.

"No problem," Nathan said. "I can set that up in a matter of minutes."

After that, we ate in silence and then stacked our dishes in the kitchen. Tilly and Alfonso went to their rooms while Nathan took a couple of minutes to satisfy Kelly's request.

I just sat at the table, too keyed up to think about sleep. When Nathan turned the communications array over to Kelly, he came looking for me. He stood behind me kneading my shoulders, which felt heavenly.

"You're way too tense to fall asleep, aren't you Jana?"

"Yes."

"Do you want to talk about it?"

I shook my head, "You have to experience the Star Stone for yourself."

"Okay, then to hell with sleep. Let's make a run on the Star Stone right now."

"Not yet, Nathan. I've been thinking about how to ensure your safety while we're inside the Star Stone. I know how to get out, but I'm not sure I can teach you how."

"If you think I'm going to let you make another run on the Star Stone by yourself, you've got another think coming."

"I wasn't suggesting that. I just think it would help if you and I were more closely connected before we made the run."

Nathan stopped kneading my shoulders, "There aren't that many ways I can think of to form that kind of connection."

"I can only think of one. Fortunately, it's also a very good way to release tension." I stood and kissed Nathan gently. "Which room has the biggest bed?"

Later, with my head resting on Nathan's chest and my hand idly caressing his side, I murmured, "That was fun. And relaxing."

Nathan ran his fingers through my hair, "I'm feeling much more closely connected to you, too. *Much* closer."

"Same here." I was quiet for a moment as I tried to impose logic on my mind, which had been running on pure emotion lately. I only partially succeeded, which is why I said, "Maybe I should be the only one to make another run on the Star Stone."

"No way. Either we both go or neither of us goes."

"But—"

"No. Way. You're not going back in there alone."

"You don't fully comprehend the dangers, Nathan. I... Don't want to finally find the right man and then lose him to the Star Stone."

"So, I'm supposed to just stay here and accept the risk that *I* might finally find the right woman only to lose *her* to the Star Stone?" Nathan tightened his arms around me, "I don't think so. You're just going to have to do your best to prepare me for the run on the Star Stone. Start by telling me how you got out."

"When the Star Stone told me I'd never leave, my brain began spinning so fast that I couldn't actually think. When that happened to me in the past, I would sit down with my parents and talk about what was bothering me or what I was trying to figure out. It wasn't that they would offer exactly the right advice that solved my problem—most of the time, they didn't really follow most of what I said—it was that they *listened* to me. I'd usually solve my own problems just by talking through them with Mom and Dad."

"I know exactly what you mean," Nathan said. "I did the same thing with my parents and, after I moved out, with Alfonso."

"I thought you'd understand." I lifted my head and kissed him gently before continuing, "That's when I realized that I only wanted to see my parents for logical reasons. It wasn't because I loved them and missed them. I didn't feel any love for them. I didn't feel love at all. I can't explain it, but that realization let me see my mind's connection to... I guess 'soul' is as good a word as any. And once I saw it, I just sort of asked my soul to bring me home. And it did."

"So, when we get inside the Star Stone, all I have to do is think about my parents and how I feel about them and I should be able to find my soul connection?"

I shrugged, "It worked for me, but I don't know if that will work for anyone else."

"Or I could think about you and how I feel about you. Since you'll be right there with me and since it will be so soon after this *extremely* close connection of ours, it ought to be even easier."

"God, I hope so. You've got to promise to tell me if that

works, though. Because if it doesn't, we need to turn around and get the hell out of the Star Stone immediately. I just hope I can pull you out of there if I have to."

"Don't worry, Beautiful, I have full confidence in you, and at least a little confidence in myself. We'll get out."

We got dressed and went to our new slicing station. The equipment wasn't quite as good as what we left behind in Nathan's apartment, but it was more than adequate for the job. We plugged into the systems, ran a few tests, settled into comfortable positions on the couches, and jacked into the system.

We had already selected our route to the Star Stone. It was a twisting, turning, complicated pathway, and we had to bypass more cutting-edge security than either of us had ever seen. But, just because we hadn't seen that much security didn't mean we couldn't handle it. In a surprisingly short time—I doubted more than fifteen minutes had passed in the real world—we cleared the last security barrier and the way to Star Stone was open to us.

I pulled up short of the interface into the Star Stone, "Are you sure you want to do this, Nathan?"

"Do you want to go back, Jana?"

"No, but maybe you should. I'm not positive we'll—"

"I've already said 'No' to that and never want to hear you suggest it, again. *We* go forward or *we* go back, but there's no way in hell I'm letting *you* go in there by yourself. Got it?"

"Got it," I sighed.

I wasn't surprised by Nathan's declaration but I felt I'd had to try. I was terrified that he would get stuck inside the Star Stone and I'd find myself forced to leave him behind. And I wasn't sure I could do that, not even if it meant sacrificing my own life.

"Do you remember everything I told you about the Star Stone?" I asked.

"Yes, Beautiful, I remember. It was only a few minutes ago

and I'm not feeble-minded. So, are we going into the Star Stone or not?"

"We're going."

Together, Nathan and I entered the maelstrom that is the interface with the Star Stone.

I was ready for the maelstrom between the net and the Star Stone and had done my best to prepare Nathan for it as well. Even knowing what was coming, I found the currents and swirling colors disorienting. I stayed as close to Nathan as the maelstrom allowed, hoping my presence would ease the effect it had on him. Just being close to him made my second trip through the interface a lot easier than my first time. I could only hope I did the same for Nathan. Eventually, we emerged into the impenetrable darkness of the Star Stone.

I still had nightmares about my first time here, my struggle to see or feel anything, and remembered the relief I felt when I saw that first window showing what someone else was seeing. The darkness was just as bad this time, only I was trying to find Nathan, now. As before, the darkness was so complete that I could see nothing. I flailed about me, hoping I might find Nathan. Hoping I could hold onto Nathan if I found him.

I didn't find him.

I couldn't see him.

"Nathan? Can you hear me? Are you there?"

I listened intently for a reply but heard nothing.

Had he come through with me? Had the interface routed us to different...facets...of the Star Stone? If only I could see something!

Then I remembered forcing those windows into order during my last visit. I remembered imposing my will on what I saw inside the Star Stone. And I found myself wondering why I was spinning around in the darkness when it should be within my power to turn on the lights.

Pushing down my fear of the darkness and of being alone, I

drew on my experience as an elite slicer and said, "Let's have a little illumination!"

And just like that, there was light. And with that light, I saw Nathan. He wasn't that far away. From his wide-eyed expression, I could tell he hadn't cared for primal terror blackness, either.

"There you are," he said. He tried for a nonchalant tone but completely missed it. "I was about to light things up, myself. Thanks for saving me the trouble."

I arched my left eyebrow. "Do guys really think women believe them when they say things like that?"

"The smart ones know better but we say stuff like that, anyway." Nathan shrugged, "It's a guy thing."

"Whatever. On a more important topic, can you see it?"

Just in case Nathan was still a little disoriented and had forgotten what 'it' was, I made a kissy face, reminding him that love was the key to find his lifeline.

"Um..." Nathan craned his neck, "I think so?"

I shook my head, "That's not good enough. If you can't give me a definitive 'yes', then we need to leave right now."

Nathan stopped moving and took a moment to bring himself under control. When he looked my way again, his eyes were calm and his countenance was collected. Once again, he looked around himself. This time his eyes tracked something back toward the maelstrom.

"Got it." He looked my way, "You know, this whole place is really odd."

"Yes, it is. Now it's time to find—"

"Miss Ward, what a pleasant surprise." The Star Stone, still appearing as the nondescript man I'd seen during my last visit, suddenly stood before us. "And you brought a guest. How very thoughtful of you. I hope you told him he'll never leave and will fade away to nothing within a matter of days."

"I told him more than that, Star Stone, though I also warned him of the consequences if he can't get away. Fortunately, he can."

The Star Stone smiled, "Are you so certain, Miss Ward? After your unexpected departure, I have been very busy working out how you did that. Would you believe that I've succeeded and can now block your departure?"

I folded my arms, tapped my foot—which seems a little odd since I was basically hanging in space, but it worked—and said, "You'll excuse me if I don't believe you?"

"What reason have I to lie?"

"You probably want one of us to return while you're watching for it. I assume you hope you can figure out what we're doing if you watch closely enough."

"That's a very reasonable guess, Miss Ward. But why are you so resistant to the idea that I might have figured it all out?"

"You had thousands of years to figure out how that religious guy got away and couldn't do it. Am I supposed to believe that you managed to discover the answer in the few weeks since I got away?"

"When the time comes, Miss Ward, you'll discover your belief has no power here."

Nathan chose that moment to join the conversation. "If you have figured it out, tell us how she did it."

The Star Stone regarded Nathan askance, "Why should I share my secrets with you?"

"You won't be sharing a secret with us," Nathan said. "We already know it. You'll just be proving to us that you know it, as well."

The Star Stone clapped its hands slowly, "Bravo. That's very logical of you. I can see why Miss Ward chose you to accompany her this time. I believe the three of us are going to have quite a good time—until the two of you fade away."

"Well threatened, sir," Nathan riposted. "As you can see, we are quaking in terror."

"I grow tired of this banter." The Star Stone clasped its hands together as if in supplication and asked, "What may I do for you, Miss Ward?"

I thought about claiming we were only interested in learning more about such an ancient, alien artifact but knew the Star Stone wouldn't believe me. Instead, I told the truth.

"We want to learn what your ulterior motive is. Why did your creators send you to humanity? What did they hope to gain and how can you help them achieve their goals? Oh, and where are they? Humanity has expanded a lot since you showed up and we haven't found any ancient alien races."

"What is it the characters say in those insipid adventure vids you humans seem so enamored of?" the Star Stone asked, drifting closer to me. "Oh yes, I remember. I could tell you the answers to all your questions, but then I'd have to kill you."

Nathan snorted, "I thought you were going to kill us, anyway."

The Star Stone stopped right in front of me, so close our noses almost touched. Without taking its eyes from mine it answered Nathan, "I'll certainly kill Miss Ward this time, but must simply hope you prove incapable of utilizing her escape method. If that is the case, I'll kill you next."

Suddenly, the nondescript body the Star Stone wore morphed into something shapeless and black and enveloped me.

As soon as I realized that the Star Stone was trying to trap me, I ordered my soul connection to bring me back. I gave that order a few picoseconds too late because nothing happened. Terrified my connection was severed, I looked for the glowing thread back to my body. It was still there but only extended a short distance before... I'm not sure what happened to it. All I can say is I couldn't see the glowing thread beyond that short distance. It wasn't flopping around as if it'd been cut, at least.

I tried moving to my right, hoping to see whether my soul connection moved with me or stayed anchored at that... 'Cut off point' was not the phrase I wanted to use and 'endpoint' wasn't much better but I'm going to go with endpoint. Anyway, I tried moving while watching the thread back to my body hoping I'd feel myself moving while the endpoint stayed in one place. That would tell me... I *think* it would tell me that I was still connected to my body, only the thread was snagged or tangled or simply caught tightly and unable to reel me back in.

What I hadn't considered was how hard it was to judge movement when everything around you is black. I think I moved to the right, but I also may have pivoted about the endpoint. In other words, I couldn't tell a damned thing. Since I was almost certainly dead if my soul connection was severed, I decided to work under the theory that it was still intact.

"You appear agitated, Miss Ward," the Star Stone's voice boomed from all around me. "I'd have thought you would be thrilled to have finally reached my core."

"I'm not agitated, just surprised at how quickly my plan worked." That even sounded lame to me, and I'm the one who said it. Still, I wasn't going to give the Star Stone the satisfaction of panicking. "Now that you've brought me to where I wanted to be, I'll plunder your memories, programming, and everything else I can think of, and then I'll leave. Just like last time."

"You sound as if you are trying to convince yourself rather than me, Miss Ward. Are you succeeding?"

I ignored its question and asked, "If this is your core, where was I before you engulfed me?"

"I'll humor you and answer that question. What lies outside are my monitoring systems. They gather data, sort it, prioritize it, store it, and feed the most important information to me. From a human perspective, you might consider them the equivalent of your five senses and this core is the equivalent of your brain. It's far more complicated than that but—"

"It's so far beyond me that I will never, ever understand," I snapped. "You are a condescending pain in the ass, Star Stone. You do realize that, don't you?"

"I must admit your defiance is quite endearing, Miss Ward. I will miss it—and the rest of you—when I finish picking you apart. I mean that quite literally, of course. I'm not going to make the same mistake I made with those who came before you and let you simply wither away. It seems like such a waste, especially when you consider I can't gently pry you apart and sift through everything that makes you who you are. I think I'll learn quite a lot from this experience, though. I do hope it won't prove too unpleasant for you, but I can't say."

Well, crap. That didn't sound good, but I refused to give the Star Stone the satisfaction of showing it just how terrified I was.

"You're just going to digest me slowly without first proving your vast superiority by telling me what the hell you've been doing with humanity for the last several thousand years?"

"That is my plan. Why would I bother assuaging your curiosity when there will be nothing left of you a day or two from now?"

That was a very good question, and I needed a very good answer. Any kind of delay might give Nathan the chance to do something. I have no idea what that something might be, but if anyone could come up with an idea, it was the best slicer in the Star Kingdom. That's assuming he hadn't gotten the hell out of the Star Stone when it grabbed me. I wouldn't blame him if he had done that, but it just didn't strike me as something Nathan would do. Not where I'm concerned, at least.

"Why would you tell me your ultimate purpose? How about because I'm human and you're not?"

"We've already been through this, Miss Ward. Have I failed to convey my opinion of humanity during any of our conversations?"

"No, you've been quite clear about your disdain for us. Despite that, you've spent thousands of years preparing us for... Something. Obviously, you need humans for whatever it is. Has it ever occurred to you that one of us might provide a useful viewpoint? One you are incapable of seeing?"

"Come now, Miss Ward, even you know the average human rarely thinks about anything beyond his or her daily needs. How could I gain anything useful from someone such as that?"

"Okay, you've got me there. The average human wouldn't be

particularly useful to you. But *I* am not an average human. I am about as far above average as it's possible for a human to be."

"You raise an excellent point, Miss Ward. Besides, I do enjoy our conversations and see no reason not to extend this one a bit longer. After all, once I start taking you apart you're not going to be much of a conversationalist."

"So, you're going to reveal your nefarious plan? Tell me the ultimate purpose you've been working towards over the last several thousand years?"

"I am."

Color me surprised. I didn't expect my appeal would work. I also didn't expect what the Star Stone said next.

"I have been breeding superior humans. Due to the strange emotional attachments humans develop to their breeding partners and offspring the task has been vastly more difficult than my creators anticipated. Many promising lines have been lost as a result of unexpected infatuations with inferior genetic specimens. Worse, I have not always been able to bring the best your species has to offer into my program. Take yourself, for instance. You came into existence by random chance, yet you would be an extraordinary addition to my breeding program. Alas, you have never been Recognized nor ever would have been."

"Gosh, that must be truly frustrating for you."

The Star Stone did not catch the sarcasm in my tone. "You are quite correct, Miss Ward. I will greatly regret your loss as I would dearly love to find some way to get you Recognized and drawn into my gene pool."

"Considering some of the idiots I've met among the aristocracy, I can see your point. Tell you what, why don't you let me go? Once I'm out, I'll get myself Recognized. Princess Olivia is looking for me, so I could agree to join her side in exchange for a barony or something like that. Hell, even a knighthood would do, right?"

The Star Stone laughed, "Very clever! So much so that I'm tempted to grant your request."

"Great! Just toss me back out into your monitoring area and I'll go back to my body. You have my word that I'll turn myself in to Princess Olivia first thing in the morning."

"I said I was tempted, Miss Ward, not stupid."

"A girl can hope, can't she?"

"Anyway, as I was explaining, my breeding program has taken far longer than it would have had I been working with a reasonable species. Had humanity been anything like my creators, I could have achieved my goal in well under a thousand years. But you humans have such delicate genetic structures that my creators' methods were destructive rather than constructive. I was forced into a lengthy period of genetic trial and error, exploring the boundaries of what your weak species could survive. Worse, due to various constraints built into me, my experimentation time was severely limited. At long last, I believe I have both the knowledge to properly perform the manipulations I require and the conditions necessary to prove it."

I did not like the sound of that. "And what do you have now that you haven't had before?"

"I have two extraordinary females who have both been Recognized and are of prime breeding age. Very soon, I shall have the opportunity to verify the techniques I have developed over the previous four thousand years."

Without the Star Stone even saying it, I knew who it meant. "You're talking about Jeanine and Olivia, aren't you?"

"Very good, Miss Ward."

"And Olivia's baby is the one you're going to experiment on?"

"I am beyond the experimental stage. I shall, instead, transform her fetus."

"What are you going to do to the child?"

"I shall grant her the greatest honor ever bestowed upon any human. Through her—or through Jeanine's daughter, it depends on which one survives their confrontation—my creators shall return. One of them shall be the queen of a reborn race!"

As the Star Stone's words sank in, a strange and terrible idea entered my mind. "What happens during a Recognition ceremony?"

"Come now, Miss Ward, everyone in this little Star Kingdom knows the answer to that question. During Recognition, the Star Stone—God's instrument of truth and justice—judges whether the person in question is worthy to serve humanity."

"I never imagined you were one for fairy tales," I sneered.

The Star Stone laughed, "Who am I to deny the human race their myths and legends?"

"Since you've been toying with us for the last four thousand years, I'm going to guess you're the one who created those myths and legends."

"No, Miss Ward, that's all on you. More properly, it's all on your ancestors. Mankind is extraordinarily adept at crafting stories that explain what they don't understand. I merely provided a mystery. Poets, bards, and storytellers did the rest." The Star Stone paused for a moment as if it was thinking. "Your species is singular in their predilection for stories. My creators never did anything like it, nor did any of the other species they... dealt...with. That, combined with your race's unfortunate collections of evolutionarily superfluous emotions, has severely handicapped me."

"Uh, come again? If the stories are just for us lowly humans, how do they make your exalted existence difficult?"

The Star Stone paused long enough for me to begin worrying it wasn't going to answer. "Somehow, the command structure in my central core can be shaped by human belief. The whole system of Recognition was born from your race's belief that I was an instrument of your God. The concept aligned closely with my purpose even if it restricted my work. Though, to be fair, one anomalous aspect of Recognition was a boon."

"Which part is that?"

"If you are as superior as you claim, Miss Ward, you should have little trouble deducing the answer."

Offered more time to temporize, I said, "You raise a good point, Star Stone. Let me think about this..."

And I *did* think about it, along with everything else the Star Stone had revealed. If human belief could reprogram the Star Stone, could I simply *believe* my way to freedom or did that require many people all believing the same thing? I bent my entire mind to the belief that the Star Stone was releasing me. My belief pushed almost everything else from my mind, and maybe that's why I failed. Or maybe one person couldn't reprogram the Star Stone. Whatever the reason, the Star Stone didn't release me. But I did figure out the anomalous aspect of Recognition.

"You're talking about Recognized Knights, aren't you?" I asked. "People believed the knights should obey every command given by their lord and master and that effectively gave you a way to experiment on humans who weren't in the womb."

"Very good, Miss Ward! I knew you could do it."

"Great. Maybe you can mark my homework with a gold star. Mom will be so proud."

"I do not understand your reference."

"Never mind, then. But I guess you've learned the true power of stories, right?"

"Power? Bah! Mankind's stories have been no power over me. If they did, my true purpose would have changed. These stories have hindered, but they have not obstructed. Over the next one thousand years, I believe we'll discover just how powerless humanity's stories are. Perhaps your descendants—not yours personally, of course, as you shall not survive to reproduce your species—will invent songs and stories to explain the ascension of my creators. No doubt your kind will hail them as gods. Your stories will only exert power over humanity—and that power will do nothing but ensure humans become docile servants of my creators reborn!"

I got the idea that statement was how the Star Stone planned to end our conversation. I was still trapped, so needed something to keep it talking. "That discussion was an interesting diversion but why don't we return to my original question? Since you're certain I'm going to die, why not answer it? What happens during a Recognition ceremony?"

"What do *you* think happens, Miss Ward?"

"Has anyone ever told you that you're the most irritating AI in the galaxy? Must you answer every question that way?"

"As before, I'm testing you."

I sighed in frustration. "Fine, we'll do it your way. During the Recognition ceremony, I think you send microscopic organisms or nanobots—probably both—into the body of the person requesting Recognition. I think it occurs when your red glow envelops them. If I'm right, that's how you keep track of every Recognized person and, though I have no idea exactly how it works, see and hear everything a Recognized person sees and hears. I suspect some of those nanobots and organisms even infect sperm cells, which lets you track people who have a Recognized father but not a Recognized mother. People like Jeanine."

I heard the sound of one person clapping. "Bravo! Once again you've proven yourself an amazing specimen of humanity, Miss Ward."

Unable to resist taking the Star Stone down a few pegs, I said, "Just think, you had absolutely nothing to do with my creation. I happened through random chance. Meanwhile, *you* spent over four thousand years trying to produce Olivia and Jeanine. Both of Olivia's parents were Recognized, so I guess you can take some minor credit there. On the other hand, only one of Jeanine's parents was Recognized, and he had nothing to do with her beyond his role as the sperm donor. Tell me again why these creators of yours put such faith in you?"

"Very droll, Miss Ward." It might have been my imagination, but I thought the Star Stone sounded rather petulant at the moment. "I grow weary of this infantile repartee and, quite frankly I grow weary of you."

I laughed in triumph. "Poor little Star Stone, it simply hasn't got the imagination required to win a battle of wits against a mere human—just like your creators and their alien friends."

"*Enough!*" the Star Stone roared. "Goodbye, Miss Ward. I shall find your screams entertaining."

I steadied my nerves, swearing I would never give the Star Stone the satisfaction of screaming. "Do your worst."

"Rest assured, Miss Ward, I—"

Suddenly, the darkness was rent asunder and a bright, golden light blinded me.

IT ALWAYS ENDS IN BLOOD

Tilly

Insistent banging on my bedroom door pulled me out of my dream. The images in my head melted away, leaving behind nothing but a vague feeling of unease. I didn't need those feelings to tell me I'd had a bad dream—the sheen of sweat covering my body told me the same thing. Ignoring that sticky-sweat sensation, I climbed out of bed.

"I'm coming."

The door slid aside, revealing Kelly standing in the hallway. "It's Jana! Come on."

I tried to make sense of Kelly's words, but she turned and hurried down the hall before I could speak. I trotted after her, calling, "What do you mean? Is something wrong?"

Kelly didn't stop or look back but she replied, "I think so. Jana sure as hell doesn't look okay."

"Where is she?" I asked reflexively since the answer was obvious once my brain got itself in gear. "I thought she and Nathan weren't doing any slicing until tomorrow."

"You and me, both," Kelly said. "It's pure luck I found her. An uneasy feeling woke me up, so I decided to do a security sweep of this place."

She led the way into Nathan's and Jana's slicing lair. That's what Jana has taken to calling it, so I'm just copying her.

Kelly moved to the side so I could see Jana and Nathan, "This is what I found."

Nathan looked perfectly normal, comfortably reclining in his seat and connected to his bleeding-edge equipment. Jana was reclining in a seat and connected to the equipment as well. That's where the similarities between her and Nathan ended.

Sweat covered Jana's face and, from the damp patches on her clothes, the rest of her body. Her eyes moved rapidly beneath her eyelids, her head jerked back and forth, and her knuckles had turned white from the force of her grip on the chair arms. Jana's legs twitched spasmodically and a soft moan escaped her lips.

Kelly's hand moved tentatively toward Jana's connection with the equipment, "Should we disconnect her?"

"*No!*" I leapt forward and slapped Kelly's hand down. "We might lose her forever if you do that!"

Kelly's eyes widened, "I had no idea."

"I know," I sighed. "Jana and I should have told you all about this days ago. It's just been... A bit hectic, lately."

Kelly waved her hand vaguely at Jana, "What should we do?"

I scrubbed a hand over my face and shrugged, "I don't know if there's anything we *can* do besides wait. If Nathan comes out of it, maybe he can tell us something. Or maybe Jana will just suddenly come back."

"I haven't felt this helpless since Drake and the rest of us patrollers came back to our mining colony and found everyone dead," Kelly muttered.

God, I'd forgotten Kelly had been part of Drake's crew. I couldn't even imagine what it must have been like for them, excited to be heading home only to find their home's dome slagged and all their family and friends slain.

I gave Kelly's shoulder a squeeze, "Jana is really good at this stuff. We're just going to have to hope she's good enough to take care of whatever is doing this to her."

As if on cue, Jana gasped and sat up. Her eyes flew open and darted wildly back and forth. Shaking hands reached for her connection with the network, "Get this off of me! Get it off! Off, dammit!"

I caught Jana's fumbling hands while Kelly disconnected her from the network.

"Sssh! It's okay, Jana," I said in what I hoped was a soothing tone. "Kelly is disconnecting you now. You're home. Do you understand? You're home."

Jana's eyes swung my way, "Is it really you, Tilly? You're not some kind of Star Stone trick?"

I had no idea what Jana was talking about but replied, "Yes, it's really me. If you're not sure, just ask me something only you and I would know."

Jana shook her head, "No, I don't need to do that. You feel too real to be a network construct—even one created by the Star Stone."

"What happened to you? Your whole body was quivering."

"The Star Stone had me and was about to... I don't know, I guess 'devour' is the right word for what it was going to do to me."

I pulled Jana into a hug, "My God! How did you get away?"

"I didn't. There was a sudden flash of golden light and then I was here. I guess Nathan—," she broke off and looked at the other chair. "Nathan! Why isn't he back?"

I thought that was a very good question, one I didn't have a very good answer for. But I could feel Jana's body tensing so said, "I'm sure he's fine. He's looked just like that—normal—the whole time. I'll bet he's just giving that Star Stone a piece of his mind."

I regretted saying that as soon as the words left my mouth. Jana told me how those who entered the Star Stone before her had just faded away or been absorbed by the Star Stone. Now I had stupidly put that idea in Jana's head.

She gave a short sob and said, "No, Nathan, don't sacrifice yourself for me!"

"Well, if you insist, Jana," Nathan said. He quickly disconnected himself from the network but his eyes stayed on Jana. "Are you okay? Did that thing hurt you? Did it take anything from you?"

Jana shook her head, "No, I'm fine. Was that golden light you?"

"I guess," Nathan said.

Eyes wide with wonder, Jana asked, "What did you do?"

"When the Star Stone swallowed you up, there was nothing left but this big, roiling darkness where you had been. I know everything already was dark, but this thing was darker than dark. That doesn't make any sense but—"

Jana waved that off, "Don't worry about that."

"I tried going into the roiling mass, but I just bounced off of it. I couldn't grab it, either. Honestly, I was at my wit's end when I felt something tugging at my back. It was the lifeline back to my body. Although from what you said about it, maybe I should call it my love line. Anyway, without any conscious thought, I grabbed hold of my line and pulled."

"Nathan! You could have broken it and stranded yourself in the Star Stone," Jana cried.

"What would be the point of coming back if it meant leaving you behind?"

Nathan said that with such simple and deep sincerity that I found myself blinking away tears even though he was talking to Jana. She was doing the same thing. So was Kelly.

Oblivious to the effect he'd had on the three women present, Nathan continued, "The lifeline or love line or whatever you want to call it stretched. I reeled in a lot of extra line and started whipping the roiling darkness with it. Somehow, the lifeline affected it. The line stripped away layer after layer until you appeared. I flicked my line at you and it wrapped itself around you. Then I yanked you back toward the Star Stone interface. Once you vanished into it, I followed."

"But why didn't you come back at the same time I did?" Jana asked.

"My lifeline had a lot of slack in it. It took a little while to reel it all in."

Jana pulled free of me, went to Nathan, and gave him an extremely passionate kiss. After a few seconds, Kelly and I grew so uncomfortable that we just stared at each other.

A few seconds after that I folded my arms and said, "There's a room with a great big bed in it nearby. If you two want to keep this up, I suggest you move it in there."

The two slicers broke their lip lock. Jana, her cheeks reddening a bit, said, "I wish we had time for that."

"What's the rush," I asked. "Have you and Nathan got someplace to go?"

"No, Tilly, you do."

My eyebrows rose in surprise, "I do?"

"Most definitely. It's going to be dangerous, it's going to take a lot of planning, and you're going to need my help."

"What am I doing—stealing the crown jewels?"

Jana shook her head, "I wish it was that easy."

My mouth fell open, "What the hell do you want me to steal?"

"A sample of Princess Olivia's blood."

I stared at Jana trying to make sense of her words. After failing utterly, I said, "Would you repeat that again and this time use words that don't sound crazy?"

Jana rose from her place on Nathan's lap and headed for the hallway. Over her shoulder, she repeated, "We need to get a sample of Princess Olivia's blood. Maybe two of them though I'll have to think about that."

As the three of us hurried after her Kelly murmured, "Are you sure all of her mind came back from the Star Stone?"

"I heard that," Jana called. "I know this all sounds ridiculous but it will make sense after I've explained everything to you."

"Oh, good," I said. "Knowing it makes sense will make it *so* much easier for me to slip into the Royal Palace and take a couple of blood samples from the Crown Princess. The *pregnant* Crown Princess. The pregnant Crown Princess with the large, muscular, overprotective husband. Not to mention an army of overzealous guards who are probably just itching to shoot someone like me."

"I'm not saying it won't be dangerous, Tilly," Jana said, flopping onto the sofa. "I'm saying we don't have any other choice. I'll do everything in my power to keep you safe while you do this."

I dropped into a chair opposite the sofa. Nathan joined Jana, sitting close and watching her with worried eyes. Kelly took a seat more or less between us. I got the idea she hoped to moderate the argument she thought was coming. Since I didn't want to put Kelly in that position, I forced myself to calm down.

"You know I'll do everything I can to protect you, Tilly," Jana said, her voice was still tight with stress. "I'm sorry I sprang all of that on you without leading up to it but what I learned from the Star Stone this time really rattled me. It didn't help that it was about to kill me when Nathan pulled me out of there."

Jana suddenly had another case of the shakes. Nathan pulled her into a tight embrace and whispered quietly into her ear. Whether it was his words or his presence that did the trick, Jana's shivers slowly subsided.

"Why don't you take some time to rest and recover?" I asked. "Whatever happened inside the Star Stone has really shaken you up. Don't make yourself re-live it right now. I can wait a while to have my questions answered."

Jana shook her head, "I wish I could wait, but this is just too important. We have to move fast before it's too late."

"If you say so. Why don't you start at the beginning and build up to why I have to get that blood sample?"

Jana took a deep breath and began, "I've learned the Star Stone's true purpose. It is an artifact from an extinct sapient race. Those aliens created the Star Stone for one purpose—to ensure the rebirth of their race. Everything about Recognition serves that purpose."

"Are you telling me the Star Stone really does put nanobots or something like that into people during the Recognition ceremony like you originally guessed?" I asked. "That's...disturbing."

Jana gave a humorless laugh, "You have no idea, Tilly. 'Disturbing' doesn't even come close to the truth. It puts nanobots and alien genetic material into everyone who gets Recognized. That's how it sees and hears what they do. It can even mark the children of Recognized adults. That's easy when the mother is Recognized because the Star Stone's little helpers have access to the child for nine months. It's a little more tenuous when only the father is Recognized, but every one of the father's sperm cells carries a nanobot rider."

"That's how the Star Stone knew about Jeanine, right?" Kelly asked. "Her mother was never Recognized but her father was a Recognized Duke."

"Yes."

I waved away that subject, "Yeah, that's really interesting but it doesn't explain why I need to steal some of Olivia's blood."

"Okay, I'll skip a lot of the back story and get to the point. The Star Stone has been performing genetic experiments on babies growing inside Recognized mothers for thousands of years. The alien programming gives the Star Stone its purpose but also imposes certain restrictions on it. The most stringent of those conditions is only met once every few hundred years, but right now is one of those rare times. We've got two intelligent, strong-willed, powerful, fertile, Recognized women in the Star Kingdom."

"Jeanine and Olivia?" Kelly asked.

"Jeanine and Olivia," Jana agreed. "Using its nanobots and alien genetic material, the Star Stone will begin genetically engineering Olivia's baby soon—maybe in the next few days. It's going to turn that little princess—the Star Stone will ensure the child is a girl—into something that looks human but is really the first of its creators' race reborn. When Jeanine gets pregnant, her daughter will get the same treatment."

I felt a shiver of horror run up my spine. "You can't be serious. Please, tell me you're not serious."

"I wish I could, Tilly. But I can't."

"Can't what?" Alfonso asked, stumbling into the room. "And why didn't you guys wake me up if you were going to have a serious discussion?"

"It's a long story and I'll fill you in later," Nathan said. "For now, just sit down, shut up, and listen."

Alfonso shrugged and lowered himself into a chair, curiosity written all over his face. But he followed Nathan's instructions and kept quiet.

"If you're right about this, Jana—and I don't doubt that you are," Kelly said, "we have definitely got to do something about it. Drake and Jeanine have been through too much already. I will be damned if I'll let something happen to the child they haven't even conceived yet!"

Alfonso's curiosity turned to confusion, but he didn't interrupt. I'd have been firing questions left and right if I were him.

"I know we all agree with Kelly," I said. "But how can a blood sample from Princess Olivia help?"

Jana ran a hand through her hair, "I'm kind of shooting in the dark here, but I think a xenozoologist can test the blood for alien biological matter. If he finds the nanobots or the alien genetic material, we'll have all the proof we need to get Olivia and William to listen to us."

I felt a wave of relief wash over me. "If that's all you want to do, I can just arrange to visit my great-grandmother and get a blood sample from her. She's been Recognized."

Jana shook her head, "If we had more time I'd agree with you. But we've got the RIA breathing down our necks. If they capture us, we may not have a chance to talk to the Royal family until it's too late to save the baby.

"And even if the xenozoologist finds alien material in your great-grandmother's blood sample, you know the Royal family would insist on performing the same test on Olivia's blood. By then the Star Stone will know what we're doing. Maybe it has a way to keep the nanobots and genetic material out of a blood sample. If we get Princess Olivia's blood without her realizing we're doing it, the Star Stone won't have a chance to do anything. And we will have incontrovertible proof that something strange is going on."

"I know I'm supposed to shut up and listen," Alfonso said, "but I think Jana is on to something. If the Star Stone couldn't keep its stuff out of blood samples, surely someone would have found some evidence of this alien crap during routine blood tests. I mean, the Star Stone has been around for thousands of years. That adds up to a lot of blood tests."

"That's why I keep Alfonso around," Nathan said. "Every now and then he says something really smart."

"And he makes a damned good point," Kelly added.

"Yeah, he does," I muttered. "Add it to everything Jana has said, and it makes a pretty compelling case. Or maybe it doesn't and I'm just too frazzled to see it any other way. Regardless, it looks like I'm going to break into the Royal Palace and pretend I'm a vampire."

NIGHTMARES

Olivia

I ran, chasing...something. Something I desperately needed to catch. Something of unimaginable importance. Something that could destroy me. Something I wanted to destroy. But it was always just beyond my grasp. Even when I thought I held it, it turned to mist and slipped between my fingers.

Still, I ran, chasing the thing I wanted—no, *needed*—more than life itself.

Still it eluded me.

And then it was gone. Escaped. Beyond my reach.

Fearing its loss would cost me my very existence, I screamed in agony and frustration.

I bolted up in bed, eyes wide as a cry swept away the last vestiges of sleep. Then, I realized the cry was my own and silenced it. Only then did I notice William was also silencing a cry, too.

Our bedroom door burst open and four guards rushed in. Light flooded the room as they searched for threats to our safety.

"Is there an intruder?" the senior guardsmen asked.

"No. There's...nothing," William responded. "Just a horrific dream."

The man turned his attention to me, "What of you, Your Highness? Did you see anything?"

"No, nothing. I had a nightmare, too. I'm sorry we disturbed you."

I suddenly realized my throat was parched beyond endurance. Without thinking, I threw the covers aside and rose from the bed. The four guards suddenly averted their gazes, and I remembered I was naked.

The senior guardsmen, a man old enough to be my father, snatched up a robe I had tossed across one of the chairs. Holding it up while still averting his eyes, he advanced toward me.

"Let me help you cover up, Your Highness. We wouldn't want you catching a chill, what with you carrying the Royal heir and everything." The man whipped his head around toward the other three, much younger, guards. Satisfied that none of them were sneaking peeks at their naked princess, he barked, "That will be all, men. Resume your stations."

Keeping their eyes firmly locked on the bedroom doorway, the men marched quickly out of the room. As the last one exited, he asked, "Shall I shut the door, Sergeant?"

"Just keep your eyes fixed on the far wall, Tibbs. I'll close it in just a moment."

I slid my arms into the robe and shrugged it on. Keeping my back to the embarrassed guardsmen, I closed the front and tied the belt. The robe was a translucent black, so I was only slightly more modestly attired than when I'd been stark naked. For that reason, the guardsman kept his back to me as I turned around.

"Please forgive the lack of respect implied by showing you my back, Your Highnesses."

"There's nothing to forgive, Sergeant," I said. "You and your men have behaved with gallantry."

Speaking for the first time, William added, "Indeed you have. My compliments to the four of you for your vigilance and the alacrity of your response."

"'Tis but our duty, Your Highness. If you won't be needing anything else, I'll return to my station and close the door."

"Of course," William said. Once the door closed William flashed a lopsided grin at me. "Well, my dear, you've given our four guardsmen a night to remember!"

The dream-induced fear had faded, replaced by a certain thrill at what I'd done. I could never be so brazen as to put myself on display purposefully, but giving the guards an unintentional eyeful of bare royal flesh made me feel rather naughty. From the way the sheet over William's lap rose, he felt the same way.

I walked to the water pitcher and poured myself a drink. Turning to face William, I tilted my head back, elongating my neck, and drank. Putting the cup down, I licked my lips and sauntered back to the bed, slowly opening the robe. Reaching the bed, I let it slide down my arms and puddle at my feet. Flicking the sheet off of William, I gave a low growl and crawled toward my husband.

"Why, Olivia, you heard what the guard said. We might catch a chill without any coverings."

I straddled William, "Then we'll just have to share our body heat. It's for the baby's well-being, after all."

For a brief moment, my mind wandered back to the nightmares. Why had we suffered from them tonight? Why had our dreams wakened us at the same time? Why—

Then, William began nibbling on my neck. I gasped and forgot all about the dream.

William and I slept late the next morning. We enjoyed a leisurely breakfast and were reviewing our morning schedules when Dr. Edwards arrived. Neither of us had an appointment or were due for a checkup so we were both surprised to see her.

"Good morning, Your Highnesses," she said. "I hope you'll forgive my intrusion but this will just take a moment."

The doctor wore a friendly smile but I read tension in her eyes. As an expectant mother, my first concern was for the baby. "Is there a problem with my pregnancy?"

William took my hand and gave it a gentle squeeze. "I'm sure everything is fine, my dear. Isn't that right, Dr. Edwards?"

"Quite right, Prince William," Dr. Edwards said. Turning her attention to me, she added, "This has nothing to do with your pregnancy, Princess Olivia. It is proceeding normally, and the baby is developing as expected."

The doctor waited as I absorbed her reassurances. I smiled my thanks, "I apologize for my reflexive and emotional response, Dr. Edwards. Please do continue."

"Your response was perfectly understandable, Your Highness. I should have begun by telling you I was not here for anything associated with the pregnancy."

"Water under the bridge, as they say." William gave a nonchalant wave, dismissing the matter entirely. "What does bring you here this morning?"

"I received a copy of your guardsman's report of last night's incident. I wish to ask you a bit about that."

My cheeks warmed as I blushed. "It was nothing, Doctor. I simply forgot I wasn't wearing pajamas. I didn't mean to—"

Dr. Edwards shook her head, "No, Princess Olivia, I don't wish to ask about anything quite so personal as that. However, rest assured you're hardly the first member of the Royal family to accidentally reveal more of yourself than you intended. Why, Queen Charlotte must have done the same thing a dozen times or more. We all do unintentional things when surprised or startled."

I tried to imagine my mother-in-law doing anything unintentionally and failed utterly. Even so, Dr. Edwards words did ease my embarrassment. "My apologies for interrupting, though I can't think of anything about the incident that requires your attention."

"As I understand it, the incident began when both of you awoke screaming at the same time. Is that correct?"

William appeared as surprised as I was by the question, but he responded, "That's correct. Why is the Royal physician taking an interest in our nightmares?"

"If you'll bear with me for just a moment longer, I'll explain everything, Your Highness. Have the two of you had simultaneous nightmares before? Have either of you ever awoken screaming since the marriage?"

Puzzled, William and I both shook our heads.

Dr. Edwards nodded as if our response meant something to her. "Do either of you remember your nightmare?"

"Barely," William mused. "I recall chasing something and being unable to catch it. Whatever I was chasing was dangerous, important, and catching it was vital to my survival."

I stared at William in stupefaction. "I had the same nightmare."

William's eyebrows rose in surprise. Looking at Dr. Edwards, he asked, "What are the chances that Olivia and I had the same nightmare at the same time and both awoke screaming?"

The smile was gone from Dr. Edwards face. "Slim, Your Highness. Exceedingly slim, given what else I know of last night's events."

"What does that mean?" I asked.

"I've had several reports of nightmares last night. In all cases those suffering from the nightmare awoke screaming and, many times, their spouse and children awoke screaming at the same time. Every one of them awoke at exactly the same time as the two of you." Dr. Edwards was silent for a moment, letting her news sink in. "I could explain away your nightmares by blaming Princess Olivia's pregnancy and declaring Prince William suffered from a sympathetic nightmare. That explanation is illogical and unscientific, but I might have convinced myself it was true. *This* situation, though..."

"Am I correct in assuming we all shared the same nightmare?" William asked.

"I'm afraid you are, my Prince," Dr. Edwards sighed. "That is one of three distinct similarities shared by all cases."

"The actual nightmare and the time we all awoke are two of the similarities," I said. "What could the third similarity possibly be?"

"It was so subtle that I didn't even notice it, myself. My lab assistant made the connection but dismissed it as irrelevant. It only came out when he made an offhand comment. After we received our sixth call about simultaneous nightmares, he said, 'I'm glad I'm not Recognized.' It was only then that I realized the nightmare had only affected Recognized individuals and many of the children of Recognized parents."

"Many?" I asked. "Not all children were affected?"

Dr. Edwards shook her head, "At the moment, I'm baffled by that discrepancy. I'm certain we will eventually discover a logical reason why some children were spared the nightmare, but that reason has eluded me thus far."

I recalled one of Jeanine's wild accusations concerning the Star Stone and children of Recognized parents. "Dr. Edwards, about the children who did not have the nightmare—were they born to unrecognized mothers?"

The doctor's eyebrows rose in surprise and she turned her attention to her data pad. She tapped diligently on the pad for a bit before muttering, "I'll be damned."

"Is my suggestion correct?"

Dr. Edwards gave me a respectful nod, "It is, Your Highness. May I ask how you thought of that connection?"

"It was something from a recent conversation."

William gave me a concerned glance, "What does it all mean, Dr. Edwards? This sounds rather worrisome."

It was the doctor's turn to wave nonchalantly—a gesture I

doubted was sincere. "No, not at all, Your Highness. I'm sure everything is fine."

"Then why are you here?" I asked.

"I had to make sure your story matched the others I've received. I also know how things such as this can throw off a person's equilibrium. Considering the stresses of your daily duties, I'm prescribing a sleep aid for both of you. It's entirely safe for the baby, Princess Olivia, so I want each of you to ingest it before turning in tonight. It will ensure you both enjoy a full night's sleep, one free of nightmares."

Dr. Edwards gave the medication to us, smiled reassuringly, and left. It was a masterful performance. Had I not seen increased tension reflected in her eyes, it would have set me at ease. As it was, I was more worried than ever.

But I was no longer certain I knew what I should be worried about.

TOYING WITH EMOTIONS
Jeanine

Baron Oswald leaned back in his chair, "And that is why your predecessor instituted the current plan of taxation."

As much as I wanted to criticize Olivia's financial plans for Gaunner, I couldn't. Her taxes were reasonable, balancing the need for ducal income against the needs of the people and the businesses who employed those people. Hell, I liked her approach so much I'd probably use it on Neert, too.

"Thank you, Baron, your explanation was both succinct and clear. I—"

My thoughts were blocked as a wave of triumphant rage swept over me. I found myself wondering who allowed such a sad and pathetic little man into my presence? Why should I listen to his defense of Olivia's gutless plans? *I* ruled on Gaunner. *My* word was law. *I*—

"My Lady?" the little man bleated. "Are you all right? Did I say something to upset you?"

Drawing upon everything Grandfather had taught me, I fought the inexplicable rage. I concentrated on the small part of my mind screaming, *Get a grip, Jeanine! This isn't your rage or triumph.* I drew strength from that distant voice and pushed back against the surging emotions.

"My Lady?" the little man repeated and his name—Baron Oswald—returned to me.

I waved a hand at the Baron. The gesture was supposed to appear nonchalant, but it took so much effort I'm certain it looked peremptory. The words I forced from my mouth grated on my ears, "I am... Fine, Baron... Leave me. *Now!*"

Without another word, the Baron jumped up and fled my office. I heard him babbling something to Edward, my assistant, before my office door slid shut. Beyond that, I paid no attention to anything except the struggle to control my own emotions.

Gripping my head with both hands, I moaned, "Grandfather, please help me."

You don't need my help, Jeanine. You know what to do.

Even though the words and the soothing tone were nothing but memories, they had an effect on me. Strengthened by them, I found the will to resist the alien emotions in my head. And, with sudden clarity, I realized what was happening.

The Star Stone. Through whatever means it used to see and hear everything I saw and heard, it was twisting and toying with my emotions.

Screw that!

"Get out of my head you pathetic AI. My mind is not for you!"

I felt myself gradually turning back the wave of emotion, forcing it from my mind. But in the last seconds of my battle the alien emotions mutated. The triumph vanished, replaced by confusion and then rising fear. Unprepared for the sudden shift, the Star Stone's emotions ripped through my mental wall. I screamed long and loud and then fell into darkness.

The murmur of voices sifted through the lancing pain in my head. My eyes fluttered, but the light beyond my eyelids was too bright. I turned my head before trying again.

"She's waking!"

I knew I should recognize that voice, but couldn't quite place it.

"Jeanine?" the same voice asked. "Come on, babe, answer me!"

Drake! He's the only one who ever called me 'babe.' I turned toward the voice and fluttered my eyes again. The light wasn't as bad this time, so I opened them all the way. My husband loomed over me, his eyes filled with concern. He was also blocking the light, which is why I could keep my eyes open. While Drake's face filled my vision, I saw several others standing above him.

"Don't worry, I'm fine," I said. "If you could all back away, I'll get off this floor."

Drake gently pushed me back down. "I think you should stay here until the doctor arrives."

The carpet was thick and comfortable, so I did as Drake suggested. "The show's over, everyone. You can all go about your business. Is Baron Oswald still here?"

"What may I do for you, my Lady?" he asked.

"Please accept my apologies for my behavior at the end of our meeting."

"Give the matter no further thought, my Lady. I am simply relieved you appear to be on the mend."

"Thank you, Baron."

The doctor arrived just as everyone but Drake turned to leave. The man checked me over thoroughly before allowing me to sit up. "Call me if this happens again, Captain Haral."

"Or," I growled, "I could call you myself, Doctor. I *do* know how to operate a comm."

"She's definitely feeling better," Drake said as he helped me to my feet. "One of us will call you if this episode repeats itself."

The doctor bowed, suggested I schedule a complete physical, and excused himself.

As soon as the office door slid shut, Drake demanded, "What the hell happened, Jeanine?"

My head hurt like hell but I couldn't help smiling, "I'm pretty sure Jana has seriously pissed off the Star Stone."

"And it did this to you in, what, retaliation?"

I shook my head and immediately regretted it as the pain hit me again. "Ow... I think this attack was unintentional. The Star Stone probably doesn't even know it did it to me. I'm probably not even the only person it hit."

"Still, if it can do *this* to you without trying..."

"Yeah," I sighed. "What else can it do?"

"Do you have any idea what Jana did? Did the wave of emotions give you a clue?"

"No, but whatever she did scared the Star Stone. And I'd really like to know what that was."

"Is that a not-so-subtle hint for me to send a message to Kelly?" Drake asked.

"You are a very smart man, Drake."

"Obviously. I married you, didn't I?"

"Yes, you did. I guess that makes you an extraordinarily smart man. Now, genius husband, find out what's happening on Xapreathea. Whatever help they need, tell them I'll send it. Anything at all. Got it?"

"Got it, babe."

Drake gave me a quick kiss and left. I closed my eyes. Unbidden, the feel of the Star Stone's fear rose up in my memory. My lips curled up in a predatory smile.

"I think your days are numbered, Star Stone, and the number is very, very small."

SCOOP

Jana

The five of us discussed our next moves for close to an hour. Since we were trying to figure out how to do the all-but-impossible on a truly impossible deadline, more than one argument broke out. To my surprise, Tilly wasn't the one who argued most vociferously against the break-in.

"This whole idea is crazy!" Alfonso declared. "Chic Thief or not, what you're asking Tilly to do is impossible. Come on, Nathan, would you try slicing the most secure systems in the Royal Intelligence Agency with less than twenty-four hours to prepare? What about you, Jana? What you're asking Tilly to do is the burglary equivalent of that."

Nathan held his hands up in a placating gesture, "I understand the difficulties facing Tilly—"

"I don't think you do," Alfonso growled, leaning forward for emphasis. "If anything, my comparison underplayed the dangers Tilly will face. On a slicing run if things go to hell you just disconnect. During a burglary if things go to hell the burglar is in real danger. And I mean physical danger not 'oh no, someone might learn my identity' danger."

I looked into Alfonso's eyes and saw fear reflected there—fear for Tilly. I offered a small smile, "Tilly is my best friend in the whole galaxy, so I truly understand your concern. I wouldn't ask this of her if I thought there was any other way. We *need* that blood sample and she's the only person I know who can get it. If you know a better way, I'm all ears."

Alfonso calmed down somewhat, "No, I don't have any better ideas. It's just..."

He trailed off and gave Tilly a misery-filled look. I can be oblivious to emotional situations, but even I knew what Alfonso's look meant.

"It's just what?" Tilly asked as she took his hand.

Alfonso lowered his eyes, "I haven't even had a chance to ask you out, much less introduce you to my parents."

Tilly's eyebrows shot up in surprise. "You want to take me home to meet your mother?"

"Oh yeah, she's going to love you."

"Even though I'm a thief?"

"So was Mom when she was your age. But we don't have to tell her about you if you don't want to."

"Well, I wouldn't want to disappoint your mother." A silly grin spread across Tilly's face, "So, I promise I won't get caught. Besides, I'm a little better equipped for this than most of you think."

Alfonso looked up, his curiosity piqued, "How?"

It was Tilly's turn to look away. "I...uh...lived in the Palace for a month. With William."

"Were you casing the Palace for a potential job?" Alfonso asked.

Still not meeting Alfonso's eyes, Tilly shook her head, "No, William and I were an item for a while."

"Okay," Alfonso mused. "But you *did* case the palace while you were living there, right?"

"Of course."

"I knew the Chic Thief was too smart not to take advantage of that situation," Alfonso said. "That makes this job a bit easier. Tilly just has to get inside the palace and Jana has to help her get past the alarms. But once she is inside, she'll know the exact layout. Don't get me wrong, it's still a hard job but if the queen of thieves can't pull it off, who can?"

"It's sweet of you to call me that, Alfonso, but I'm not a queen of anything."

Alfonso waved off Tilly's protest, "You will be after you pull off this job."

Tilly rose, "Then we'd better get some breakfast. We've got a long day of casing the Palace ahead of us."

"I'll check in with Drake and find out what's happening with our ride out of here," Kelly said. Her stomach rumbled, so she added, "After breakfast, that is."

Nathan took my hand, "And Jana and I will go to The Club and see what information we can turn up. *Someone* among the elite slicers must have made a run against the Palace network."

I felt a surge of adrenaline when Nathan suggested we make a slicing run. I knew it was an aftereffect of my latest run-in with the Star Stone. But recognizing that wasn't enough to quell the fear I felt at the idea of returning to the net so soon—even if we weren't going anywhere near the Star Stone.

Nathan sensed my churning emotions and put an arm around me, "You don't have to go. I'm pretty good at this slicing stuff and can probably take care of it by myself."

I smiled gently, "Don't worry about me, I'll be fine once we get in there. Besides, we'll get twice as much done with twice as many slicers. It's simple math."

Then we got up and joined the others in the kitchen.

When I brought Tilly with me to The Club—it seemed like ages ago but was only last week—she'd been awed by the deference paid to me by those within The Club. I found myself wishing she was here to see the reception Fox and I got when we arrived together.

The wannabes outside The Club parted before us in mute wonder. Inside, the elite of the slicing universe did much the same, though the susurration of quiet speculation arose as they closed ranks behind us. Paths opened to my table and Fox's while all present waited to see our choice.

If we sat at my table, we gave notice that Fox was helping me. That was hardly unheard of considering Fox is the best slicer in the Star Kingdom. If we sat at Fox's table we would proclaim I was helping him—a far rarer thing. So, Fox did the one thing none of the other slicers expected—he steered us to a new table.

Activating a macro so his voice carried to all in The Club, Fox said, "This table now belongs to Dreamwalker and me. We no longer need our old tables."

Slicers around us gaped in silence for almost an entire second before the clamor of voices rose as they debated the meaning of Fox's announcement. Were we a team, now? Or were we an item? Most importantly, what did it mean to the balance of power within the slicing community?

Watching the uproar, I mused, "What difference does it make whether we're a team or a couple?"

"A lot," Fox replied. "Teams can still work together after a personal falling out. Couples, not so much. If you and I had an acrimonious breakup, it could cause chaos at the top of the slicer food chain."

"So, everyone here is hoping we've just teamed up, right?"

"Yep. I think we should dash those hopes immediately."

Fox leaned over and kissed me on the lips. We both had macros running to simulate physical sensations, so the kiss felt pretty good, but real-life kisses were a lot better. Fox's gesture had its desired effect on the crowd and we heard more than a few muttered curses. Apparently, many of our slicing colleagues feared either our combined abilities or the possible fallout from a breakup—probably both.

"Enough fun and games," I said. "We're here for information."

"I know. That's why I sent a message to Scoop right after we got here."

I nodded in appreciation. Everyone in the upper echelons of the slicing community has their specialties. Scoop is the go-to-slicer for news and gossip. If anyone could tell us what was happening across the Star Kingdom—from the meanest streets to the most secure palaces—it was him. Or her. You could never tell with Scoop. He—or she—used an androgynous avatar and switched between male and female clothing as the whim took him. Or her.

We didn't have long to wait. Scoop slipped through the crowd and approached our table. Or maybe it was Our Table since no one in The Club would dare sit here anymore. At the moment, Scoop's avatar wore a very elegant, male business suit. I always based my pronouns on Scoop's clothing, so it was 'he' and 'him' this time.

"My, my, my. Look at you naughty darlings getting all lovey-dovey and cozy-wozy. I didn't have a *clue* you silly slicers were an *item*! Do you have any *idea* what this will do to my reputation? Only the *juiciest* slicer tidbit in years—*years*, darlings—and I completely missed it." Scoop folded his arms and glared down at us. "I'm tempted to stalk off in high dudgeon. It would be just desserts for your temerity. Just desserts, indeed!"

Smothering a smile, I said, "Please accept our most humble apologies, Scoop. If it makes you feel any better, this development surprised us, too. One minute we were talking and the next..."

Scoop brought a hand to his mouth in astonishment, "Did you darlings make the beast with two backs?"

"That's a little too personal, Scoop," Nathan growled.

Thinking the other slicer would enjoy an exclusive, I triggered a blush macro. As my cheeks reddened, I offered a shy smile. Scoop's eyebrows climbed right off his avatar's face, not stopping until they were floating above his head. As his eyebrows returned to his face, Scoop sat down and leaned toward me, propping his chin on one hand.

"Tell me *all* about it, darling. And don't leave out a single detail!"

Ignoring the surprised look Fox gave me, I leaned toward Scoop. In a conspiratorial whisper, I said, "Let's just say that slicing isn't the only thing Fox excels at."

"Oooooh!" Scoop playfully slapped Fox's shoulder, "Did she ascend to the heights of ecstasy under your masterful control?"

I caressed Fox's arm, "Under *and* above, Scoop."

"Now *this* is more like it!" Scoop purred. "You haven't told anyone else?"

"No," Fox growled. Glaring at me, he added, "And *I* wouldn't even have told you."

"That's fine, dearie. Your smarter half knew better." Scoop looked thoughtful. "I've always wondered whether your avatars matched your real-life sexes. I don't have to wonder anymore."

"You don't?" Fox asked.

"Absolutely not, darling. *You* are male and the lovely Dreamwalker is female."

"What makes you say that?" I asked.

"Simplicity, itself. A *man* will tell the most outrageous lies about his sexual history but wouldn't *dream* of discussing real sex with a real woman he loves." Scoop smiled triumphantly at me. "Whereas a *woman* is just the opposite. *You* talked. *Fox* growled."

"Yes, you're very smart," Fox growled. "Can we shut up about our love life now?"

"Certainly, darling. But you really *should* thank Dreamwalker. She gave me such a yummy morsel that I've completely forgiven you for keeping your surprising relationship a secret."

"Does that mean you'll answer our questions?" Fox asked.

"That's what I just said, dearie." Scoop smiled at us, "How may I be of service?"

I asked, "Have you heard of any...odd...developments over the last couple of days?"

"Besides the news that a *mysterious* slicer tops the Royal Intelligence Agency's most-wanted list, darling? I *do* so hope it isn't one of you. I'd miss both of you *terribly*. Quite terribly indeed!"

I shouldn't have been surprised Scoop knew about that, but I was. "Yes, I'm sure everyone in The Club hopes the slicer—whoever he or she is—evades the authorities."

"That is *so* true, darling! I *do* hope they don't catch either of you. Oopsie—I mean *if* it's one of you. Budding romances simply should *not* be nipped by government agents."

"On that, we agree wholeheartedly," Fox said, "but we aren't the ones the RIA is looking for."

"No doubt, Foxy. No doubt, at all." Scoop's eyes unfocused, "But you want news of the strange, the odd, and the unusual. I believe I have just the thing!"

Fox and I thought Scoop would go ahead and spill the news, but he just sat there with an expectant look on his face.

After a couple of seconds, I realized Scoop wanted us to ask for the information. Widening my eyes, I asked, "What could it be, Scoop? Please *do* tell us."

Damned if Scoop didn't look away as if embarrassed, "Oh, I couldn't, darling! I *swore* I'd keep it secret."

Before Fox could growl again, I wheedled, "Oh, Scoopsy, you simply *must* tell us!"

"Well, if you insist!" Once again leaning toward us conspiratorially, he said, "*Something* happened among the nobility last night. I don't know exactly what caused it, but *every* Recognized noble on Xapreathea had a strange nightmare—the exact *same* nightmare, darling! Can you imagine? They all awoke at the exact same time, all of them crying out and frightening the servants. As you might guess, many of them called their medical practitioner for advice."

"What about the nobles who were awake?" Fox asked. "Like the ones on the other side of the planet. Most people don't have nightmares when they're awake."

"You are quite correct," Scoop replied. "They got...testy. Irritated. Even angry. And all for no reason. *And* all at the same time as the sleeping ones had their nightmare."

Fox and I exchanged glances, then I asked, "You don't happen to know what time that happened, do you?"

"Of course, darling! I *am* Scoop after all. It was—"

"Two twenty-six in the morning, local time," I said.

This time Scoop's astonishment wasn't feigned. "*How* did you know, darling? Unless... Are *you* Recognized?"

No, I thought, I caused the nightmares. Or, more accurately, Fox and I caused them. I almost said as much, but Fox spoke first.

"No!" he blurted, his denial much too forceful. He pretended a laugh, "Heh, that's one you sure got wrong, Scoop."

"Well, you can't fault a slicer for trying," Scoop said. Struggling to hide a self-satisfied smile, he added, "I *do* hope my news proves helpful, but I simply *must* be going. News doesn't collect itself, you know!"

"Of course, Scoop," Fox replied. "You've been very helpful."

"Tootles!" Scoop sang before sashaying off into the crowd.

"That was quick thinking, *darling*," I said. "Though Scoop may never forgive you for sending him sniffing down a false trail."

"That's his problem. I think we've got what we came for, though."

"I agree. Let's go see what the others have found."

Once again, the crowd parted before us. Soon after, we disconnected from the network.

One advantage to slicing is you can do almost everything you want to do from the comfort of your home. Or secret lair, in our case. That wasn't the case for Kelly, Tilly, or Alfonso. Our three friends had been gone for less than thirty minutes when we returned from The Club.

"It's going to be hours before any of them get back," Nathan said. He gave me a sidelong glance and asked, "Whatever shall we do to occupy the time?"

I rolled my eyes, "Why does potential danger make men so horny?"

Nathan surprised me with a serious answer. "I suspect it's an evolutionary impulse to extend our genetic line before risking our lives."

"Okay, except *I'm* the one who will be risking her life."

Nathan's eyes widened, "You're not planning another run on the Star Stone, are you?"

I shuddered, "Hell no! But I will have to go with Tilly when she breaks into the Palace tonight."

"Why? What can you do there that you can't do here?"

"Connect to the Palace's internal network. That's the only way I can help Tilly."

Nathan nodded his understanding. "I should go instead of you."

I bristled, "Why, so you can be all manly and protect li'l ol' me from danger?"

"No." Then his lips turned up in the ghost of a smile, "Well, yes, but not *just* for that."

Crossing my arms, I glared at Nathan, "Then that other reason had better be a damned good one because I will *not* be anyone's damsel!"

"It's because Fox is a better slicer than Dreamwalker, especially when it comes to security systems."

Ouch. That assessment stung. My face must have shown some of that because Nathan reached over and caressed my cheek.

"Hey, Beautiful, you're one of the absolute best slicers in the galaxy, but your specialty is data retrieval. And if this was a data mission, I'd unhappily stand aside and let you take it. But it's a security job, and that's *my* specialty."

I nodded in reluctant agreement, "I'll concede your point, but what if there's a data retrieval element to the mission? I think the royal family has more information about the Star

Stone than is available to the public and was going to search for it while also keeping an eye on Tilly."

Nathan shook his head, "Security requires constant attention. Once you got into the system, you'd realize you couldn't split your attention like that. You can help us best by staying right here and doing what you do best—searching the net for any hint that Tilly and I are in any danger."

I did the same thing when Jeanine and Olivia were captured and even intercepted a clue to their whereabouts. We didn't find them from that clue, but that wouldn't be the purpose of my search this time. I'd just need to alert Nathan and Tilly if I discovered anything.

"Fine. I'll stay here and play nursemaid. But this whole job was my idea, so you'd better not get caught! I don't think I could stand the guilt."

Nathan raised his right hand, "I solemnly swear I shall do everything in my power to avoid capture."

"And keep Tilly safe, too."

Keeping his hand raised, he repeated, "And keep Tilly safe, too."

On a whim, I added, "Or you will never get laid again."

"Whoa," Nathan protested, lowering his hand, "that's going too—"

"*Say it*," I growled, grabbing his right hand and pulling it up again.

"Or I will never get laid again." When I released his right hand, he reached around me and pulled me close. "To make sure I appreciate the gravity of my oath, don't you think you should give me a taste of what I'm putting at risk?"

He kissed me and I felt the passion building in him. Apparently, women also have an evolutionary impulse to grab one last chance to extend their genetic line with the man of their choice because an answering passion welled up inside me. Nathan must have felt it, too, because he picked me up and carried me to the bedroom.

Then the galaxy went away, and we were as one.

HOW DID YOU KNOW

Olivia

Malaise gnawed at me throughout the morning. I found myself snapping at servants, aides, and even William. From their expressions, the aides and servants assumed my ill temper was associated with my pregnancy—hormones and lack of sleep with a bit of petulant princess thrown in for good measure. God, how I wished that was the case, but I knew it wasn't.

William was far from his usual, easy-going self. He actually shouted at one of the servant girls, something he *never* does. Sara, a grandmotherly woman who had worked in the Palace since King Bernard was a boy, took the poor girl aside and comforted her. I overheard just enough of Sara's words to realize she attributed William's behavior to "a man's needs" going unfulfilled while I was with child. Wrong though Sara's explanation was, it calmed the girl which was all that mattered.

I dithered until lunch before coming to a decision. Elizabeth, my personal assistant, came promptly when called. Her face betrayed none of the trepidation I'm sure she felt at my summons.

"How may I assist you, Your Highness?"

"Place a subspace call to the royal yacht. I need to speak to the Queen."

"I'll see to it at once," Elizabeth bobbed a curtsy and left.

"Why are you bothering Mother?" William groused. "Is there some dire emergency of which I was not informed?"

I almost answered in kind but caught myself. Taking time to soften the tone of my voice, I answered, "It's nothing, William. I just feel the need for some maternal advice. Mother to expectant mother."

For a moment, the old William—*my* William—broke through the irritation. He flashed an affectionate smile, "I'm so very glad you and Mother have grown close since our marriage."

I took William's hand, "As am I, darling."

We held hands until a servant told me the subspace connection was established. A moment later, I sat before the screen. Marie, Mother's assistant, nodded at me in greeting.

"I'll tell Her Majesty you're ready."

While Marie fetched my mother-in-law, I dismissed Elizabeth. I struggled to order my thoughts before Mother arrived and mostly failed. The brief moment of peace I'd shared with William was gone, once again displaced by the malaise of the morning.

My thoughts were still whirling when Queen Charlotte appeared on the screen. Her eyes narrowed, her lips turned down into a frown, and she demanded, "*What* is so important that you felt the need to interrupt my journey home?"

Her tone took me aback. I'd expected the calm, collected, and caring woman I knew and had come to love. Dimly, I realized she was the first Recognized noble other than William I'd spoken with since the nightmare. Being dozens of light-years away, I'd felt certain *she* would be unaffected by the events on Xapreathea.

Mother hardly gave me time to respond before she snapped, "Really, Olivia, you're a grown woman. You shouldn't require hand-holding nor should you expect it from someone of my station."

"Your pardon, Mother, my thoughts are a jumble. Please give—"

"Why did you bother me if you weren't ready for the conversation? Really, Olivia, I thought you were more level-headed than this."

Her words stung and my few gathered thoughts fled. But when Mother reached toward the control board, obviously intent on disconnecting the call, I blurted the first thing that came to mind. "Did you and the King suffer nightmares last night at two twenty-six?"

I knew my parents-in-law kept the royal yacht on Xapreathean time and would follow the same sleep schedule William and I did. Mother's eyes widened as my question registered and she sat back with a contemplative expression.

"How did you know?"

"William and I woke from nightmares at that time. Our dreams were identical." I had Mother's full attention now. "We found ourselves pursuing someone vital to our survival who always eluded our grasp."

"Yes... Bernard and I had the same nightmare. We assumed the similarity was attributable to some strange hyperspacial effect. Since the four of us were affected, it's obvious there is more to the story."

"I'm afraid it wasn't just us. Every Recognized noble on Xapreathea suffered the same nightmare. They all awoke at two twenty-six. Nobles who weren't asleep suffered from extreme and unfounded irritation or anger for several minutes. Many of their unrecognized children had the nightmare as well."

Always one to spot a discrepancy, Mother asked, "*Most* of the children? Why not all?"

"Dr. Edwards wondered the same thing. But I recalled something Jeanine said to me during a recent subspace call. I asked the Doctor if the children who were not affected were born of unrecognized mothers. To her surprise that held true for every unaffected child."

For the first time in my life, I saw Queen Charlotte at a loss for words. After a few seconds, she simply asked, "But why? How can that matter? What did Jeanine say to you?"

Scrubbing a hand over my face, I said, "I am far from convinced by her theory, but she believes the Star Stone uses the Recognition ceremony to...infuse...us with alien genetic material and nanobots to tend to that material. She claims it allows the Star Stone to see and hear what Recognized individuals see and hear. I know the whole idea is preposterous but the Star Stone is the *only* connection to every person who had the nightmare."

"Yes... Preposterous, indeed." Mother spoke thoughtfully and her tone was far from the dismissive one I'd expected.

"Mother, you don't actually believe what that woman told me, do you?"

Lost in thought with her eyes unfocused, she didn't answer my question. Instead, she asked, "When you and William returned from Gaunner, I suggested that you read several private reports concerning the Star Stone. May I assume you haven't done that yet, dear?"

"I've been busy and haven't gotten around to it."

"As soon as we disconnect, go to our private library and get the documents. Please finish reading them before Bernard and I return home."

"Of course, Mother. Do you actually give credence to Jeanine's story?"

"No. Or, rather, mostly not. But..." She waved her hand vaguely. "Just read the reports."

"Jeanine was worried the Star Stone would...modify...my baby's DNA to serve some strange purpose. Is that—?"

"That idea is absolute rubbish, my dear. Your mother was Recognized, Olivia, and so was mine. Do you think we're not human?" I slowly shook my head and Mother continued, "The Star Stone is the symbol of our power within the Star Kingdom.

God only knows what would happen if that symbol was discredited, but I'm certain the resulting events would play directly into the hands of that rebellion Jeanine associates with."

I nodded, relieved by Mother's words. "Sowing doubt over the King's divine right to rule would serve her well."

"Quite correct, dear. Now, why don't you start reading those reports?"

"I will. May I take them to our suite?"

"By all means. The chairs in the library provide too little back support for a pregnant woman—even one still in her first trimester."

"Thank you. I look forward to your return, Mother."

"As do I. Goodbye, dear."

After disconnecting the call, I fetched the reports and took them back to our suite. The information within was illuminating and surprising, but it was also deadly dull. I was relieved when William interrupted me later that evening.

"Olivia, it's time to take the sleep aid Dr. Edwards left for us."

Putting the report folder on my bedside table, I rubbed my eyes. "These reports are doing a fine job of putting me to sleep, already."

"Even so, drink up!" William handed me a glass containing cloudy liquid before emptying one of his own.

I did as instructed. Soon we were both fast asleep.

THE PALACE JOB

Tilly

Never in my life have I been so happy to get on with a dangerous job. Waiting is always the hardest part of a job but waiting with my friends was *much* worse.

Jana went back and forth between manic bouts of friend-consoling—even though I wasn't distraught and just wanted to relax—and deep dives into the net in search of any information she thought might help me break into the Palace. Her behavior was the complete opposite of the Jana I know so well. I'd have been worried about her if I hadn't understood what was driving her.

The job was her idea, yet she was not one of the people doing the dangerous part. Jana thought she would be the slicer coming with me. She thought her life and freedom would be on the line along with mine. Then her new boyfriend rained all over that parade by insisting *he* was the one who should go with me. He pointed out he was the best security system slicer in the Star Kingdom and that made him the best person to support me.

I thought using logic was playing pretty dirty, but it showed Nathan knew exactly how to handle Jana. She could have waved aside his emotional desire to protect the love of his life. That kind of argument would have warmed her heart, but it wouldn't have swayed her. But irrefutable logic is Jana's one weakness—that and security systems. No, that last bit isn't fair to Jana. There are only a handful of people better qualified to slice security systems than my best friend. Since she's sleeping with the guy at the top of that very short list, she bowed before his superior logic.

Then there was Alfonso, who surprised the hell out of me hours ago by proclaiming his love for me. Or maybe it's just a deep infatuation with a mysterious woman. Who can tell with a guy you've only known for a couple of days? I'm sure my looks have a lot to do with it—guys are nothing if not visually oriented, especially when it comes to the initial attraction—but I think Alfonso is even more attracted to me for my profession than he is to my looks.

And he wants to take me to meet his mother. He hasn't even asked me on a date and he's already thinking about that. I'm in unknown territory there, especially since the other guys I've dated rarely thought about anything except getting me into bed. I don't even know how to react to a guy who wants to get to know me as a person first. But I'm a damned sight more flattered by Alfonso's earnest desire than by all the smooth compliments I've gotten from the usual bed jockeys I end up with. And, assuming we all get out of this with our skins intact, Alfonso and I are going on a real date and then he'll take me to meet his parents.

Thank God for Kelly who, beyond her offer of whatever assistance she could provide, left me alone. Three times she distracted Jana from friend-coddling by sending her into the net for data.

So, like I said, I was thrilled when the three of us left for the job. Yes, three of us.

Me to do the actual breaking, entering, and blood-drawing.

Nathan to keep a digital eye on me.

And Alfonso to keep a physical eye on Nathan while the slicer was deep inside the Palace's network.

Our underground trip to the Palace was longer than the tunnel crawl Jana and I went on all those weeks ago. We didn't dare use the same approach as before. Jana and I barely got away from security patrols last time, and it was a good bet security was even stronger around those tunnels now. But working with two of the best slicers in the galaxy has its benefits. With Nathan opening paths through security systems and Jana mining the data, we had our route into the Palace mapped out before lunch. That's why Jana had so much time to coddle, so call their combined skill a two-edged sword.

I led the way through the tunnels, watching for physical security—alarms, cams, even simple trip wires—but the tunnels we used were so old the Xapreathean authorities probably didn't even know they still existed. Even so, we took our time and had Jana riding networked shotgun, watching for anything out of the ordinary.

Our way was clear until we came to the wall. That wall is why everyone forgot about this old set of tunnels. Back when the government built the new tunnel system—God knows how long ago that was—this old system was blocked off with a then-impenetrable polymer. Now? All it takes is a little chemistry and —*voilà*—we had a solution that dissolved the polymer. That, by the way, is why I studied chemistry in college.

This is one of the big secrets of the burglary trade. Building materials that were once impassible are rarely a match for hundreds of years of scientific advancement. The people who originally installed the super-secure walls had every reason to feel confident their homes couldn't be breached through those walls. That confidence was passed down to subsequent generations, even after the confidence was sorely misplaced.

Imagine my surprise that the royal family suffered from the same overconfidence as the other nobles. *Not*.

I sprayed the chemical solution over a section of the blocking wall. Within seconds the old polymer was flowing down the wall and puddling at our feet. All it took was time—which we had built into our schedule—and patience. I had to spray the stuff on the wall six times but we were through in less than an hour.

Without Nathan, I wouldn't have a hope of getting through the new tunnel undetected. As he and Jana planned, we were close enough to the Palace that he could pick up their network signal. He needed some super-sensitive equipment, signal boosters, and a lot of skill to do it, but there's a reason he's the best of the best. Even better, he set up a relay that let Jana get in, as well.

While the slicers cleared my path of digital dangers, Alfonso and I performed one last check on our equipment. When he gave me the okay, I turned to go. Then, on impulse, I spun around and kissed Alfonso long and hard.

Pulling away, I murmured, "For luck!"

And then I headed into the Palace and the burglary of a lifetime.

Do you know the difference between talented amateurs and true professionals? Professionals keep their nerves in check and their mouths shut when they're on the job. Despite working with Jana on several jobs—including the test-run burglary that led directly to our problems with the Star Stone—I'd been afraid she would get nervous and chatty. Staying safe and sound while your friends and lover attempt a daring and dangerous crime would do a number on anyone's nerves.

So I was prepared for the worst—and didn't get it.

Connected to the palace network through Nathan's link, Jana immediately went questing after the information she assumed the Royal family had concerning the true nature of the Star Stone. The logic behind her assumptions seemed reasonable to me. Then again, I'm the woman who finds breaking into the homes of rich nobles and taking their stuff incredibly exciting. So what do I know about reason? At least Jana had something to occupy her mind besides worrying about Nathan, Alfonso, and me.

And that left me free to wiggle and wriggle my way through the tunnels beneath the Palace. I estimated I had another forty meters to go when Nathan spoke through our comm link.

"Freeze."

I froze and waited for further instructions.

After several seconds, Nathan spoke again. "Someone in the Royal family's security corps is very clever. They had a whole array of sensors installed in the tunnel floor just ahead. Weight, heat, motion, light—you name it and they layered it into the next few meters. That's why it took me so long to clear your path. Sorry about the delay. You're clear to move again."

I hadn't even been frozen in place long enough for my nose to start itching and Nathan was apologizing for being slow? When this whole save-the-galaxy stuff was over, I'd have to see about getting a top-notch slicer as a partner. Or maybe I'd just retire and have some babies.

Whoa! Where did *that* thought come from? Not that I don't want to retire and have children someday, but that day is supposed to be far in the future. Was my subconscious trying to tell me something about Alfonso or was this just one of those danger-induced evolutionary impulses Jana talked about while sharing not-so-enigmatic smiles with Nathan? I firmly pushed aside both questions, along with thoughts of miniature humans, and focused on the job.

By the time I climbed out of the tunnel and into the lowest Palace level, I'd dealt with ten physical alarms. On top of that, Nathan disarmed half-a-dozen sensors and shut down or intercepted at least seven alarms. In all honesty, I'd never have made it through the tunnels without him. I doubt *any* thief could have made it. And I had a feeling only one or two other slicers in the galaxy could have done what Nathan did. He also made the next step of the job a lot easier, too.

Nathan gave me the layout, "Laundry room cams two, four, and five are the only ones without any staff in them. I've got them running loops showing the empty areas. You're in the section covered by cam six. Cam five's area is about five meters away. You should be fine if you stay down on the floor and crawl. Wait for my signal."

A voice called out requesting help. A man no more than three meters from me answered.

Two seconds after that, Nathan said, "*Go!*"

I triggered my catsuit's low-friction setting and slithered from behind the machine hiding the exit from the tunnel. Sliding easily across the floor, I covered the distance in three seconds.

"I'm there," I whispered, turning off my suit's slither mode.

"Stay down for a few more seconds... And...you're clear. No one is in any position to see you."

I stood and walked quickly but casually toward the storage area for this part of the laundry. It's the section dedicated to cleaning and maintaining Palace staff uniforms. The storage room held literally thousands of them in every size imaginable and the door didn't even have a lock.

The others assumed I learned about the laundry room during my month living with Prince William, and they were right. They also assumed I'd included the laundry room when casing the Palace for a possible break-in. That was completely wrong, but I saw no reason to tell them about William's brief infatuation with having sex in semi-public places. The risk of being caught made it more exciting for him. It did the same for me if I'm being honest.

Actually *getting* caught—which happened twice, once in the very storage room I was approaching—put a serious damper on the fun. The poor servant who walked in on us just about had a heart attack. Terrified, she backed from the room stammering apologies. William, in a rather endearing bit of idiocy, ran after her hoping to calm her down and assure her everything was fine. He forgot he was naked and still...excited.

Pushing aside that brief bit of nostalgia, I slipped into the room and glanced about. As expected, it was empty. Seconds later, I pulled two Royal-quarters uniforms from the shelves. Dropping one uniform on the floor, I walked all over it, scuffing it across the less-than-sparkling floor. Once it was appropriately mussed, I tossed it in an empty basket for dirty uniforms. I doubted anyone would ask me anything when I left, but if they did, I could tell them I had to change out of a dirty uniform.

That's another thieving trick, by the way. *Always* make sure your story will stand up to inquiry. You'd be amazed how many overconfident thieves get caught because they assume no one will check out their stories.

Satisfied my story had verisimilitude—I learned that word from a pretentious noblewoman with literary ambitions—I pulled the second uniform on over my catsuit. Checking myself in a viewer, I was satisfied with the fit and the look. As long as I didn't run into anyone who remembered me from my time in the Palace—it was a year and a half ago, but Royal servants are damnably good with faces and names—I should be free to wander the Palace.

My biggest worry was the guard team outside William's and Olivia's suite. I wasn't going to take them out with fancy martial arts moves. Hell, I wasn't even going through the door they guarded so closely. But if just one member of the team when I lived with William was on duty tonight I was in serious trouble. Any of them would recognize me if they saw me. I prayed they'd been rotated off guard duty or at least moved away from the night watch.

Quelling my concerns, I boldly walked out of the uniform storage room and toward the exit. None of the laundry workers even gave me a passing glance. Passing a table piled with linens and towels, I scooped up a large stack of both.

"Hey," a man called, "what do you think you're doing?"

Without breaking stride, I said, "Lord and Lady Bilton spilled wine in their bed. I get to clean up after them."

Yes, Lord and Lady Bilton were guests in the Palace. Like I said, verisimilitude.

The man barked a laugh, "Better you than me, honey."

And then I was out the door, wandering the Royal Palace freely and virtually invisible in my servant's livery.

This was both the easiest and riskiest part of the break-in.

It was easy because there are always servants going about their business in the Palace—even in the middle of the night. I was just one among many. As long as none of the real servants paid too much attention to me—and I was just as invisible to them as to anyone else—I was golden.

It was risky because I'd known quite a few servants and guards well by the time William and I parted ways. A servant's position in the Royal Palace is a *very* good job, complete with a certain level of status, good pay, great benefits, and the Royal family's well-known tradition of providing sizable retirement gifts to loyal servants. It was extremely likely my friends among servants and guards still worked here. If I ran across any of them I could be in serious trouble.

That's one reason I carried the towels and linens. I had my left hand propped beneath the stack and brought my right hand across to balance it. Servants always walk next to the walls, leaving the middle of the hallway free for nobles and government officials. The stack of cloth blocked my head entirely from most people using the hall while my right arm blocked much of my face from anyone in front of me. It was far from a perfect disguise but it was the best option available to me.

Despite looking as if both hands were busy, I had little trouble lifting a key card from another servant wearing the same livery as me. If Palace security followed the same protocols as before the card would unlock any door in the living area except for the Royal quarters.

I was most fearful of the servants' stairway. Lift chutes were *the* location for servants to exchange gossip, so there was no way I would risk using one of them. Still, the stairs were comparatively narrow, meaning passing servants quite close to each other. With my big pile of stuff, I'd have to turn sideways to let another servant go by. And that's exactly what I did each time I passed someone. It worked great until, suddenly, it didn't.

Trudging up my fifth flight of stairs, I heard the quick footsteps of another servant descending. They were too light to belong to a man, which was unfortunate. I knew many more female servants than male. I also couldn't count on my body below the neck—shown to good effect by the curve-hugging uniform—to distract a woman as easily as it would a man. Still, as the other servant drew near, I turned to face the wall and continued up the stairs sideways. My worst fears were realized when the servant slowed her descent as she approached me.

"Well now, who have we here?" The voice was husky for a woman, a tone I knew most men found extremely sexy. "You must be new because I know I'd recognize *that* ass if I'd seen it before!"

Did I mention one of the downsides to a servant's position in the Palace? Some senior servants considered the younger members of the staff fair game for sexual conquest. Many of them were open about their interest to the point of discomfort among other servants. Everyone who could put a stop to the whole thing tended to look the other way as long as the senior servants never got overly familiar without permission. It did make life uncomfortable for anyone who ended up attracting unwanted attention though.

Like now.

I kept moving but knew a reply was required. Hoping to sound younger than I was, I pitched my voice higher than normal, "I prefer men, miss."

A hand caressed my butt and gave it a gentle squeeze. "You're young. I bet I could change your mind. Why don't you turn around and let me see the rest of you?"

"No, miss."

"Why not, little girl?"

"Because I don't want you grabbing my tits, miss."

A throaty laugh exploded behind me and she gave my butt another squeeze, "Cheeky, aren't you?"

She released me and resumed her trip downstairs. Her last words floated up, "I'll wear you down eventually, little girl."

I passed several more servants on the stairs, but none of them spoke or even slowed down. Finally, I reached the level with the Royal quarters and exited, happily putting the confining stairway behind me.

My relief was short-lived. Approaching the corridor to the Royal quarters and the quarters reserved for special guests, I heard two voices coming from the direction of William's and Olivia's suite.

One protested, "I did *not* say I was fantasizing about Lady Jeanine!"

A second replied in a calm tone, "Sure you did."

"No, Rob, I simply asked if you had seen the vid about her abduction and rescue."

"And then you pulled out your pad and offered to show it to me, Josh."

"So?" Josh asked. "Offering to show you a vid doesn't mean I've been fantasizing about her!"

"She's a beautiful woman, Josh."

"So is Princess Olivia, but that doesn't mean I imagine myself having my way with her."

"You don't?"

"You do?"

Josh and Rob could go on like that for hours. Josh would say something that sounded benign and then Rob would respond with a non sequitur that no one saw coming. Josh would demand an explanation but never accepted the one Rob gave. To be fair, Rob's logic was twisted in the extreme. But it was also logical—if you turned your head just right, closed one eye, and squinted through the other one. I never figured out if Rob's mind was as twisted as his logic or if he just liked pulling Josh's chain, but he always got a rise from Josh.

A year and a half ago, I thought they were hilarious. When William was busy with affairs of state, I sat in the hall and listened to them bicker for hours. Of all the guards in the Palace, Rob and Josh were the worst ones to find outside the Royal heir's rooms.

Before I reached the intersection with the Royal corridor, I switched the towels and linens from my left side to the right. It blocked my face from them as I walked through the intersection, never once even hinting that I might turn into the Royal corridor.

Once past the intersection, I keyed my comm and whispered, "Problem."

"What?" Nathan replied.

"Guards. Two."

We'd worked out some simple phrases to keep our comm exchanges short. I'd just told Nathan that two of the guards could recognize me. I just hoped there was something he could do about it.

Nathan was silent for a few seconds, then asked, "Alarm?"

Triggering an alarm would clear the corridor for a brief time while the guards went to protect the Royal couple. And by 'brief' I mean twenty to thirty seconds, max. Once the false alarm was discovered, the Palace would be crawling with guards looking for whoever triggered it. It would also disable all key cards except those carried by security. That meant I would have to sprint to the suite next door to William and Olivia, spoof the lock, and slip inside. In less than thirty seconds. No thief alive could do that.

"Lock?" I asked, hoping Nathan had discovered a way to unlock doors within the Palace security system.

"Wait," he replied.

Seconds ticked by and I kept walking down the hall, farther and farther from my actual goal. Finally, Nathan came back.

"Yes."

I released the breath I hadn't realized I was holding. Turning around, I replied, "Signal."

"Roger."

Approaching the Royal corridor at a steady walk, I once again heard Rob and Josh arguing. Five meters from the intersection with the other corridor, I whispered, "Go."

Alarms sounded throughout the Palace. Praying the guards wouldn't hesitate, I dropped my camouflaging burden and sprinted around the corner.

SLICING THE PALACE

Jana

Logic is, without a doubt, the least comforting concept in the universe. It is cold, shedding no warmth for basking. It is calculating, granting no solace for raw emotions. It consoles not. It cares not. Logic is either correct or incorrect. Under its harsh glare nothing else matters.

Logic is why I'm safe and sound in our current hidey-hole scanning the net for alarms. Logic is why people I love are breaking into the Royal Palace while I sit here.

Long ago, logic was my friend—a refuge from a universe that confused a teenage girl. Logic was structure. Logic was sensible. Logic was safe.

But now?

Logic is a stone-cold bitch and I am her thrall.

Kelly, the only member of our little gang who wasn't putting herself in danger at my behest, sat quietly nearby. I think she's deeply empathic because she let me wallow in misery just long enough to do justice to my feelings but not so long that I became maudlin.

"All right, you can stop pissing and moaning inside your head," she said. "You've got work to do."

Not quite willing to abandon my self-pity, I spat, "Screw you."

"No thanks, Jana, I like men. And unless I misinterpreted the sounds coming from the room with the big bed, so do you."

I felt a blush climb my cheeks. "You heard us?"

Kelly grinned at my embarrassment. "It must have been quite a while since you got laid, honey, because you screamed like a banshee."

I buried my face in my hands, "Oh God, I'll never be able to face any of you again!"

"Why not?"

"Why do you think?"

"Do you think so little of your friends, Jana?"

That question surprised me. "Um, what?"

"So what if you got a little loud in a moment of ecstasy? You're in love and, unless I miss my guess, the guy you love is the one you're going to spend the rest of your life with. Don't you think your friends are happy for you?"

"But you all know that Nathan and I...you know."

"Did what lovers have done since the beginning of time? Oh dearie me." Kelly's tone lost all inflection, "I. Am. So. Shocked."

To my surprise, I burst out laughing. "When you put it that way, I guess it's not such a big deal."

"Exactly." Kelly let me laugh a bit longer before asking, "Are you finished with your pity party?"

"Yes. I guess I should connect to the network and do my part."

"I guess you should."

Rising, I caught Kelly's gaze with my own. "Thank you."

She waved if off. "That's what friends are for. Now, go watch over our other friends and do everything in your power to bring them back safely."

"Aye aye, Cap'n Cutthroat, ma'am!"

By the time Nathan gave me access to the Palace network I was all business, focused and ready to do my part. It's a good thing, too, since it took all my concentration to ignore the terse exchanges between Tilly and Nathan. I made sure I had a clear reception from the bots I left monitoring communications for the police, specialized agencies, the RIA, the military... Let's just say I had bots monitoring anyone who might remotely be summoned if my friends were discovered. Satisfied I'd know if anything came up, I dove into the Palace network.

I found the Royal family's private database quickly—and it took all my willpower to keep myself from screaming in frustration. The data was disorganized! No, that word was insufficient for the mess I found. I considered calling it haphazard but not even that word captured the true horror I beheld.

This database was *random*!

God above, how did anyone find anything in that database? I knew the answer, of course. Whoever tended the files had their own method of organizing the information. I'd seen it before, where someone completely undeserving of the title Database Administrator arranged the data to suit themselves, ignoring the possibility that others might go searching for information. The worst part is the pathetic excuse these faux DBAs used to explain away their disorganization.

"My system makes it impossible for slicers to steal our data!" they claim.

As if slicers had any interest in the data they made impossible to find. Except this time was the exception, dammit.

Figuratively gritting my teeth, I sent waves of seething hot hatred toward my opponent. Dreamwalker was the equal to any master of disinformation technology and superior to most. Drawing a deep breath I dove into the mess and searched for a key.

I tried the most obvious option first, sorting the files alphabetically and then looking for one marked 'catalogue.' No such luck, but I hadn't thought it would be that easy.

'Directory' was next—and another bust.

Maybe 'listing' was it? No.

'Key?' Uh uh.

Next up was 'map.' Nope.

I tried a dozen more options and none of them worked. Backing out of the database, I calmed my frantically spinning mind and considered other approaches. It dawned on me my database nemesis might not have the key in this database, at all. But where would they have it? Maybe if I knew who the admin was, I'd have a better chance figuring that out.

Slicing the Palace employee records database was a piece of cake. Like all such systems, this data was meticulously maintained and arranged. It took no time at all to find the person I was looking for. Skimming the man's file I discovered I wasn't the only person who disapproved of his data sorting methods. The personnel manager, noting how important the Royal family's personal data was, handily included the key to the database.

Score!

Two seconds later I had a perfectly sorted, perfectly decipherable database. One second after that, I had the information I most wanted—the Royal family's personal map of the Palace, including secret rooms and passages, and the contents of their private library. And in that private library? The very report I desperately wanted to read.

Except there was no digital copy of it. The Royal family had just one physical copy of the thing. Of all the rotten luck! Hoping for a miracle, I examined the reader log for the report.

And discovered my miracle. The miracle even had a name— *Her Royal Highness Princess Olivia*. She had the report in her suite *right now*! The very same suite Tilly was breaking into soon. Surely a thief of her caliber could grab the report along with a blood sample, right?

Thinking my success boded well for our plan, I turned my attention to Tilly's progress. That's when every alarm in the Palace went off.

THERE'S NO DUST

Tilly

With my heart hammering harder than it ever had on any previous job I dashed around the corner and ran towards the suite next to William's and Olivia's. I caught a fleeting glimpse of a guard's uniform before their door slid shut, leaving me alone in the hall. The short sprint gave me just enough time to decide this job was more thrilling than even *I* liked. I touched the door control and slid through as soon as it opened enough for me to fit. Slapping the inner control, I leaned against the wall and caught my breath as the door slid shut again.

"In," I said. "Lock."

I heard a soft 'clack' as security locks slid into place inside the door.

"Done," Nathan replied.

Confident no one could walk in and surprise me, I donned my headlamp and turned it on. Dim light spread out before me. That's when Jana joined the conversation.

"According to the Royal family's plans for the Palace, all rooms in that area are soundproofed."

"Keep short," I snapped. "Possible intercept."

"Oh, please, do you think I'd take unnecessary risks? I'm monitoring everything happening in and around the Palace. No one is looking for transmissions right now, not that they could intercept the beyond-the-bleeding-edge shifting-frequency ones Fox set up for us."

I took a second to calm my frazzled nerves and, taking Jana's cue about using avatar names, said, "Sorry, Dreamwalker. The last couple of minutes have been very adrenaline-intensive."

"Understood, Smoke. I wouldn't have spoken at all if I didn't have something important to say."

I didn't even have to think about what that meant. "Besides finding the Palace floor plans—"

"Including the hidden room and passage plans," Jana interrupted, her tone more than a little smug.

"You must have discovered the Star Stone report you were looking for."

"I did. Unfortunately, there's no digital copy."

"So you want me to steal the physical copy."

"I do."

"Instead of getting a blood sample from Princess Olivia?"

"No, I still want that."

"Dammit, Ja- Dreamwalker, after the alarm Fox just set off there is no chance I can safely get from here to the King's personal library!"

"I don't expect you to."

"Huh?"

"Her Royal Highness, Princess Olivia is currently in possession of the report. It's probably sitting on her desk in the suite next door."

"Oh. In that case, consider it done. Now, if you don't mind, I need to concentrate on getting into the ventilation ducts and crawl to Their Highnesses' suite—all without being heard."

Smug self-satisfaction fairly dripping in her tone, Jana asked, "Why not use the hidden door, instead?"

"*There's a door?*"

"Two doors, really. According to these plans, there's a narrow passage hidden in the walls between the two suites. I'm guessing it's probably an escape route for royalty. A place to hide in case of a peasant uprising or assassins—you know, the stuff of royal nightmares. Go into the suite's bedroom and I'll tell you where to look for the hidden door."

"Does your floor plan include instructions for opening the door?"

"Sorry, no. I guess it's a good thing we have the Chic Thief on hand to figure it out."

Even knowing where the door was, I couldn't find a single seam or hint that the door existed. I appreciate good work as much as the next thief, but this level of craftsmanship was astounding. Maybe even excessive. Without the floor plans Jana discovered I'd never have known it was there.

Whoever installed the door was just as careful disguising the switch to open it. It took me twenty-three minutes to find the damned thing. I suppose it was just as well since I would have to wait for the Palace to calm down from the alarm, anyway. Still, I felt a lot better after I was hidden away in the passage.

My relief lasted about two seconds.

My voice dropped to a whisper, "Guys, there's no dust anywhere in this passage."

"Dammit," Jana said, her voice dropping low in response to my whisper. "Someone still uses it."

Without conscious thought, I turned off my headlamp. Then my ears probed the darkness, alert for the slightest out-of-place sound. A faint and distant sound reached my ears. A couple of seconds later, it came again. Less faint. Less distant. I heard it a third time, clearer and closer than before. And this time I identified it.

It was the sound of a shoe scuffing against the floor.

Someone else was in the passage with me—and they were coming my way!

Mentally kicking myself for not finding the door control on this side of the door as soon as I went through it, I pulled out my night vision goggles. I slipped them on and examined the door. As I'd hoped, the button was right next to the door. There's no point in hiding a control *inside* the secret hallway, after all.

The door slid aside without a sound. I reentered the room as the door softly closed behind me. With a wall between me and the other person—God, please let it just be *one* person—I brought my friends up-to-date.

"Someone else was in the passage and they were heading my way," I hissed. "I've returned to the suite. With any luck, whoever it is will just keep walking. Considering the alarm Nathan set off, I'm not counting on that."

"What can we do?" Jana asked.

"Keep quiet until I say otherwise. Clear?"

"Yes," Nathan and Jana responded.

Alfonso remained quiet. Some women might wonder about that. I'm not one of them. As a fellow practitioner of the intrusion arts, my potential man understood my on-the-job needs far better than our friends. It was also his job to watch Nathan's back, something he couldn't do while paying attention to me.

I'd given the suite a cursory inspection before looking for the way to open the secret door. It was remarkably free of useful hiding places. I couldn't even take the cliché hide-under-the-bed choice since the humongous thing rested directly on the floor. I couldn't curl up in any of the dresser drawers—yes, I can and have done that but God was it uncomfortable—because they were way too small for it. Someone could fit underwear and multi-million credit baubles in the drawers but lithe thieves were right out.

I gave the closet a quick look. If I'd had William's closet available I'd have been in great shape. He has tons of clothes hanging in his and I was certain I could have hidden myself among his copious collection of black formal wear. Of course, no one was staying in this suite, which meant no clothes in the closet.

Or so I thought.

Don't get me wrong, the closet wasn't full of clothes. Every single hanger was empty. But a row of hooks along the near wall weren't. Bathrobes, each bearing the royal family's coat of arms on the left breast, dangled from the hooks. The robes ranged from tiny child sizes up to ones large enough for the most corpulent noble in the Star Kingdom.

I hurried down the line, rearranging several of the robes so they hung as much as half a meter out from the wall. Reaching the last one—a truly massive garment large enough to engulf three normal-sized people—I slipped under it and put my back against the wall. Grabbing the hook, I offered a silent prayer to the goddess of wardrobes asking for a hook that could hold my weight. Then I lifted my feet off the floor.

My prayer was answered. The hook held.

Putting my feet down, I waited and listened.

I didn't have long to wait. Usually, less waiting is a good thing. Not this time. Worrying replaced waiting when I heard the soft sigh of the hidden door sliding open. I'd never have heard it at all if I hadn't concentrated on that exact sound. Not that I doubted myself, but the quiet scuff of a footstep that followed removed all possibility of doubt. I can't say what stroke of good fortune put the foot scuffer in the hidden passage, but I was thankful for it.

I lifted my feet from the floor, this time bringing knees all the way up to my chest. I wrapped my left arm around my legs, hugging them close, and dangled with all my weight supported by my right arm.

A minute later, the foot scuffer came to the closet. I held my breath as a bright light swept the small room. Then it played along the floor beneath the robes. The light flicked up to the ceiling. Seconds later, it flashed beneath the robes again. Then the foot scuffer moved into the hallway and headed towards the living area and the suite's entrance.

I could have lowered my feet after that. It was a safe bet whoever was out there—a guard, almost certainly—would scuff his or her feet when they returned. But a smart thief—that being one who hasn't been captured—doesn't take safe bets when her freedom is on the line. I kept my legs pulled tight against my chest and left all my weight on my right arm.

I keep myself fit and trim for all sorts of reasons, both personal and professional, but I'd never taxed my arms this severely before. I listened as the foot scuffer searched the rest of the suite. Doors opened and closed. The suite's lights came on when the guard reached the entrance. Then the guard searched each room again. He or she only gave the closet a cursory second look before moving on.

Finally, minutes after my right arm descended from a dull ache to torturous pain, a male voice said, "This is Davis. I've searched the suite thoroughly. It's empty and the door's security seal is active. Is the servant sure she saw someone duck into this suite? I'll bet she was just flustered by the alarm."

The man was quiet for a bit, obviously listening to a reply, and then said, "All I can tell you is this place is empty. With the activity in the main hallway, anyone leaving that way would have been spotted and they couldn't have set the security seal, either. If this mythical intruder went through the hidden door, they'd have run into me or Watkins. And we know no one besides the Prince and Princess's guards entered their room."

Another few seconds passed, then he said, "That's what I've been saying. The girl just misinterpreted something she saw while she was running for her designated emergency station after the alarm sounded. Make sure you tell her no one blames her and we're glad she told us what she thought she saw. No one wants to take any chances with Their Highnesses' lives, especially with an heir on the way."

No longer trying to walk quietly, Davis went back to the suite's entrance and turned the lights off. As he walked back to the bedroom and the hidden door, he said, "I'm returning to my post. Davis out."

I heard the soft sound of the hidden door opening and closing. It took all my willpower to keep my legs off the floor, but I held my position for a slow count to one hundred. I heard nothing else during the count so finally put my feet down and let my trembling right arm fall to my side.

Sliding down the wall, I rested my legs and left arm, too. Then I keyed my comm, "I'm clear. A guard searched the room but didn't find me."

"Are you okay?" Jana asked.

"Where did you hide?" Nathan added.

"I'll be fine after some rest and I hid behind a bathrobe. I'll tell you the whole story after I get out of here." Taking a deep breath, I added, "Getting away isn't going to be easy, though. The hidden passage is guarded and the whole Palace is on alert. Hell, for all I know, William and Olivia are wide awake right now. I certainly would be in their place."

Blinking back tears of fatigue and frustration, I said, "I'm sorry, guys, but I don't see how I can finish the job."

THE STAR STONE REPORT

Jana

I heard something in Tilly's voice I'd never heard before—defeat. She sounded as if she blamed herself for the current predicament and *that* was something I most definitely would not tolerate.

"So what if we ran into some unexpected obstacles?" I asked. "No job this complex ever goes according to the plan."

Tilly gave a bitter laugh, "You got that right, but this job went from smooth sailing to mangled beyond all recognition in record time."

"Are you telling me that's never happened to you before?"

"Of course it's happened before," Tilly muttered. "But this is the first time I've found myself completely surrounded by hyper-alert, heavily armed, and highly trained guards when things went to hell."

"That just means it's time for some serious improvisation."

"You don't get it, Jana," Tilly was so upset she forgot protocol and used my real name. "I don't even see how I can escape the Palace. Finishing the job is completely out of the question."

Much as I hated to do it, I decided my friend needed a metaphorical slap on the cheek to break her out of her defeatist mood. "Huh, I never figured you for a quitter."

"Why you goddamned bitch!" Tilly snarled. "I'm the one putting my ass on the line while you sit safe and comfortable next to your data rig and you *dare* to call me a quitter?"

Okay, that hurt—mainly because it's true. I wanted to protest, point out how I planned on going with them to the Palace. To remind Tilly *she* was the one who insisted I stay behind. But I didn't do that because I *was* safe and comfortable next to my data rig. And it was up to me to make sure Tilly got back to me.

I reached into my school memories and tried channeling all the mean girls I'd known. "I'm not the subject of conversation. We're talking about the quitter who's ready to give up at the first sign of trouble. We're talking about the woman who's willing to let the Star Stone win rather than get up off her ass and *do her job*!"

"Um, ladies?" Nathan said. "Why don't we just calm—"

"*Shut up!*" Tilly and I both snapped.

Then Tilly burst out laughing. It wasn't deep, joyous laughter, but it was a damned sight better than what I'd been hearing from her. "Okay, Dreamwalker, you win. I'm ready and willing to listen to anything you suggest." She paused for a few seconds before adding, "And, thanks, I needed that."

"You're welcome, Smoke. I hated doing it even if it was necessary."

"So, after all that, do you have any bright ideas for getting me out of here?"

"Of course I do. We can probably even finish the original job —or at least part of it."

"Uh, no offense Your Geniusness, but I can't think of any possible way to get that blood sample."

"I know, but you *can* get the Star Stone report."

"How?" Nathan asked.

"That depends on you, man of my dreams. Can you spoof the Palace's aerial alarms?"

"Maybe. What do you want them to show?"

"I don't exactly know. Some kind of threat that Palace security simply can't ignore. Something they'll act on even after the false alarm you triggered earlier."

"Like a squadron of starfighters on their way to attack the palace?" Nathan asked.

"Or an out-of-control freighter or an asteroid or…whatever. If you can't spoof the aerial alarms, try a fire or radiation leak. It doesn't matter what it is. Just make sure the guards have to evacuate William and Olivia."

I could hear dawning comprehension in Tilly's voice, "They'll evacuate the entire Palace once the royal couple is on their way to safety! Then it will be simple for me to grab the report and slip out in the mass confusion."

"I don't know about simple," I countered, "but at least it will be possible."

"All right, then," Nathan said, "let me see what I can do to those alarms."

"While you're at it, can you give me access to the security system?" I asked. "I want to dig up the evacuation plans so we'll know exactly who is going where."

A few seconds passed before Nathan said, "Done."

I found what I wanted quickly. Nathan's work, on the other hand, took over an hour. What can I say, he's detail-oriented and very thorough. In *everything*—there's a damned good reason Kelly said I screamed like a banshee.

By the time he was ready, Tilly had her escape route memorized. When she said she was prepared, Nathan activated his alarm, and all hell broke loose in the Palace. Three minutes after that, the Chic Thief slipped into the royal couple's empty suite. Olivia obligingly left the report sitting right out in the open on her bedside table.

While Alfonso sealed the hole in the tunnel and Nathan packed his equipment, Tilly slipped into the flood of people evacuating the Palace. Two hours later, everyone was safely back with Kelly and me.

Tilly handed the report to me. Before I opened it, I offered up a quick prayer the report held something we could use against the Star Stone. Because there was no way we could ever pull off another Palace job.

∼

Tilly and Alfonso had a sweet reunion with lots of hugs and kisses and even a little publicly appropriate caressing. Even so, Tilly shivered in a good way when Alfonso ran a hand down her spine. Then she took him by the hand and pulled him towards her bedroom.

"Don't disturb us unless the RIA is breaking down the door," she called.

Grinning, Kelly asked, "Banshee time?"

Tilly leered. Alfonso laughed. Nathan looked confused.

"What does that mean?" he asked.

"You're a smart boy, I'm sure you can figure it out," Kelly said. "If not, maybe you can coax your girlfriend into showing you again. And again. And, unless I miscounted, again."

Comprehension dawned and Nathan's face turned bright red. "I'm, uh, sorry we disturbed you."

Kelly waved it off. "Just make sure it happens again."

Confused, Nathan asked, "Don't you mean 'make sure it *doesn't* happen again?'"

"Jana's my friend and I like it when my friends are happy. Ecstatic is even better." Nathan's face, which had almost returned to its normal color, flared red again. Kelly rolled her eyes and said, "Lord, boy, you are such a newb. One week of Space Patrol training would wring that out of you quick-like."

Nathan glanced at me and asked, "Why aren't you blushing, too?"

"She's already had this talk with me," I replied, and then my face warmed.

Kelly laughed, "My work here is done!"

That reminded me of what I held in my hands. Holding up the Star Stone report, I said, "Mine isn't, so please keep quiet while I'm reading."

I thought Kelly would suggest Nathan and I engage in an enthusiastic round of...stress relief before I dove into the report. But when serious subjects arise Kelly gets serious fast. She just nodded, "I'll fix some breakfast and bring it to you when it's ready. Any requests?"

"Coffee," I said.

"And bacon," Nathan added.

Then Nathan and I sat next to each other and began skimming the report together. While Nathan is a better slicer than me, I read a lot faster than him. I quickly shifted from skimming to in-depth reading within the first few pages and I still kept up with him. The report's tone was dry and academic but the information it contained made fascinating reading. Not to mention illuminating.

About an hour later, with the remains of breakfast discarded on a side table and a hot mug of coffee in my hand, my subconscious suddenly put part of the puzzle together.

"Son of a bitch!" I said, surprise and disgust warring for dominance in my tone.

"What?" Nathan asked.

"They *knew*!"

"Who knew what?"

"The Royal family. They knew the Star Stone was performing genetic experiments on the nobility!"

"I must have missed something, Jana."

I shook my head and flipped back to an earlier page, "It's all between the lines stuff. The report doesn't come out and say it, but I'm sure no one could have gotten most of this information without going into the Star Stone and talking to it."

"But you told me Queen Charlotte said no one who entered the Star Stone ever got out alive."

I couldn't stop a derisive snort, "And the nobility are such paragons of virtue that they never, ever tell lies, right?"

"Okay, you've got me there. But why would the kings and queens of the past cooperate with the Star Stone if they knew it was messing with their DNA?"

I flipped to another page and pointed to the text, "Because the Star Stone lied to them. Or didn't tell them the entire truth, anyway. If I'm interpreting this correctly, the Star Stone convinced the Royal emissary that it was experimenting on nobles and would only use successful procedures on royalty. It implied it was turning them into superior beings. Hell, from the Star Stone's point of view, it was even telling the truth."

"Okay, but if you're right, it also means the Star Stone doesn't date back to pre-technological times. Not that I'm surprised the myth of the Star Stone is completely fabricated."

"It pretty much told me as much just before you rescued me. I haven't had much time to think on it, but it claimed it had been working on humanity for four thousand years. That means it appeared on the scene at the beginning of the space age—probably no more than a couple of hundred years after the first spaceflight."

"If humans were already using primitive spacefaring technology and had begun making real scientific progress, how did the Star Stone end up at the center of an interstellar kingdom?"

I shrugged, "Your guess is as good as mine, not that I care very much. I can live without that knowledge as long as we can find a way to stop the thing."

Nathan and I went back to reading and were quickly absorbed in the report. At some point, Kelly put sandwiches in front of us. We ate them without really noticing what we were eating. Sometime later I noticed Tilly and Alfonso settling into the couch across from us.

"Did you scream like a banshee?" I asked.

Tilly nestled up to Alfonso, "You didn't hear me?"

I shook my head, "Sorry, the report had my full attention."

"Tilly's voice doesn't go as high as yours," Kelly said. "Otherwise, your performances were remarkably similar."

I gave Tilly a thumbs up, "Good for you."

Smiling smugly, Tilly replied, "*Very* good for me, indeed!"

"Don't you have a report to read, Jana?" Alfonso asked.

"Huh," I said, "it looks like Scoop was right about men and sex talk."

"He was also right about women and sex talk," Nathan muttered. "Can we please get back to the report?"

Bowing to the wishes of the men, I returned to reading. Thirty-four minutes later, we turned the page and discovered the answer to my prayers—six small chips from the Star Stone and a detailed scientific analysis of them.

Handing the report across to Tilly, I said, "You studied chemistry. Do you understand any of that?"

Tilly scanned the analysis, flipping pages back and forth as she did. "Some of it is clear, Jana, but most of this is way over my head."

"Damn. I was sure that analysis could tell us how to destroy the Star Stone."

"You may be right," Tilly agreed. "*I* can't understand most of this stuff, but I know someone who can."

TRUE NEEDS
Olivia

I gradually emerged from sleep's comforting embrace. When consciousness reasserted itself I found myself longing for the hazy half-awake state where problems do not exist and life is wonderful. But sleep's shelter was gone, banished to the hidden recesses of my mind by harsh reality. My eyes fluttered open, and I found William silently watching me, his mouth stretched into a gentle smile.

When several seconds passed without him speaking, I asked, "What?"

"Have I told you how much I love you?" he asked.

"You tell me all the time, dear—not that I'm complaining." I scooted toward William and kissed him. "I love you, too."

"For which I am profoundly grateful."

"Is something wrong, William? You seem pensive."

"Last night's double alarms, especially that harrowing evacuation, coupled with your recent kidnapping sent my subconscious off in morbid directions. My dreams have faded, thank God, but they shared one horrible theme. You were gone from my life."

"You can't get rid of me that easily, William."

"*I* know that, it's my subconscious that's being difficult about this."

Looking into William's eyes I realized his nightmares truly bothered him. That made my decision simple. I grabbed William's comm—since I was snuggled up to him, his was closer—and called his assistant.

Peter answered, "Yes, Your Highness?"

"Peter, after such a trying night, William and I are spending the day together. Please reschedule all his appointments. Also, contact Elizabeth and have her do the same for my appointments."

Despite the mountain of work I'd just dumped on our two assistants, Peter simply replied, "At once, Your Highness!"

"And Peter?"

"Yes, Your Highness?"

"William and I understand just how difficult we've made your day. We'll find a way to make it up to you."

"That's not necessary, Your Highness. This is my job after all."

An idea occurred to me. "You have a teenage daughter, don't you? Katrina, I believe?"

Peter couldn't keep the surprise out of his voice, "Yes. She's quite a fan of yours."

"Do you think she'd enjoy spending a day with me? I could take her shopping—my treat, of course—have lunch at one of my favorite restaurants, and then she could join William and me for a private dinner."

"That... That is most generous of you, Your Highness. Katrina would love that."

"Excellent! Could you arrange that with Elizabeth? And tell her I'll think of a way to make this extra work up to her, also."

"I will, Your Highness. And thank you. Thank you so very much!"

"It is the least I can do, Peter."

I disconnected the call and put William's comm back on his bedside table. Meeting William's stunned gaze, I said, "I believe you were about to have your way with me."

"I was?" He suddenly grinned, "Yes, by God, I was!"

I was so wrapped up in my husband that I didn't realize the Star Stone report was missing until after dinner. Even then, I merely assumed someone had moved it. It wasn't until the following morning that I discovered it had vanished completely. I alerted Palace security, of course, but their attention was rightly focused on hardening the Palace's network security.

I had only read part of the report, but I couldn't imagine it would be useful to whoever took it. Even if it ended up in the hands of Jeanine's pet slicer, what could Jana possibly learn that she hadn't already discovered when she accessed the Star Stone directly?

I put it out of my mind and turned my attention to the true needs of the Star Kingdom.

PLANNING

Jana

Nathan and I made several copies of the Star Stone report and handed them out to everyone on the team. We gave Tilly an extra copy of the analysis of the Star Stone fragments, along with one of the fragments.

"Maybe a piece of the Star Stone will help your friend with his analysis," I said.

"He's not just a friend, Jana," Tilly told me, "he was my mentor in college."

"Even better," Alfonso said. "Don't college profs love it when beautiful former students visit and ask for their help?"

"It wasn't like that," Tilly protested. "Dr. Kristof was interested in my mind, not my body. He and his wife treated me like a granddaughter during my college years."

"I'm not saying he had designs on your body, Tilly," Alfonso placated, "but no matter how old a man is, he still enjoys looking at a pretty woman."

"Whatever," Tilly muttered. She grabbed a fashionable-yet-floppy hat from her room and headed for the door, "I'll be back as soon as possible."

"Hold it," Kelly commanded. "I'm coming with you. I can

help watch your back. I also want to check for messages from Drake."

"You can do that from here," Nathan said.

"Yeah, but I hate using the same access method more than two times in a row and I've done my last five checks from here. I'm just too paranoid to push my luck any farther than that."

After Kelly and Tilly left, Nathan and I returned to reading the Star Stone report. Alfonso kept an eye on our security cams and alarms, leaving Nathan and me free to give all our attention to the report.

Since I was the faster reader, I was the one who discovered the biggest surprise in the report. "Holy crap!"

"What?" Nathan asked, looking up from his reading.

"You remember the holy man the Star Stone told me about? The only person before us who escaped from the Star Stone?"

"Sure. He thought he was meeting God, or maybe God's instrument in the real world, right?"

"That's the one," I replied. "Only he wasn't a holy man. He was deeply religious, which is why he discovered his soul connection and escaped, but the 'holy man' story was a cover story."

"Maybe I'm a little dense, Jana, but what's the point in an undercover mission to the Star Stone? Wouldn't the Stone already know all about the guy?"

I shook my head, "He was a commoner so never came in contact with the Star Stone before or after his visit. He was also the Royal Intelligence Agency's top data analyst and network system specialist. Apparently, he theorized the Star Stone was some kind of alien computer and convinced the king to let him investigate it."

"Did they even *have* networks four thousand years ago?"

"Primitive ones, but yes. The thing is, this guy—they don't give his name—entered the Star Stone less than two thousand years ago. By then, half the planets in the Star Kingdom were settled, and the throne was well-established on Xapreathea."

"Okay," Nathan said, flipping to the agent's findings in the report, "but the two of us aren't slouches when it comes to networking and data systems. We didn't learn anything useful about that stuff while we were in there."

"We were concentrating on other things. Besides, the Star Stone basically gave the RIA agent a guided tour of its workings."

"Say what?"

"That's what it says in this report."

"But why would the Star Stone do something like that?"

"I don't know, Nathan. Maybe it was lonely? Maybe it wanted to show off? Maybe it was certain there was nothing a mere human could glean from the tour? Maybe it thought it was crushing the man's religious beliefs? Regardless of the reason, it's a safe bet the Star Stone assumed the 'holy man' would never return to his body. So maybe it was just toying with the guy." I caught Nathan's eyes with mine, "The important thing is the man spent *hours* of real time inside the Star Stone."

By now Nathan was flipping through the agent's report, his eyes moving rapidly over the information. "Assuming any of this information is correct, that analyst was *very* good at his job. I wonder how he convinced the Stone to divulge all this information?"

I waved that off, "Tricking the Star Stone isn't hard. Or maybe the Star Stone is just so insufferably arrogant that it *wants* to tell us mere humans how magnificent it thinks it is. Besides, it always assumes anyone accessing it will never leave. For all I know, it's watched too many adventure vids where the villain tells his entire plan to the supposedly helpless hero. Whatever the reason, I think the agent's report is as accurate a description of the Star Stone's inner workings as we'll ever find."

"Maybe, but the jargon in here is way out of date. How long will it take to bring it up-to-date?"

"Not long. I researched a lot of that stuff before building the interface that let me access the Star Stone the first time."

"Have I told you just how amazing you are?" Nathan asked.

"Not since we put our clothes on last night."

A snort of laughter came from behind me. I'd forgotten Alfonso was still in the room! Before I could hide my face in chagrin, Nathan leaned over and kissed me.

"You're amazing, Jana," he said. A wicked grin crossed his face, and he added, "With or without clothes."

Alfonso laughed harder, gasping out, "Get a room, you two!"

"We already have a room," Nathan replied.

"Then use it."

Pushing aside my embarrassment, I said, "Maybe later. Right now, we've got work to do."

"You do, anyway," Nathan said. "I'd probably just slow you down if I helped."

"Don't worry, I've got something I want you to do while I'm working on this."

"Name it."

"Arrange a meeting at The Club with the fifty best slicers you can reach. If you even suspect any of those slicers are Recognized, don't invite them."

"I can do that. What should I tell them the meeting is about?"

"Saving the human race. We'll tell them about destroying the Star Stone once they've all gathered."

"Uh, isn't that what Tilly is taking care of right now?" Alfonso asked.

I nodded, "If we're lucky, yes. But it's always a good idea to have a fallback plan."

"Do we have a fallback plan for the fallback plan?" Nathan asked.

I shrugged, "There's always my original idea of dropping the Stone in the nearest star, but doing that will probably start a galactic civil war."

"Yeah," Nathan said, "let's not do that."

He went back to his data rig while I got busy updating the language in the agent's report.

SKULKING

Tilly

As we drove onto the university, my eyes never stopped moving. They alighted on potential threats, only moving on after I decided that specific threat was harmless.

I eliminated groups of four or more people almost automatically. Surveillance personnel avoid gathering in large clusters because they stand out, even more so when those involved must pay attention to everything around them *except* the people they're with. Loners are the biggest worry and they were all over the place.

A man guiding a baby floater caught my attention immediately. He stopped and bent over, supposedly comforting the infant. His attention stayed on the floater, but what if he had monitoring screens inside it? Then he lifted a real child from the floater. Dismissed.

My eyes flicked to a young woman listening to an earnest young man. Head-to-toe, she wore the latest fashion and from the almost-pleading expression on the young man's face was well out of his league. She was pretending to listen but not looking at him. Her eyes were just like mine, darting all around and never focusing on the same thing for more than a second or two. RIA agent. The young man probably was, too, or she'd have gotten rid of him with a suitably scathing remark. By the time she focused on our car, I was having an animated—and entirely silent—conversation with Kelly. The woman's eyes slid to someone else, dismissing us.

Next was a tense man talking on his comm. His tension and the comm made me suspect him immediately. Then his face contorted in anger and he dashed his comm on the sidewalk. Curious behavior but no longer suspicious. Dismissed.

Never taking her eyes from the road, Kelly says, "We're entering the campus, Tilly. Keep an eye out for RIA agents. You can spot them by—"

"Do I tell you how to pilot starships?" I asked, never taking my eyes from our surroundings. "Or even how to drive the car?"

"Right. Sorry. I'm not used to working with professionals. So, have you seen anyone suspicious?"

"We just passed a couple of agents."

Kelly glanced at me in alarm. "Why didn't you tell me?"

"Watch the road, Kelly, and wipe that alarmed expression off your face. It looks suspicious," I admonished. "I didn't tell you because the agents didn't notice us."

"Dammit. Sorry, again."

"Don't worry about it. In fact, we should keep a running conversation going for the rest of the drive. It doesn't matter what you say, just act animated."

Kelly did just that, keeping a running commentary going until we reached the car park. I spotted two more agents, both wandering the campus by themselves.

As Kelly pulled into a parking spot, I told her, "They're watching Dr. Kristof pretty closely. Getting in to see him won't be easy."

"Should we abort?"

"Not yet, but you should stay near the car in case I need a fast exit."

"Won't that look odd?"

"That depends on how well you can act."

Kelly sighed, "Let me guess—I'm dropping my girlfriend off and waiting while she runs an errand?"

"Exactly." I showed her a data stick. "I'm dropping off my application for grad school and you're wishing me luck."

"Why bring it in person when you can submit it over the net?"

"For some odd reason, the university's application process isn't working right now."

"Ah. Jana's handiwork, I assume?"

"Of course."

Kelly and I got out and met in front of the car. She kissed me softly, though quickly, on the lips. "I'll wait for you here."

I nodded, "Okay. Wish me luck!"

"Good luck, honey."

With that, I turned and sashayed away. From the way I walked, anyone watching me should assume I had nothing to hide. *Should.*

An experienced agent wouldn't fall into that trap, but I'd only seen young, minimally experienced agents so far. They didn't stand out from the students. Plus, watching Dr. Kristof had to be a long shot from the RIA's perspective. Sure, I'd been close to him during my student years so they had to keep an eye on him. But I hadn't visited him since my graduation six years ago and I wouldn't be visiting him now if it wasn't for the Star Stone analysis in the Royal report.

Heading straight for the graduate admissions office, which is on the opposite side of campus from the chemistry department, I passed within a few meters of one of the wandering agents. He watched me, all right, but his eyes never left my swinging hips. I still flashed a bright smile at his attention, confident my hat hid the rest of my face from him. Since half-a-dozen other women around me wore similar hats it didn't arouse his suspicions.

Fashion is your friend, ladies.

As are inexperienced and bored agents.

I found the door to graduate admissions, entered, and spoke to the first person I saw. "I tried submitting my application over—"

"It's down," the man interrupted. Pointing to a basket on a nearby desk, he said, "Drop your data stick in there."

"Uh, thanks," I said and added mine to the growing pile of data sticks in the basket.

The man nodded, already turning away from me. "We'll contact you once we've processed your application."

I left the office but turned away from the building exit. I wandered, as if looking for someone or something. When I reached the drop chute to the basement, I stepped into it. As I descended, I switched from my fashionable-but-loud heels to comfortable-and-quiet soft-soled shoes.

As a student, I'd snuck in and out of almost every building on campus, including this one. Its basement was usually deserted and today was no different. I found the door to the maintenance tunnels, picked its lock with practiced ease, trotted down an ancient stairway and entered the university's tunnel system. Minutes later, I entered the chemistry department's basement and rode the lift chute up to the first floor.

Dr. Kristof had been in the same office for decades but I checked the department directory all the same. He was right where he'd always been, on the third floor. I kept scanning, though, verifying the same professors occupied the offices around his. Nothing had changed since I was here last but something just didn't feel right.

Repressing a sigh, I entered the restroom and locked the door. Then I climbed onto one of the cabinets and gently removed the grill for the antique ventilation system. I quietly slid my bag into the duct, unlocked the restroom door—nothing is more suspicious than a locked door when no one is in the room to respond to a knock—and pulled myself up and in. Replacing the grill, I set off for the third floor.

The biggest problem with old ductwork isn't moving from

floor to floor. It's moving quietly. That's why it took me twenty minutes to reach the grill above Dr. Kristof's office. I heard him get up and shut his office door. His chair gave that old, familiar squeak as he sat down again. Then he surprised me by speaking.

"Stop skulking in the ducts, my dear. We don't have much time before the RIA checks on me again."

He never told me how he always knew when I came creeping through the ducts, but he knew. I *think* it's because Dr. Kristof has been in this office so long he knows every background sound by heart. As such, the minor sounds I make don't fade into that well-known collection of creaks and sighs. That's my theory, anyway.

"Be right down, sir."

"*I'll* be right down," Dr. Kristof said. "That is what you meant to say, is it not?"

I lifted aside the duct grating and rolled my eyes at my former professor. "The 'I' is implied and my grammar choice is perfectly acceptable for casual conversations."

Grabbing the lip of the opening, I tucked and dropped into the office below. Landing lightly, before Dr. Kristof, I added, "You're a chem teacher. Why do you care about my grammar? Besides, I graduated years ago."

"When you stop learning, you stop living, my dear." Dr. Kristof opened his arms wide, gave me a big hug, and then held me at arm's length. "It's good to see you, girl! How are you?"

"I need help, sir."

"I rather assumed that, Tilly. The RIA rarely pays visits to mere chemistry professors. They claim you are part of some great threat to the Star Kingdom."

"From their point of view, I suppose I am."

Dr. Kristof's eyebrows rose in surprise. "They also told me you're some kind of thief?"

To my surprise, I felt heat in my cheeks from a blush.

My old mentor offered a gentle smile, "To which I told them,

'I bet she's a damned good one!' You always could do anything you truly set your mind to."

"You aren't...disappointed in me?"

"It's not the career I'd have chosen for my favorite student, but following that path has let you put a burr up the RIA's backside. That's no small accomplishment."

"You sound as if you're proud of me."

"I am. Back in my youth, I was quite the republican. I even met Rebecca—the future Mrs. Kristof—at an anti-monarchist protest. I could have sworn I told you about that."

"You did. It's one reason I came to you."

"I'm glad you did, Tilly. But, as I said, we don't have much time before the RIA checks on me. They do so with distressing, though unpredictable, regularity. What may I do for you?"

I pulled the analysis from my equipment pouch and handed it to Dr. Kristof. "I can only understand part of this. Can you interpret it for me?"

He took the copy from me and flipped through it. "It will take a while, but I think so. What are you looking for?"

"A way to destroy the item described in the report."

"Will you tell me what the item is?"

"Are you certain you want to know, sir?"

"I'm a scientist, my dear, of course I want to know."

"Okay." I met his gaze and said, "It's the Star Stone."

As my old professor's eyes widened, we both heard footsteps out in the hallway. Dr. Kristof flicked his eyes up to the duct. I leapt and caught the lip of the opening. As I pulled myself into the duct, Dr. Kristof stuffed the report in a pocket and then walked to his office door. As I lifted the grating into place, I heard the door control beep.

"Dr. Kristof?" a woman's voice called. "Open this door, immediately."

I scooted as far from the grating as possible while still giving me a narrow view of the door. Dr. Kristof unlocked it. Before he could do anything else, the door slid aside and revealed a trim woman a few years older than me. She wore a no-nonsense expression on her face.

"You were told to keep your door open and unlocked," she said as she glanced about the small office.

Dr. Kristof backed out of the doorway. "I *always* close my office door when I'm preparing an exam. One can't have students wandering into the office and discovering the questions, can one?"

The woman entered the office, looked under the desk, and then opened the door to the small closet. "Why did you lock the door?"

"I didn't realize I had until you asked me to unlock it. It's the result of decades of habit, I suppose. You'd be amazed how ill-mannered many students are these days. They think nothing of simply barging through a closed door without requesting entry permission." Dr. Kristof shook his head at this appalling lack of manners. "In *my* day, none of us youngsters would have dared—"

The RIA agent turned back to Dr. Kristof. Her eyes glanced at his shirt, narrowed, and then returned to normal so quickly I almost missed it. Turning to the door, she said, "You may shut, but not lock, your door."

"But what of the students who charge through—?"

"I'll station myself outside the door until you finish with the exam. That should deter your mannerless students."

Dr. Kristof shut the door and turned back to his desk. I looked at his shirt and saw what caught the woman's attention—a small dusty smudge over his breast pocket. Glancing down at my frictionless catsuit, I spotted a dust smudge over my own breast. Dammit, this is why I wear a new catsuit on every job. Every job except this one since I couldn't risk contacting my usual suppliers. If only I hadn't let Dr. Kristof give me that hug.

Pushing that thought aside, I considered my next course of action. Through the ducts, I heard the soft murmur of the agent's voice. I couldn't make out what she was saying, but it was bound to be some variation of, "She's in the ducts."

I had to clear out, and fast—but not before I warned Dr. Kristof. Carefully lifting the grating again, I waved. When he looked up, I pointed at the dust on his shirt. He saw it immediately and turned a questioning look my way.

Thinking solely of Dr. Kristof's safety, I pointed at the pocket with the report and indicated he should give it back to me. Reluctantly, he stood and handed it back to me. Once I had it secured in my pouch, I replaced the grating, waved, and scooted back toward the vertical duct I'd used to climb to the third floor. Reaching it, I used a fiber-optic cam to glance down the shaft. An RIA agent crouched at the bottom of the shaft, a blaster ready in his hands.

Damn.

I carefully scooted away from the shaft. I didn't bother heading for any of the other ventilation shafts. If the RIA had one covered, they had them all covered. I couldn't go down, but I also couldn't go up since I'd have to use the same shafts. So much for leaping to a neighboring building and escaping through it.

That really only left one choice. I stopped at the first grating I came to and peered into the office. Dr. Calloway—the chemistry department's least favorite professor—sat at his desk studying something on his data pad. His door was shut, at least. Without giving myself time to think too carefully about it, I quietly removed the grating. Calloway didn't look up from his pad though that was about to change.

I swung down into the office, landing in front of the door. Dr. Calloway recoiled in surprised terror as I locked the door.

Catching the front of his desk, I shoved it hard toward the professor. The thing was big and heavy but I had plenty of adrenaline pumping through my veins. It pushed Dr. Calloway against the wall, knocking the wind out of him and trapping him against the wall.

As I opened his office window, I said, "That makes us even for the 'D' you gave me in organic chem."

Dr. Calloway just stared at me as I leapt from his third-floor office window.

Wishing there was a tall and majestic tree outside the window, I dropped three stories and into the hedgerow surrounding the chemistry building. Branches stabbed and poked me while rough leaves scraped my exposed skin, but the hedge also broke my fall. Students stared at me in slack-jawed stupefaction as I pulled myself free of a now-mangled bush. From the open window above me, Dr. Calloway's voice rose in panicked indignation.

"Help! A madman attacked me! Help!"

A mad*man*? Could this be the same professor whose eyes never strayed north of my breasts when I was a student? Putting that thought out of my mind, I sprinted toward a nearby courtyard that should be crowded with students at this time of day. While running, I ran a hand through my hair and brushed away leaves and twigs caught in it.

Behind me, Dr. Calloway must have found his bearings because his cries turned demanding, "You, woman, come away from that window and pull this desk away from me!"

I could only assume the agent outside Dr. Kristof's office responded to Calloway's shouts, though not in the way the old bastard hoped. Fighting down the urge to look over my shoulder, I cut to my left and, two steps later, cut back to the right. I heard the crack of the blaster at the same time a bolt splashed against the walkway. It barely left a mark. At least the agent had her gun set to stun.

Another bolt flew wide as I zigged when the agent expected a zag. That shot clipped a student's leg. He fell to the ground, clutching his leg and screaming far more than the shot deserved. Mass panic swept through the students. With cries and screams, they scattered in all directions. That helped me some but hindered me almost as much.

With people dashing madly all around the courtyard the agent would have trouble hitting me from her window vantage point. But I was slowed by the unpredictable mob running wild around me. Despite my best efforts, people caromed into me and knocked me off my stride every few seconds. Worse, a couple of the bigger ones sent me crashing to the ground. I recovered before anyone trampled me but lost precious time doing so.

The center of the courtyard was clear when I reached it, giving me the chance to sprint ahead and also contact Kelly over the comm. "Red!"

That was short for 'condition red,' which meant I'd been spotted.

Kelly's reply was immediate, "Blue?"

That was a pickup location on the southeastern edge of the campus. I, of course, was running north. "Green."

The 'green' pickup was on the north side of campus—about as far from the blue rendezvous spot as possible. I thought I detected a slight sigh when she replied, "Five."

Could I avoid capture by RIA agents for five minutes? I didn't have any other choice, so I said, "Roger."

By then I heard authoritative shouts coming from behind me. The agent in the window must have gotten her fellow agents out of the ducts and on my tail. I risked a glance over my shoulder and saw three men, blaster pistols held high, ordering panicked students from their path. Anyone who moved too slowly was unceremoniously shoved aside.

Because of their rough tactics—not to mention their guns—the men were gaining on me. I, on the other hand, was almost to the other side of the courtyard. The physics department was less than twenty meters ahead of me. Once inside it, I could disappear into the tunnels and wait until the furor died down. I'd also give Kelly the code to come back for me in six hours.

I finally got free of the mob of students. My escape path lay just ahead of me. Then, to my right, I saw them—the hot female agent and her earnest suitor from our approach to the university. They must have rotated stations while I was working my way into Dr. Kristof's office.

Like the other agents, they had their blaster pistols in hand. Unlike the other agents, they had a close, clear shot at me.

Dammit!

I sent a last message to Kelly. "Abort."

The agents leveled their guns. I saw a bright flash as they fired. Then everything went dark.

OUR TARGET IS THE STAR STONE

Jana

I was so deeply engrossed in updating the language in the Star Stone technical report that I didn't hear my comm buzzing. My first hint that something was wrong came when Alfonso shook me. I looked up and opened my mouth to ask him what the hell he thought he was doing. That idea died as soon as I saw his face.

"What's wrong?" I asked.

Alfonso headed for the back room where Nathan was connected to the network. Over his shoulder, he snapped, "We leave in five minutes."

I gathered up the report and my data pad, "Okay. But *what happened?*"

"The RIA captured Tilly."

A cold knot of fear sprang into being right where my heart used to be. "Kelly?"

"She's ditching the car. I gave her a rendezvous time and place. She'll alert us if it's safe to pick her up."

I followed Alfonso down the hall, "And if it's not?"

"We leave her, go to Nathan's final safe house, and finish the job."

"We're just abandoning her?"

"If we have to. Keeping you and Nathan safe so you guys can destroy the Star Stone is all that matters." Alfonso punched a key on one of Nathan's data rigs and said, "Fox, condition yellow."

Seconds later, Nathan sat up and disconnected himself from the network. "Status?"

"They got Tilly," I said.

"Dammit!" Standing, Nathan activated his system destruction routines. He took a second to glance at Alfonso and me, "We'll get her back. I don't know how, yet—"

"I do," I said, "but it will mean moving our schedule up a lot."

Alfonso headed back up the hall, "I'll grab our go-bags. We leave when I return."

Nodding, I turned to Nathan, "How many slicers turned up for the meeting?"

"Everyone we invited and a few we didn't."

"Did you block the uninvited from the meeting?"

Nathan shook his head, "Someone—probably Scoop—has been spreading rumors about us and a truly momentous job. The uninvited must have heard the rumors and decided they'd crash the party. In all honesty, I think we should have invited them first."

"Hackers?"

"Yep." Nathan verified his data rigs were rapidly destroying themselves. "And if there was ever a time to embrace the destructive slicer fringe, this is it."

I couldn't argue with that. A little hack-and-slash action was precisely what we'd need against the Star Stone.

Alfonso called, "Are you ready? If so, get up here."

We didn't have a hidden escape tunnel like the one we used when the RIA crashed our party back at Nathan's apartment. Instead, we just dashed out the door. I followed Alfonso and

Nathan to a car we'd never used before. Alfonso had us merging into city traffic two minutes later. He drove for several more minutes, all the while keeping a watch on the car's various cams, while Nathan worked with his data pad.

"Anything?" Alfonso asked.

"No sign of an alert. At least, not yet," Nathan replied. "What about you?"

"We're clear." Alfonso relaxed a bit. "Call Kelly and set up a rendezvous."

While Nathan did that I worked on the details of my plan to get Tilly back. Calling it a plan seemed grandiose when I considered it objectively. Still, it was the best bet we had. By the time we picked up Kelly I knew what to do.

"I need an untraceable subspace connection, Nathan."

"It'll take me close to an hour once we get to the last safe house, Jana."

"That'll do. While you're working on that, maybe I can go back to the club and push our case with the slicers and hackers."

"Slicer. Hacker. What's the difference?" Kelly asked.

"Slicing is precise and careful," I responded. "A slicer gets in, gets what she wants, and gets out again—all without being discovered. Hacking is brute force. A hacker enjoys the destruction as much as he enjoys getting what he's after."

"One is a surgeon, the other is a thug with a club. Got it." Kelly considered that for a second or two, "So, you think attacking the Star Stone is more of a thug-and-club mission?"

"Absolutely."

"You're the expert. Once Nathan sets up the subspace line, who are you going to call?"

"Jeanine."

"Why?"

"I need her to negotiate Tilly's release."

Kelly raised an eyebrow. "Olivia isn't going to give Tilly up just because Jeanine asks her to. Hell, she'll probably throw Tilly in the deepest dungeon just because Jeanine is the one asking for her release."

I shook my head, "Jeanine will offer her a trade—one I'm certain Olivia will go for."

Kelly considered that and before asking, "What have we got that the Princess of the Realm wants more than Tilly?"

"Me."

The response from everyone else in the car made me feel warm and well-loved.

"Absolutely not!" Kelly protested.

"Tilly wouldn't want you doing this," Alfonso claimed.

I'm biased, but Nathan's was the sweetest protest. "How can we spend the rest of our lives together if you're stuck in a Royal dungeon?"

"I appreciate everyone's concern—especially yours, Nathan—but it's my fault Tilly is in trouble," I replied. "If I'd finished reading the report before telling her about the chemical analysis of the Star Stone, she wouldn't have put herself at risk."

"Time was running short—*is* running short," Kelly said, "we didn't have time to wait for you to wade through the whole report. You know It. Tilly knew it. She also knew the risks."

"Besides," Nathan added, "we need you for the Star Stone hack. If you give yourself up—"

"I won't give myself up until after the Star Stone is... Is 'dead' the right word?"

"Won't destroying the Star Stone kill the whole deal?" Alfonso asked. "Why would Olivia bother keeping her end of the agreement if it meant she'd already lost the Stone?"

"How will she know?" I countered. "The Star Stone is only active during Recognition ceremonies. They won't figure it out until Tilly is long gone and maybe even after Jeanine has negotiated my release. Now, would you all please shut up and let me finish updating the data analysis of the Stone?"

To my surprise, they did as I asked. By the time we reached

Nathan's third safe house, I had a document any slicer or hacker could understand. And, once we had a working data rig, I connected to the Network and headed for The Club.

As I'd expected, the slicers were still there waiting for more information. Most of the hackers had gotten bored and wandered off. At my request, those who waited called those who left.

I added, "And invite anyone else you think would enjoy getting in on the single most important hack in human history. That goes for you slicers, too."

That got their attention—enough so it got the slicers muttering among themselves. Finally, Scoop voiced the slicers' concerns.

"Just thinking about a large, coordinated slice like the one you're planning sends shivers up my spine. But, darling, your friends and colleagues in The Club find your lack of exclusivity extremely vexing."

"Yeah," someone hidden in the crowd called, "we don't need help from that bunch of byte trash!"

Angry shouts rose from the gathered hackers. Equally angry shouts from the slicers answered them. Great, I'd barely said anything and my potential allies were already at each other's throats.

I tried shouting over them, "If you'll just quiet down, I'll explain."

I'm not even sure anyone heard me over the din. Hell, *I* couldn't hear myself. Certainly, no one responded to my request. Having no other choice, I took drastic measures and activated one hundred and eighty-six versions of my isolation routine— one for every hacker and slicer in meeting with me. A nanosecond later, all was silent. The crowd still shouted but no one else heard them.

I watched the avatars before me, waiting for the realization to sink in. It didn't take long—idiots don't master slicing or hacking. As faces turned my way, I said, "You can hear me but this isolation routine is one-way. I can't hear you unless I choose to. You can either sit quietly and listen to what I have to say or you can leave. My routine will delete itself as soon as you leave The Club."

My gaze swept over the avatars before me, giving any who wanted out time to leave. No one did. I smiled, "Good. Before I tell you about this job, I'll address Scoop's concern. Fox and I included hackers because their skills are perfectly suited to this particular job. Our goal is nothing less than the utter destruction of a data system unlike any you've ever seen."

I saw the hackers' eyes quite literally light up at that. Apparently, glowing red avatar eyes were a thing in the hacker community. Combined with their more monstrous avatar designs, it actually looked badass. I grinned at the hackers, showing I appreciated their enthusiasm.

Not to be outdone, the slicers closest to hackers made on-the-fly adjustments to their own avatars. Scoop was the first, and I had to admit smoldering white eyes gave his avatar a menacing demeanor. Shortly, a sea of bright white eyes stared back at me. More importantly, the hackers nodded and grinned at the slicers, forging a tenuous link between the two groups.

"I'll get to the details of this job in just a minute. First, I have one more extraordinary thing to add." Activating my avatar's most solemn expression, I said, "Some of us could die doing this job. And not because we're breaking into a heavily secured system with deadly, brain-melting feedback, either."

As I'd intended, that drew a laugh. We'd all seen the adventure vids where the slicer's head explodes because of a new and fatal security system. It's a load of crap, but one we in the community let stand. It buffs our reputations as daring risk-takers, lets us charge more for our services, and discourages those who don't have the dedication required to learn the trade.

I only let them laugh for a couple of seconds. "But this job *is* potentially deadly. I know we're all familiar with the theory that a person's...essence, soul, whatever you want to call it...is nothing more than electrical impulses working within an organic operating system. And that it's theoretically possible to draw that essence out of a person and trap it somewhere else."

I had their undivided attention now. A few avatars nodded but most just watched me, waiting for what came next.

"It's not just a theory. The system we're attacking does that to everyone who passes through its interface. I know this from personal experience. I've been inside this particular system twice and barely escaped with my life each time. Fox was with me the second time and I'd never have escaped at all if it wasn't for him."

Once again, I let my gaze sweep over the crowd. Most of the avatars were thoughtful. A few were dubious. In truth, I'd expected more doubters. Obviously, I'd underestimated Fox's and my reputations.

"I see some doubters among the crowd and don't blame you for that. Even for someone like Fox or me, it's a fantastical claim. If there's nothing I can say to convince you otherwise, I must ask you to leave now. Your doubt might hamper your ability to successfully return to your body at the end of the mission. I will not have that on my conscience."

To my surprise that simple statement convinced some doubters that I wasn't delusional. Most of them, though, did as I'd requested and left. I sealed our gathering area after their departure, blocking them from returning. And, since I definitely had everyone's attention, I dismissed the individual isolation bots.

I still had a hundred and fifty-seven hackers and slicers after the departures. But I had one more winnowing to perform.

"This next question won't immediately make sense to you but if you can't answer 'yes' to it, I want you to leave. Once again, it's for your own safety. Do you all agree to this?" Avatar heads nodded all around, so I continued, "Do you have someone you love at least as much as you love yourself?"

Startled expressions appeared on most avatars and then

morphed into puzzlement. Realizing I couldn't just leave it at that, I said, "Love for another is the key to a rapid escape from this system. Whatever gives us the capacity for love is not included in the part of you that will be drawn into the target system. When you're inside it, you'll have complete access to logic and intellect. You'll also feel fear since that's usually a rational response to a threat to your existence. What you won't feel is love of any kind. That ability will remain within your body but also forge a link to your logical self. You can use that link to pull yourself back to your body."

I let that sink in for a few seconds. "So, I'll ask again, do you have someone you love at least as much as you love yourself?"

Only six avatars left this time. Less than I'd expected. Once again, I sealed our meeting area so no one else could enter.

Smiling, I asked, "Have I piqued your curiosity with this lead-up? Are you ready to learn about our target?"

Heads nodded and since I'd removed the isolation bots, a lot of them called, "Yes!"

I raised my hands, calling for silence. To my surprise, I got it immediately.

"Our target is the Star Stone."

My announcement was met with stunned silence from slicers crowded before me. That was what I'd expected and was about to launch into my persuasive arguments. The hackers reacted differently.

A roar of approval rose from them. I waited for it to crest but the roar just kept going on and on. All along the dividing line between hackers and slicers, the hackers shared their enthusiasm. Some simply nudged their slicer neighbors in friendly enthusiasm. Some slapped their chests, a hacker gesture of solidarity. A few even wrapped arms around slicers.

And the enthusiasm spread. At first, it was just a few slicers who joined in—the ones next to the hackers. But their rising cheer infected those next to them. It was like watching a wave roll across the slicers. Within seconds everyone was stamping their feet, waving their arms, and roaring their approval.

I didn't even notice Fox appear outside my privacy shield until he sent a private message.

"Knock, knock."

I extended the shield, including Fox, and waved him forward. The cheering eased as the crowd parted just enough to let him pass through to me. When he reached the front, Fox swept me into his arms and kissed me deeply. The crowd reacted with another roar.

"The secure subspace connection is set up," he told me when our lips drew apart. "What did you say to get everyone so excited?"

"I told them our target. Credit the hackers for the rest."

Keeping an arm around Fox, I faced the crowd again. They quieted when I raised my free hand. "Fox will begin your briefing. I have one thing I must do before we make our move against the Star Stone."

Assigning control of my privacy shield to Fox, I slipped free of him and walked into the crowd. As with Fox, they parted before me. Hackers grinned and slapped their chests. Slicers smiled and gave me a thumbs up.

Once outside the shield, I wasted little time returning to the real world and placing the call to Jeanine. I kept it brief, telling her nothing about our planned attack on the Star Stone. After all, the damned thing could still hear and see everything she heard and saw.

Jeanine hated the idea of trading me for Tilly but I cut the call before she could try talking me out of it.

As I connected myself to the network again, Kelly said, "She won't trade you for Tilly. You know that, right?"

"I didn't leave her any choice."

"That you know of."

"What else does she have to bargain with?"

"Damned if I know, but don't underestimate Jeanine."

"I hope you're right, Kelly, but don't get your hopes up. I will *not* abandon Tilly."

I activated my connection and merged into the network. I had an attack to lead with the fate of humanity hanging in the balance.

I pushed my concern for Tilly from my mind and rejoined my attack force.

NEGOTIATIONS
Olivia

A serious young man in a well-tailored Royal Intelligence Agency uniform saluted from my office doorway. "She's awake, Your Highness."

"Thank you, Lieutenant." I kept my tone formal but offered a warm smile, "Please escort Miss Smythe-Warrington to my office."

The young man's eyes betrayed just a hint of surprise but his response was prompt. "At once, Your Highness."

As my door slid shut, I tapped the interoffice comm, "Elizabeth, I'm expecting a subspace call from Lady Jeanine. Alert me the moment it comes."

"Of course, Your Highness," came the surprised reply. "I'm afraid I don't have anything on my schedule."

It wasn't on Jeanine's schedule, either. "It's an unscheduled call."

"Very well, Your Highness. Shall I clear your schedule?"

"Yes. After the RIA delivers a woman to my office, allow no interruptions beyond notification of the subspace call from Lady Jeanine."

"As you command, Your Highness."

"That includes my husband."

My assistant hesitated briefly before replying, "Yes, Your Highness."

William could get past Elizabeth by simply ignoring her admonition but he'd respect my wishes for anything short of a dire emergency. Confident one of the two people capable of precipitating an emergency of that scale was on her way to my office, I began mentally preparing for the upcoming war of wits and words.

Minutes later, the same young RIA officer returned, this time accompanied by the lady thief. Disheveled and still suffering from stun shock, Tilly remained remarkably beautiful. The anger smoldering in her eyes simply added to her undeniable appeal. No wonder William was drawn to her.

Tilly met my gaze without a hint of shame or sorrow. "Olivia."

The Lieutenant backhanded Tilly's cheek. "Use Her Highness's proper title!"

"Screw you," she spat.

The officer raised his hand again, but I interceded. "That will do, Lieutenant."

"As you command, Your Highness."

Before I could send the man away, my assistant's head popped into view. "The subspace call you were expecting has arrived, Your Highness."

The call came almost an hour sooner than expected. Jeanine's people moved quickly, I'll give them that.

"Tell them I'm on my way." I turned to the RIA officer, "Come with me and bring the prisoner."

A short walk later, I left Tilly and the Lieutenant outside the subspace center's door. As soon as I settled into the seat, Jeanine's image materialized on the screen.

Taking the initiative, she said, "I assume Tilly is alive and unharmed?"

"What, no pleasantries? You didn't even ask after my pregnancy."

Jeanine's green eyes narrowed, "You wouldn't have taken my call, much less worn such a smugly satisfied expression if your baby was anything but healthy."

"True, but I'm told it's considered polite to inquire. It sets a friendly tone for the conversation and establishes a convivial rapport."

"If you want convivial, send for Tilly and let me judge her condition for myself."

I smiled, "There's no need to be so snippy, Jeanine. You had but to ask."

The Lieutenant answered my tap on the door immediately. "Send the prisoner in. You will wait out there."

His eyebrows rose, "Your Highness—?"

"That is an order, Lieutenant."

"Of course," he replied. "My apologies for my presumption, Your Highness."

I waved this off as Tilly joined me in the room. As the door slid shut, I turned back to the screen, "As you can see, Tilly is alive and unharmed."

Without asking permission to sit in the company of royalty—tsk, Tilly's lack of manners would appall her great-grandmother—the thief settled into the seat next to mine. A soft sigh escaped her lips as she drooped against the backrest.

Jeanine's gaze swung to the other woman, "Is that true, Tilly? Are you all right?"

"Besides being her prisoner," Tilly jerked a thumb in my direction, "I'm okay. Still hung-over from being stunned, though, so don't let my exhaustion worry you."

Jeanine's face relaxed a bit, "Don't worry, I'll get you out of there as quickly as possible."

I arched my left eyebrow, "How do you propose to accomplish that?"

Jeanine's attention swung back to me. "Through negotiation. You know, the way *civilized* people deal with situations such as this."

That was a dig at my past attempts to kill Jeanine. And, if I was being honest, she had a valid point. I responded with a simple nod of acknowledgment and waited for her first offer.

It took Jeanine a couple of seconds to realize I wasn't going to say anything. "You surprise me, Olivia. I expected a list of demands."

"What is the point? You'll never agree to exchange Jana for Tilly."

"Damned straight she won't!" Tilly said. "And I wouldn't let her—"

I placed a finger over Tilly's mouth and, in my most condescending tone, said, "Shush, child. The adults are speaking."

Jeanine shot a warning glance at Tilly, who swallowed her no doubt acerbic retort. Then Jeanine said, "You're quite correct, though that didn't stop Jana from telling me to offer that exchange. What I am willing to offer is the immediate removal of Jana and her compatriots from Xapreathea. Tilly included. I'll have them brought to Neert and keep them within the Duchy until you decide they may travel beyond its borders."

I put a finger to my chin as if I was considering the proposal. I shook my head, "This deal benefits you greatly. I, on the other hand, see nothing in my favor to balance that."

"I'll turn over every bit of information I have gathered concerning the secret we discussed during your last visit to Gaunner. Furthermore, I'll give my word to never speak of it again to anyone. My oath applies to Drake as well."

If word ever got out that the Queen and I planned the destruction of my own spaceship—a deadly disaster created so the Prince could heroically rescue me and fall in love with his damsel—we might face open revolt. Worse, I would lose William's love and trust. Jeanine knew her offer would tempt me.

Ignoring Tilly's curious stare, I said, "I already *have* an oath from you concerning that information. As long as no harm comes to your friends or family, you'll remain silent. With that in mind, I have a counter-proposal. Jana and her friends will surrender to me. I will hold them only until such time as they have been thoroughly debriefed. I believe the RIA will want Jana's assistance strengthening our network's security, as well. They'll be treated as guests and I'll grant them pardons afterward. You have my oath they'll be free within one year."

Tilly's head shook back and forth as Jeanine considered my offer. The thief wouldn't enjoy such confinement, of course, but my offer was more than fair. Despite that, I could tell Jeanine wasn't going to accept it. I don't know what was going on in that mind of hers but some private concern loomed large in it. Perhaps it was that odd story about the Star Stone genetically modifying my child but I couldn't fathom Jeanine truly believed that.

Finally, with reluctance, Jeanine shook her head. "No, Olivia, I can't do that to my friends."

"That's unfortunate, Jeanine. Unless you have something else to offer, it seems as if we are at an impasse. Perhaps Jana will respond to a planet-wide broadcast and exchange herself for Tilly."

I hoped that last bit would goad another offer from Jeanine. It did.

"If you allow Jana and her friends, including Tilly, to leave Xapreathea on the *Rising Star*, I will appear before the Star Stone and relinquish my claim to the Duchy of Gaunner."

A wave of triumph surged through my body overwhelming every other sensation.

"Done!" I crowed.

Jeanine gave a brief shake of her head, "I wasn't finished, Olivia. That offer comes with certain non-negotiable conditions."

Of course, it did. Damn. I quelled my elation. "Name the conditions bearing in mind that my acceptance of your terms is no longer valid."

Jeanine smiled, "I expected an emotional response to those words and agree it holds no weight in our discussion."

I'd expected a smile from Jeanine—something haughty with condescending and predatory overtones. It's what *I* would have worn in her place. The smile she offered was none of those things. It was understanding and almost friendly. A smile of superiority would have whetted my appetite for cutthroat negotiations. This unexpected and humane reaction simply confused me.

Was it an act meant to throw me off my game?

I locked gazes with Jeanine and her eyes told me her smile was sincere. Her words meant exactly what she said, hiding nothing. Raised among nobles whose every word carried concealed daggers, I habitually examined every statement for pitfalls and landmines.

But, in a flash of revelation, I finally understood that the woman on the screen before me didn't think that way.

She was quick-witted and cunning, all the more so if she felt she'd been backed into a corner. But she was also...honest. Open. Sincere. Somehow, despite her frequent demonstrations of those qualities, I'd never truly understood how different she was from every other noble I knew.

With that realization, another thought emerged from the back of my mind. Jeanine truly believed what she'd told me about the Star Stone. She truly believed it was an alien artifact—something the first few pages of the Star Stone report made clear. But she also believed it was working against the best interests of humanity.

Against the best interests of the Star Kingdom.

Against the best interests of my baby.

And that led to the most disturbing thought of all.

What if she was right?

Struggling to keep the sudden surge of concern out of my voice, I asked, "What are your conditions?"

She watched me for a couple of seconds, almost as if she was privy to my inner turmoil. "I have three conditions, two major and one minor."

I nodded, "Go on."

"First, you and I will select the next Duke or Duchess of Gaunner. We must both agree on the choice and then announce it to the public. Only then will I renounce my claim."

During my brief visit to Gaunner, I'd seen Jeanine's evident concern for the people of Gaunner. Without a second thought, I said, "Agreed."

She nodded as if she'd expected nothing less. "You won't find my next condition nearly so agreeable. You and I both know a civil war is brewing. The Star Kingdom is too large, too all-encompassing, and too intent upon controlling lives rather than governing wisely. The simmering anger has no outlet because the populace has no refuge from the nobility. Even the frontier worlds are governed by members of that chosen class. And for every noble such as Lord Lockridge and, I hope, me, there are a dozen who more closely resemble your late brother."

I couldn't deny her interpretation of the current situation within the Star Kingdom. Nor did I try. "That's why you've chosen to throw in with the budding rebellion. You do realize the Star Kingdom will crush them if it comes to a fight?"

She didn't waste time denying her association with the rebels. "Possibly, though I think you greatly underestimate the groundswell of support we'll receive should the situation deteriorate that far."

"Your second condition is obviously tied to this. Please name it."

"The Duchy of Neert must be granted sovereignty as an independent star nation."

"You know I don't have the authority to do that."

"True, but if you and William publicly support my petition for independence, it will eventually happen."

"I see two problems with that, Jeanine. First, I cannot speak for William."

Jeanine actually laughed at my protest. Waving a hand

dismissively, she said, "William will say what you want him to say. Furthermore, he'll mean every word."

I inclined my head, acknowledging her assessment. "You're probably right in William's case, but I think you overestimate my persuasive powers over the rest of the Royal family, much less the nobility."

"No, I don't. However, provided you sincerely support my request—and you've got to admit you'd rather have me as far from Star Kingdom politics as possible—I'll consider this condition met."

Out of habit, I examined her offer for hidden meaning. Then I cut myself off after only a few seconds. Jeanine's eyes still radiated sincerity and...I believed her offer was genuine. "I accept that condition, as well. You also mentioned a minor condition?"

"Yes. You know that Drake and I are planning a public wedding, one fitting for a Duchess?" When I nodded, she continued, "I'd like to use the event to further the story that you and I have put our enmity behind us."

"William and I will, of course, attend."

"That's a start, but I'd like to do the truly unexpected." Jeanine leaned forward and said, "I'd like you to be part of my wedding party."

My mouth opened and closed twice and still I couldn't quite find my voice. Tilly, forgotten by me during this discussion, didn't have that problem.

"You want her to do *what*?" she cried.

"I want her in the wedding party as a bridesmaid." Jeanine flashed a friendly smile at Tilly, "I want you as a bridesmaid, too."

Tilly swallowed her planned retort and, obviously surprised by the request, simply said, "Sure. I'd love to be in the wedding."

Finally over my own surprise, I discovered a smile spreading across my face. "By the time you hold the wedding, you realize I'll be enormously pregnant. Do you really want a waddling bridesmaid?"

"I'm certain you will waddle gracefully, Olivia. Does that mean you accept?"

"Yes."

"Excellent. As you've accepted all my conditions, I believe this negotiation is at an end. When shall I tell Jana and her friends to meet you at the *Rising Star*?"

Thinking back to everything I'd learned about Jeanine and, especially Jana, I felt certain neither of them wanted to leave Xapreathea with the Star Stone intact. Surprisingly, *I* didn't want them doing that, either.

I asked, "How much time do you think Jana will require to... um...wrap everything up and prepare for departure?"

Jeanine gave me a hard look before saying, "Why don't we err on the side of caution. How about tomorrow morning at eight?"

"Agreed. Until then, Tilly will simply be my guest in the palace." I turned to Tilly and added, "A real guest. You will not be returning to RIA custody."

After we ended the call, I sat back in my seat and considered what I'd just done. Unless I missed my guess, I'd just countenanced the destruction of the Star Stone and the partial dissolution of the Star Kingdom.

God, would Mother ever forgive me?

CRASH THE STAR STONE

Jana

Fox and I entered the Star Stone first. We had an idea for keeping it reacting to us so it couldn't act against the hackers and slicers coming behind us. My third trip through the maelstrom separating the Star Stone from the human network was almost soothing, I'd gotten so used to it.

Once we entered the Star Stone, I wasted no time imposing a little human-centric order on the place. This time I went for the look of a modern data center. The interior of the Star Stone was strange enough that I thought a little familiarity would make things a bit easier for our wrecking crew.

The Star Stone's nondescript human guise appeared before us. "Miss Ward, you astound me. I was certain I'd seen the last of you."

"Why?" I asked, "You still represent the greatest slicing challenge I've ever faced."

"Could it be you do not recall how close you came to losing your life during your previous encounters with me?"

"I suppose that's one way of looking at things," I replied. "From my point of view, you've done everything in your power to kill me and failed both times. Based on the reactions of every

Recognized noble in the Star Kingdom, you were royally pissed off when my friend pulled me out last time."

"Do not ascribe such base human emotions to me, Miss Ward. My creators left such weaknesses behind—assuming they ever suffered from them—millennia before they created me."

"Emotions are mankind's strength, not our weakness."

The Star Stone laughed, "How very amusing, Miss Ward, all the more so because you truly believe it."

"Have you figured out how I escaped from you the first time?" I asked.

For such a superior creation, the Star Stone's visage displayed human emotions well enough. Its lips compressed and its eyes narrowed in displeasure.

"Yeah, I didn't think so. What about the second time when my friend broke your grasp on me and pulled me to safety?" I didn't even wait for a reaction from the Star Stone. "Nope, you're still clueless about that, too. And you never will figure them out, either. You know why?"

"Please, Miss Ward, enlighten me. Though I deduce you shall attribute your continued existence to these emotions you value so highly."

I gave the Star Stone a slow clap. "Bravo. You're not quite as stupid as I thought you were."

"*I* am stupid, Miss Ward? Who, pray tell, just revealed her lone advantage to whom? Once I bring my full capabilities to bear on this—something already initiated, I might add—I shall discover how you utilize these emotions of yours to evade my reach."

"You know, it's almost cute how you believe that, Stony."

"Belief—another human frailty—has nothing to do with it, Miss Ward."

"Wrong. Belief has *everything* to do with this."

The Star Stone waved a hand in dismissal. "If belief is all-powerful, give me a demonstration of its power."

I flashed my best predatory smile, "I *believe* this conversation is at an end."

The Star Stone raised its eyebrows and opened its mouth, no doubt planning on explaining how wrong I was. But my words were Fox's cue to act.

While the Stone's attention was directed at me, Fox was busy drawing on his soul line. Now he looped it around the Star Stone's image, wrapping it up in the same manner Fox used to free me previously.

As the line twirled around the Star Stone, it wriggled and fought against the constricting bands wrapping it. Fox played his soul line like a fisherman fighting a big catch. He tugged on the line tight then as the Star Stone pulled back suddenly released it. Kept off balance by Fox's tactics, the Star Stone never noticed me drawing on my own soul line until I began wrapping the visage with it. With both of us pulling from opposite sides of the Star Stone, we quickly immobilized it.

It looked back and forth between us, "What are you doing? What is this...this thing around me?"

"Oh, nothing much," I said, "just a weak, human emotional entanglement."

"Good one, Jana," Fox laughed. His attention suddenly focused on the maelstrom exit into the Star Stone. "And just in time, too. The wrecking crew is here."

The Star Stone and I both looked in the same direction as Fox. Hackers and slicers poured into the Star Stone. To my relief, each one stopped and checked their soul line before heading to their assigned systems.

"*Who* are those interlopers?" the Star Stone demanded.

"We've been calling them the wrecking crew," I replied. "You should probably call them your executioners."

Having apparently accepted its current entanglement, the Star Stone gave a rueful shake of its head. "Miss Ward, do you think I am without defenses?"

"I'd be shocked if you weren't, but you've dedicated your full capabilities toward analyzing the connection between human emotions and your inability to hold me. It's Fox's guess, based on what he saw when he used this soul line trick to free me, that the line disrupts your system control. We're pretty certain you're the alien-artifact-equivalent of a control process in one of our systems. Without your direct input, I don't think you can direct your capabilities away from their current processes." My smile flowed from predatory to triumphant. "In other words, you're defenseless."

The Star Stone stared at me as if it couldn't process what I'd just said. Maybe it couldn't since all its processes were busy working away on a now-useless task. Finally, it fell back on arrogance. "I am far superior to anything created by humanity. You cannot do this."

I plucked my soul line, "If you're so superior, break free of this."

"I have no need. Mere humans cannot fathom my workings. Your friends can do nothing to affect me."

Fox and I both burst out laughing. Shaking my head in disbelief at the Star Stone's stubborn refusal to accept what was happening, I said, "Do you remember that holy man who was the first to enter you?"

"Of course, Miss Ward. My memory is perfect. Prior to your arrival, he was the one human who escaped me."

"Yeah, another case of those pesky human emotions. Anyway, did you ever figure out he was *not* a holy man? He was religious, true, but he was also the Star Kingdom's best network analyst."

"I do not see the significance of this revelation."

That actually surprised me. I thought the Star Stone would make the connection immediately. "He requested a full tour—I guess that's the best word for it—of you. Assuming he'd never understand it, much less leave, you granted his request."

"I have no idea what you are talking about, Miss Ward."

My eyebrows rose in surprise. Glancing at Fox, I asked, "Our friends?"

He nodded, "Someone is doing a good job trashing the Stone's memory."

In a monotone, the Star Stone said, "You must stop them. The rebirth of a race is at stake."

"That's why we're *not* stopping them," I snapped. "We have no interest in aiding the subjugation of the human race."

As I spoke, the Star Stone's visage gradually lost definition. When next it spoke, it appeared stiff and blocky, like something a child might create. "Who are you? Why have you accessed my system?"

"It doesn't matter. You won't remember anything I say, anyway."

The Star Stone replied, but it spoke in an alien tongue of harsh growls and clicks. Its deterioration, already rapid, accelerated. As it did, a trickle of hackers and slicers flowed toward the maelstrom, drawn back to their bodies by their soul lines. A hundred and fifty some-odd hackers and slicers working together can do a *lot* of damage. In less time than I'd dared hope, Fox and I were the only ones left in the Star Stone.

As the Star Stone's control process faded away, we let our own soul lines draw us out of the Star Stone. Behind us, the entire thing lost all systemic integrity and the Star Stone crashed for the first and last time.

IT'S OVER
Tilly

Olivia was true to her word.

"Lieutenant," she said as we rejoined him in the hallway, "I have pardoned Tilly Smythe-Warrington for all crimes, known or unknown, she has committed. The same applies to her companion Jana..."

Olivia trailed off and glanced at me, reminding me she didn't know Jana's last name. I hated divulging that without Jana's permission but was certain Jana would understand and approve. "Ward. Her last name is Ward."

"Thank you," Olivia replied. "My pardon applies to Jana Ward and companions to be named later. The manhunt for them is hereby canceled. Tell the RIA commander to recall all agents and reassign them as needed."

From the look in the officer's eyes, he was full of questions he dared not ask. He did the one thing he could do in this situation. Snapping to attention and saluting, he said, "I will convey your orders immediately, Your Highness."

"I'll put the official orders on the network once I return to my office." She offered the man a smile, "Thank you for your assistance. You are dismissed."

Entering Olivia's office, she asked me, "Are you fully recovered from the stun shot? Shall I send for my doctor?"

I shook my head, "No, I'm recovering fine. I am hungry though."

Olivia's assistant already had her comm in hand—to call the doctor, I guess—and immediately placed a lunch order.

While we waited for the food, Olivia entered the pardons into the network. Handing me a data stick, she said, "It will take several days for the pardons to work their way to all planets in the Star Kingdom. If anyone questions it before then, the data stick has the details."

"Thank you."

When the food arrived, I tore into a delicious lunch. Olivia, on the other hand, moped. There's really not another word for it. She sighed dramatically, massaged her temples, buried her face in her hands, and generally looked miserable.

Strangely enough, I found myself moved to compassion for her. Why the hell did I feel sympathy for this woman? All she'd done was make Jeanine's life hell, after all. More recently, she'd sicced the full might of the Royal Intelligence Agency on my friends and me, chasing us underground, and eventually capturing me. All to stop us from saving humanity from the machinations of an extinct alien race and their diabolical artifact.

But, in the end, Olivia backed off. She...believed us. Well, she believed *Jeanine*, anyway. And once Olivia believed, she called off her hounds and gave Jana free rein to do what Jana does best. Olivia only owed explanations to one person, but I doubted Queen Charlotte would be easily swayed. In effect, Olivia risked everything she held dear—her title, her husband, and maybe even the future of her unborn child—to do the right thing.

That didn't make me like her but it did make me respect her. I just hoped Jana could make all the sacrifices worthwhile.

And Jana did.

I can't explain it but Olivia's expression...changed. Her head lifted and her eyes darted about the room as if looking for something familiar that suddenly went missing.

"It's over," Olivia said more to herself than me. Dropping her head back into her hands, she added, "The Star Stone is gone."

"It's not the end of the galaxy unless you let it be," I said. "Hell, if you play things right this will *increase* your power, not decrease it."

"Don't be ridiculous," Olivia spat. "The Star Stone has been the arbiter of succession among the nobility for thousands of years. Now it's gone and our claim to the throne goes with it."

"Why?"

Olivia looked at me as if I was an idiot. "Because it's *gone*, Tilly. You *do* understand what that word means?"

I shook my head, "I'm pretty sure the Star Stone is right where it's always been. If it wasn't, wouldn't someone have raised an alarm?"

The princess sighed in exasperation, "Fine, the corpse of the Star Stone remains. But what made it work is no more."

"What made it work was a crimson glow that enveloped people and retreated. As the children's story says, that signifies that God and the Star Stone find the person worthy." I caught Olivia's gaze and held it. "Seems to me you just need an effect that duplicates the crimson glow and the whole Star Kingdom can just keep on handling successions the way it has for millennia."

Olivia's eyes widened, "I never considered it that way."

"I'll bet the Queen likes this change, too. After all, now the Royal family controls all successions among the nobility. If someone you don't like shows up, you just don't turn on the light show. Bam, they're rejected by the Star Stone."

"You're right! That's brilliant, Tilly!"

"It is, isn't it?"

To my surprise, Olivia burst out laughing. Once begun, she laughed long and loud and, to my relief, didn't sound psychotic at all. When she finally wound down our attitudes toward each other had changed. We still weren't best girlfriends—not even close—but we could talk to each other easily. I found myself wondering if this personable Olivia had been there all along or if she'd only just emerged from the Star Stone's captivity.

The next morning, as promised, Olivia personally escorted me to the *Rising Star*. To our surprise, Drake's favorite astrogator, Grant, was waiting for us, too. He'd only arrived the night before, prepared to help us evade Royal Navy pursuit. From the look Kelly gave him, I got the idea she thought that had been a probable suicide mission. Instead, Olivia offered us a priority escort from the system.

Less than an hour later, the *Rising Star* lifted the six of us—Jana, Nathan, Alfonso, Kelly, Grant and me—from Xapreathea. Grant set a course for Neert and we headed home.

IT'S ONLY FAIR

Jeanine

The next six months passed in the blink of an eye. Olivia and I interviewed and debated and argued and, finally, agreed on the next Duchess of Gaunner. We settled on Baroness Erin, a previously minor noble from a previously minor holding who impressed us with her deep understanding of the issues facing the Duchy and with her ideas for solving those issues. Olivia and I quite enjoyed Erin's gasp of surprise when we named her as my successor. Some nobles were upset we passed over them but most, once they got to know Erin, accepted our decision.

The Royal family's new Star Stone effects worked flawlessly during the transition of power from me to Erin. I never heard any suggestion that something was wrong with the ceremony or the Star Stone.

The Queen chose that time to have King Bernard issue a proclamation against Recognized knights. Without the alien AI forcing compliance, Recognized Knights were already free to follow their own consciences. Realizing she'd have to explain that somehow, Charlotte had Bernard claim that binding another person's will to a lord went against the Star Kingdom's newfound respect for individual rights. The simple fact that the existing

Recognized Knights had their free will returned was offered as proof that the Star Stone agreed with the decision.

Once I was free of my obligation to Gaunner, negotiations for Neert's secession began in earnest. Queen Charlotte, backed by Princess Olivia, was a tough negotiator. She was also a fair one. We had an agreement worked out by the time I returned to Neert to begin planning my official state wedding. The post-wedding festivities would also include the official secession ceremony presided over by Their Royal Majesties King Bernard and Queen Charlotte.

Jana and Nathan got married in a small ceremony before family and close friends. Jana restricted her wedding party to Tilly, her maid of honor, and me as her lone bridesmaid. I think Tilly and Alfonso will follow Jana's and Nathan's example eventually.

My wedding party, on the other hand, is huge. Besides Kelly, my maid of honor, Jana, Tilly, and Olivia, I also invited the women from Drake's Space Patrol crew and my half-sisters on my mother's side. Drake's party was equally large, including the surviving men from his crew, Prince William, and a few friends from the rebellion.

Mentioning the rebellion, with Neert's separation from the Star Kingdom they found themselves without anything to rebel against. Since the soon-to-be Republic of Neert was sorely in need of armed forces, many of the rebels accepted appointments to Neert's military. The rest accepted civilian citizenship in Neert and got on with their lives.

Lords and ladies from across the Star Kingdom arrived days before the wedding. The Neert nobility engaged in a friendly contest to see who could throw the most lavish party and enjoyed a moment in the limelight. The day of the wedding dawned clear and beautiful. Guests arrived and took their seats.

Drake and I had such large wedding parties it took quite a while for everyone to enter the cathedral. As I'd predicted, despite being almost nine-months pregnant, Olivia managed the long walk with grace and poise. At long last, it was my turn. King Bernard, who requested the honor, escorted me down the aisle and presented me to Drake. The minister droned a message of some kind, one I wasn't listening to, before finally working his way around to the important part.

"Do you, Drake," he said, "take Jeanine to be your wife? To have and to hold, in sickness and in health, for richer or poorer, for better or worse, forsaking all others until death do you part?"

Grinning, Drake said, "I—"

"Aaahhhh!" Olivia, her dress soaking wet, held her stomach and fought for balance.

William rushed to her, "Olivia, what's wrong?"

Stifling another cry, Olivia turned a beaming smile on her husband, "Nothing's wrong, dear. Your heir is tired of waiting and is on the way."

As Olivia's physician and my medical people entered the cathedral, William helped his wife sit down in a hastily cleared pew. After another contraction, Olivia found the time to look my way.

"I'm terribly sorry, Jeanine. It seems my son—"

"Or daughter," William interjected.

"My *child*," Olivia continued, "has disrupted your wedding."

I couldn't help laughing, "It's only fair, Your Highness. After all, I disrupted your wedding."

"You're right. Apology withdrawn," Olivia agreed.

With Olivia drawing all the attention, only Drake and I heard the minister ask, "What should I do, Lady Jeanine?"

"This is just a show wedding, since Drake and I are already married," I replied. "With Olivia going into labor, people have already gotten more of a show than they expected. Just pronounce us husband and wife and let's call it a day."

"As you wish, my Lady." The minister smiled at each of us and said, "I now pronounce you husband and wife."

An hour and a half later, Olivia delivered a beautiful baby boy.

IF YOU ENJOYED THE RECOGNITION SERIES...

...you might also enjoy *The Lost Planet*, a stand-alone space opera.

After reading *The Recognition Revelation*, please post a brief review. Reader recommendations are the best advertising.

ABOUT THE AUTHOR

Henry Vogel began his writing career in comic books way back in the 1980s, with the indie titles *Southern Knights* and *X-Thieves*. When the bottom dropped out of the black & white comic book market, Henry went into IT, where he worked for the next thirty-three years. Henry took up professional storytelling in 2006, and has performed all across his home state of North Carolina.

As a lifetime fan of science fiction, Henry always wanted to write science fiction novels. He began writing *Scout's Honor* in 2012, and released it to the world in 2014. He hasn't stopped writing since.

Henry makes his home in Raleigh, NC, and is hard at work on his next novel.

www.henryvogelwrites.com

ALSO BY HENRY VOGEL

Travis & Trouble

Trouble in Twi-Town

Trouble on Mars

The Fortune Chronicles

Fortune's Fool

The Scales of Sin & Sorrow

The Scout Series

Scout's Honor

Scout's Oath

Scout's Duty

Scout's Law

Scout's Training

Scout's First Mission

Hart for Adventure

The Princess Scout

Scout: The Lost Colony Adventures

Non-series books

The Lost Planet

Heart of Dorkness & Other Stories

The Connaught Family Chronicles

The Fugitive Heir

The Fugitive Pair

The Fugitive Snare

The Hostage in Hiding

The Captain Nancy Martin

The Counterfeit Captain

The Undercover Captain

The Recognition Series

The Recognition Run

The Recognition Rejection

The Recognition Revelation

Comic Books

Aristocratic Xraterrestrial Time-Traveling Thieves Complete Collection

Southern Knights Almost Complete Collection

Southern Knights Color Edition

Southern Knights: The Morrigan Wars

Southern Knights: Leaving Atlanta (prose novella)

Missing Beings

Illustrated Children's Book

I'm in Charge! and Other Stories

www.ingramcontent.com/pod-product-compliance
Lightning Source LLC
LaVergne TN
LVHW010255260326
834688LV00044B/1300